Love
IN THE
YEARS
OF
LUNACY

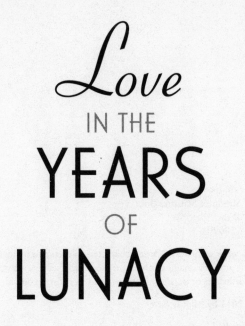

Love
IN THE
YEARS
OF
LUNACY

MANDY SAYER

ATRIA PAPERBACK

New York   London   Toronto   Sydney   New Delhi

ATRIA PAPERBACK
A Division of Simon & Schuster, Inc.
1230 Avenue of the Americas
New York, NY 10020

Originally published in Australia in 2011 by Allen & Unwin

First Atria Paperback edition November 2012

ATRIA PAPERBACK and colophon are trademarks of Simon & Schuster, Inc.

For information about special discounts for bulk purchases, please contact Simon & Schuster Special Sales at 1-866-506-1949 or business@simonandschuster.com.

The Simon & Schuster Speakers Bureau can bring authors to your live event. For more information or to book an event, contact the Simon & Schuster Speakers Bureau at 1-866-248-3049 or visit our website at www.simonspeakers.com.

Designed by Jill Putorti

Manufactured in the United States of America

10 9 8 7 6 5 4 3 2 1

Library of Congress Cataloging-in-Publication Data is available.

ISBN 978-1-4516-7846-8
ISBN 978-1-4516-7847-5 (ebook)

For Louis

*And in memory of my parents, Gerry and Betty, whose many
anecdotes and adventures inspired this story*

Prelude

Darling boy, if you're listening to this, I'm either missing or dead. The story I'm about to tell you isn't, though—yet somehow I can't bring it to life. I've always expressed myself better in music than in words. Not like you. So I want you to play these tapes one by one, and as you listen, write down the story I'm telling you. In writing our story—the story of Martin and me—you'll also be writing your own.

Aunty Pearl tried writing her memoirs many times but she never got further than the night she lost her virginity in an amusement park. She scribbled on the backs of electricity bills, scraps of paper, in notebooks filled with half-finished musical compositions, but the sentences and paragraphs didn't accumulate into much more than a string of anecdotes with too many adjectives and hardly any punctuation.

She died a year ago, two months after my father, Martin, passed away. Pearl and Martin were twins, and both played the saxophone, but it was Pearl who was the better musician. The books on Australian jazz published since the seventies note her contribution to the local music scene, particularly the fact that she introduced the new American style of bebop to our musicians. No one, not even the famous Sydney saxophonist Don Burrows, can figure out how she came to know so much, having had so little experience.

Only last week, the jazz historian Brian Jackson, an old friend of Pearl's, visited me here at the house. It was an awkward meeting because I'm having the place renovated, and that day the floors upstairs were being sanded. Over the roar of the sander, Brian told me that, just before she died, Pearl had instructed him to contact me about some archival tapes she'd left here in the house. For some reason, she wanted him to wait a year after her death before he brought up the subject of these old recordings. Why? I don't know. And neither does Brian.

"Listen," he said. "I'm writing another book on Australian jazz and one of the chapters will be devoted to your aunt."

I began to tell him that I'd already donated her papers and all the copies of her records to the National Archives in Canberra, but Brian cut me off, reminding me that it wasn't her papers he was after.

"Everything went into the archives," I told him, but Brian wasn't convinced. He cast his eyes around the parlour and into the dining room, staring for several moments at the small stuffed dog on a stand near the piano. "It's a big house," he said. He looked hopeful and a bit desperate, I thought.

"She told me she'd hidden them. Something about a toy box. Does that ring a bell?"

I thought for a moment. My son once had a toy box when he was little but that was twenty years ago and it's long since gone.

I shook my head, and then asked Brian who was publishing his book. A couple of decades ago he and I shared the same publisher—Spire—a small press in Melbourne. But after my third crime novel was a modest hit, my agent got me a four-book deal with Allen & Unwin, an independent publisher based in Sydney, and that's where my career started to take off. I created the Aboriginal detective Herman Djulpajurra, who grew up on a remote mission, learning traditional tracking techniques and how to read the complex syntax of the bush before attending Sydney University, where he studied cutting-edge forensics. When my first novel about him begins, he's twenty-six years old and is returning to Central Australia as a gun for hire. Me, I'm only half Aboriginal, from my mother's side, but over the last fifteen or so years I've become known as Australia's First Indigenous Crime Writer, a title that's taken me to writers' festivals all over the world and made me a decent living. So far there are twelve volumes in the series but since the deaths of my father and aunt last year the only words that I've written are for funeral notices and epitaphs. I've never experienced writers' block before and, to be frank, I haven't known what to do with myself. Fixing up the house has helped, and I've developed an interest in gardening, but I miss the ongoing flirtation with a blank page, the thrill of making something out of nothing. As I rattle around this big, empty house I often feel so alone in the world, unless you count an ex-wife and a son who has his own life now.

Brian didn't answer me right away about his publisher—it was too noisy, perhaps—just stood up and began pacing the room. I noticed his moustache was a little greyer and he wasn't wearing his wedding ring. When the sander upstairs abruptly fell silent, though, he said, "A university press is interested in the proposal."

I crossed my legs and nodded.

"But there's one proviso," he added.

"Yeah?" I asked. "What's that?"

Brian leaned on the mantelpiece, gazing at a photo of Martin and Pearl as toddlers, dressed in identical white dresses. "I've got to come up with some new stuff on your aunt." Then he turned and stared at me, frowning, as if I were deliberately standing in the way of his research. "She used to tape-record all her live gigs, you know."

I felt sorry for him then. He's an excellent historian, but I sensed both his personal and professional lives were stalling, as were mine. I promised him I'd do a thorough search of the house and bundled him out the door, telling him I'd ring if I found them.

I spent days looking for these secret tapes; I didn't have much else to do, after all. Even though there were no toy boxes in the house, I tried the basement, where Pearl and Martin had always rehearsed; Pearl's bedroom on the first floor; the linen cupboard; the cartons and tea chests in the attic. I found one of Pearl's old band uniforms from the fifties—black pants and jacket with red and white piping. The uniform hadn't been laundered and when I lifted it to my face I inhaled her familiar scent after all these years—a sweet, peachy odour that flashed back childhood memories: playing duets on the piano, roller-skating hand in hand (one time we ended up skating straight through the door of the local police station), the way she'd make up bedtime stories for me rather than read them from a book. But still no tapes. I felt inside the chimneys, went through my grandmother's mothballed wardrobes; I even searched my grandfather's old MG, which is standing up on blocks in the backyard.

In the glove compartment I found an old tin money box that had been mine when I was a kid. As I shook out a few pennies and sixpences, I suddenly remembered where I used to hide it—in a hole beneath the floorboards of my father's room. When I was about six or seven, Pearl and my father showed me the secret space, where, as kids themselves, they'd hidden things from the prying eyes of adults: stolen lollies, matches, money, a pet mouse. No one else knew about it except me, they said. And then I took it over for a few years, stashing in it comic books, my grandmother's chocolates, a slingshot, and a knife I once found.

I dropped the tin box and rushed back into the house. My father's old room was being renovated. The old rug had been rolled up recently and was leaning against one wall, revealing a few water-damaged floorboards. My eyes flew straight to the right-hand corner, where a tiny round indentation was grooved into one of the boards. I crouched and, for the first time in over fifty years, slipped my finger into it and pulled away a section of the floor, about a foot wide and long, like a trapdoor. In the space between the floor and the ceiling of the cellar I saw what looked like a large metal cash box covered in dust. I opened it and there they were: twenty-three cassette tapes, numbered sequentially. I was about to rush to the phone to call Brian Jackson when curiosity got the better of me. I thought I might have a listen to a few—perhaps even copy them onto CDs. Trouble was, I didn't own a cassette player. Who does these days?

I left the tradies to work on the upstairs veranda while I scoured Kings Cross for a tape deck. The Happy Hocker stocked secondhand record players, transistor radios, even an old eight-track, but not what I needed. The village markets sold scented candles, baby clothes, electric cake mixers, serviette rings, jewellery boxes, and extension cords. Nor did I have any luck at the Wayside Chapel opportunity shop—if only I'd been in the market for baggy dresses and mismatched earrings . . .

It wasn't until the pawn shop opened at 11 AM that I found what I was looking for: a large black-and-silver boom box from the eighties, for only sixty-five bucks, including batteries.

I paid the guy and turned on the radio, switching it to the local jazz station, and the sound of Duke Ellington playing "Take the 'A' Train" burst into the room. I hoisted the box onto my shoulder and left the shop. As I bobbed down the street to Ray Nance's familiar trumpet solo, I got a few strange looks, and one old lady even threw a coin at me. For such a big system, it was surprisingly light.

Back at the house, I told Omar and the boys they could take an early lunch. I wanted some privacy and silence, and retired to my study. I plugged in the cassette player, poured myself a double whisky, and settled in at my desk.

Now that everything is quiet, I open the metal box, select tape number one, push it into the plastic slot, and press Play.

I'm expecting to hear a sound check or maybe musicians tuning up before starting a gig, but after several scratchy seconds I find myself listening to my aunt's reedy voice, asking me to listen to the tapes and write up her story. "Each tape is a chapter in itself, darling. Write each one up as you go along. No skipping to the end, to the very last tape.

"Pretty it up," she then demands. "Make it sing." And when she explains it like this, I begin to understand my responsibilities. After all, I'm a novelist, not a typist. I shape and embellish; I edit and shade. It's similar to how she would improvise on a piece of music, taking the bones of a song and turning it into something startling and unique.

Yes. I'll have a crack at it.

1

A rainy day in May. Sydney was alive with swirling leaves and the cries of flying fruit bats. Afternoon showers fell on wilting flowers, sandstone buildings, vegetable stalls, a war bond rally in Martin Place. It dimpled the harbour, slicked the surface of ship decks, flooded gutters littered with condoms and cigarette butts. It sprinkled on women queuing for rations, factory workers waiting for cancelled trams, Asian immigrants who'd been interned on the grounds of a mental asylum after Japan had entered the war. In the evening, it fell on American servicemen as they picked up local women, on prostitutes out to score a greenback or two, on Australian soldiers as they brawled with GIs for stealing most of their girls.

Near midnight, it drummed a soft syncopation against the tin roofs of Albion Street. Pearl heard the rhythms as she darted beneath awnings, catching up with her twin brother, Martin, and wondered if he could hear them, too; triplets, paradiddles, shuffles, a beating heart. She was nearly eighteen, but that night was the first time she'd heard music in the weather.

"Hey!" she cried as Martin, holding his tenor sax case, dodged an overflowing roof gutter and leaped over a puddle. "Wait for me!" She, too, dodged the waterfall and jumped the puddle, but landed in another one, splattering the side of her dress with muddy water. Martin laughed.

They'd just finished performing at the Trocadero, the biggest and best ballroom in the Southern Hemisphere. Martin played second tenor in the men's big band; Pearl played second alto in the girls' big band. The two jazz orchestras alternated sets on a revolving stage backed by an Art Deco glass shell lit by hundreds of coloured lights. The dance floor was sprung, the clientele was posh, and the twins were well aware that it was the best-paid gig in Sydney. On the downside, the Trocadero orchestras performed virtually the same repertoire each night—light dance music to accompany fox-trots and waltzes; certainly no raucous jazz or swinging blues, which was why Pearl was following Martin through the storm that night, she in a white lace gown and high heels streaked with mud, her brother in black tie and tails. Martin was taking her to the only place in town where she'd be allowed to sit in with a band and play hot jazz into the early hours of the morning. At least, she hoped she'd be allowed to sit in. Martin had jammed with this particular band previously but it would be Pearl's first time.

A few months before, the first black Americans had marched off troop ships and into the streets of Sydney to bolster the country's defence force in the Pacific. Because of American segregation laws, however, they were banned from most Sydney restaurants, hotels, and, of course, the high-class Trocadero Ballroom. The Booker T. Washington Club was the only entertainment venue in the state for black GIs. Pearl had never even met a black American before, let alone played in a band with them.

As they approached the hall built onto the side of an old mansion, the trill of a clarinet escaped through the open windows and Pearl felt a flutter of anticipation in her stomach. They skipped up the front steps and onto the veranda, saxophone cases banging against their legs. She could hear the music more clearly now—an up-tempo version of "Basin Street Blues"—and couldn't believe she was about to enter an all-black club and play jazz for the very people who'd created the form. She now felt not just excited, but as if she herself were exciting.

Martin pushed open the door and almost walked into an Aboriginal girl who was serving as the door monitor. The girl's skin was a pale mahogany colour, Pearl noticed, not the near-ebony of the GIs she'd seen walking the city streets. She was wearing a grey crepe dress that was too big for her and hung off her shoulders in folds.

"Hi, Roma!" said Martin. "This is my only sister, Pearl." Then he added, perhaps unnecessarily, "My twin sister." The siblings were both tall and skinny, with heart-shaped faces and violet-blue eyes, slightly hooded. Pearl's ash blond hair was a little fairer than Martin's, though, and that night she'd piled it on top of her head and skewered the loose bun with knitting needles. The rain had curled the stray wisps into ringlets.

Roma frowned at Pearl. Technically, white women were banned from the club, but Martin had assured his sister that the ban was rarely enforced.

"She's come to sit in with the band, Rome."

Roma rested a hand on her hip and pursed her lips.

"Oohh, come on, baby!" Martin dropped his saxophone, took Roma in his arms, and began dancing her over the black-and-white tiles. Pearl was taken aback by their playfulness.

Roma threw her head back, and her black hair fanned around her shoulders to reveal a long graceful neck. She struggled to free herself, but only halfheartedly, and Martin drew her closer and held her tight. It was as if Roma had become Martin's twin and she, Pearl, were the stranger. As the music ended, he led Roma into a dip so low her hair brushed against the floor.

When he righted her and she had regained her balance, she giggled and punched him on the chest. Trying to keep a straight face, she then pointed to Pearl. "No swearing. No dancing. No fraternising with the boys." She glanced at Martin, swallowing a smile. "Is that clear?"

"Hear, hear," said Martin.

Pearl saluted her. "Aye, aye!"

"And don't fill up your dance card, Captain," Martin added, touching Roma on the shoulder. "Later on, I plan to give you a real swing around the ballroom!"

Roma giggled again and backed away toward the front door. Pearl followed Martin through a library hung with sepia-tinged photographs of stern men in suits. She recognised Abraham Lincoln with his distinctive beard, but the black faces were unfamiliar. The names on the brass plates at the bottom of the frames were equally obscure: W. E. B. DuBois, Marcus Garvey, Booker T. Washington. It was all so new to her—the portraits, her brother's behaviour—that suddenly she wanted to turn back. She caught the sleeve of Martin's dinner jacket, and he turned toward her. Her hand dropped from his sleeve, and she opened her mouth to ask him to take her home, but before Pearl could utter a word Martin linked his arm in hers and wheeled her around.

"Don't worry, Miss Willis," he said, putting on his best posh British accent. "Your prince will accompany you to the dance."

She had to laugh, which relaxed her a little. They walked arm in arm through the library, her brother so close she could smell the lemony starch of his collar. Then the door to the auditorium swung open and there were crashing waves of laughter and music and she forgot that she was nervous, that her dress was streaked with mud, that she was white. Some of the windows were cracked and the stage sagged to the left—so different from the Trocadero Ballroom, with its revolving stage and bevelled-glass wall panels. The light was dim, but through the coils of cigarette smoke she could make out the shapes of people gyrating on the dance floor, couples spinning away from each other and back again, a girl somersaulting over the back of a crouching man, the dip and swivel of hips. The GIs were all in uniform, though some had loosened their collars and rolled up their sleeves, and when she looked closer she could see sequins of sweat glistening against their faces.

Each black man dancing had a black woman in his arms. She knew that Amcross had recruited scores of Aboriginal and Pacific Islander girls to serve as dance partners for the Americans, but still she was taken aback to see so many black Australian girls in one place. She noticed a few of the dancers slowing down to stare at her. Some of the girls looked hostile, as if offended by her presence. The men leaning against the walls sipping beers nudged one another and nodded in her direction, and all at once she felt as if she were an alien. Throat dry, she glanced at Martin, who smiled and winked at her in a big-brotherly kind of way, even though Pearl was actually ten minutes older.

"Car'n, Burly," said Martin, invoking his long-time nickname for her. He cocked his head. "Follow my lead." Martin threaded his way between the dancers, head held high, and Pearl shadowed him as they made their way toward the stage. She knew the bandleader, Merv Sent, and his quartet, the Senders. In his heyday, Merv had been the first clarinettist for the Sydney Symphony Orchestra, until, the rumour went, he woke up one morning after a two-day drinking binge to find himself lying on top of the Harbour Bridge, clutching a half-bottle of rum in one hand and his clarinet in the other. He had no memory of his drunken crawl along the steep arc of metal the night before. The police had to summon the fire brigade to get him down and once it got into the papers he was fired from the orchestra. For the last year he'd been touring outback army camps in an entertainment unit, but was now on leave, along with the other three musos in the band, and was picking up some extra cash during his furlough.

The tune ended and applause rose through the hall. When it died down Pearl could hear the rhythm of the rain against the hall's tin roof, like a loud drumroll.

"Ladies and gentlemen," Merv announced, "this is Merv Sent and the Senders!"

"Where are you sending us, Merv?" cried a man from the audience, his Southern drawl filling the room.

"I'm sending you all completely mad!" cried Merv. He

wiped his clarinet reed with the hem of his jacket. "And believe me," he added, "it's not a long trip."

The audience laughed and clapped.

Merv gave the twins a quick wave, beckoning them to join the band. Martin already had his case open and was fitting his tenor sax together, but Pearl hesitated. It seemed as if everyone in the room was still staring at her, appraising her skin, her hair. She'd never felt so white, so completely naked.

Martin leaped up the stage stairs while Pearl pieced together the old alto sax that she'd inherited from her father. Aubrey Willis had taught them the basics, but since they were eight she and Martin had studied privately at the Conservatorium of Music, learning classical music, theory, and composition. Everything they knew about jazz, though, had been picked up from listening to imported records and learning firsthand on gigs.

Merv counted in "St. Louis Blues" and the band plunged into the first verse.

Pearl joined Martin under the spotlight. She sensed a slowing of the dancers again as they gazed up at her. Americans were often bemused—even amused—at the sight of an Australian girl playing jazz saxophone. To them, she was like a sideshow curiosity and, after sets at the Trocadero, she usually enjoyed being surrounded by Yanks, who'd ask her where she'd learned to blow as well as she did. But she'd never performed in front of black Americans before, and was unsure of how they'd react.

Martin gave her a nudge in the ribs and she cleared her throat, parted her feet—mirroring him—and they began to play. Gazing out at the dancers, she was astonished to see so many variations of skin colour—blue-black and mahogany, milky tea and sepia—all marbling together in swirls of rising smoke. And there were none of the waltzes and cha-chas of the Trocadero Ballroom. As the band hit the second chorus, women were sliding between the parted legs of their partners. Pleated skirts snapped in time with the music while maps of perspiration formed on the backs of the men's shirts. She caught sight of Roma, dancing around the hall with a short black American, her loose dress flapping around her like a flag in a gale.

Merv counted in "Bugle Call Rag," an up-tempo tune that Pearl didn't know very well. She wasn't sure of the melody, and the pace was so fast she could barely keep up. Martin was already on top of the beat, blowing effortlessly into his tenor as if he'd played the song every day of his life. As she struggled to keep up she sensed the reed in her mouthpiece softening between her lips; it felt like a limp, useless piece of rubber and was ruining her tone. She tried halving the tempo, then just blowing harmony, but to her dismay a couple of wrong notes escaped the bell of her sax. The band was into the fourth chorus and next it would be Pearl's turn to take a solo and she was wondering how on earth she'd get through it when there was a commotion down the back of the hall. A group of servicemen stood hooting and whistling, and then another tenor saxophone suddenly began howling.

Through the half-light, she couldn't quite see who was playing it; she could only hear the runs between the registers that were fast and sharp and accenting the back beat. The sound seemed to be coming from everywhere, up through the floorboards, from the very walls themselves, even bouncing off the pressed tin ceiling. The paper streamers on the windows shook.

The crowd parted and now she could see a glowing tenor glid-ing through the room like a beacon through fog, followed by a tall man who was blowing into it. He was playing so loudly that Pearl could hardly hear the pianist's chord changes and finally gave up. The man swayed jauntily from side to side as if the instrument were his dance partner. As he walked up the stairs to the stage the dancers slowed and then stopped alto-gether to stand and watch.

He was well over six feet, wearing standard American mil-itary trousers and shirt. Like all of the men at the club, he was clean-shaven, his black curly hair cropped short. His skin, however, was fairer than most: a pale walnut colour that shone with perspiration. Pearl stepped sideways in order to see him better as he gazed straight out into the coloured lights, a sad, pensive expression on his face.

At the end of the next chorus, the crowd was cheering so enthusiastically that he went on to play another. Soon his solo was dipping and surging between registers. At one point he was making a hard staccato sound as if he were repeatedly pecking a woman on the lips, and there was something he was doing with his diaphragm—she couldn't tell what—that allowed him to play with one long, seamless breath. Sometimes his saxophone growled, then whimpered, then soared up into a crescendo of triple-tongued high notes. Pearl had never heard anyone play like this, not even on the many American records she'd heard.

She was in such awe of him that she forgot to come in with the band; or, rather, she was too intimidated. The sensation was like stage fright, but even worse. She edged away from the other musicians, trying to be inconspicuous, but as she stepped into the shadows she lost her footing and stumbled down the stairs of the bandstand. She heard the crowd laughing, could see the smirks on the faces of passing dancers, including Roma, who had kicked off her shoes and was now dancing with a taller man.

Pearl dumped her sax against its open case and plunged into the crowd, mortified, willing herself to disappear. The band was wailing now, and above it all was the triumphant howl of that damn saxophone.

Over the music, Pearl heard her brother call her name, but she ignored him, rushing through the tobacco-coloured light toward the exit.

Outside on the covered veranda, she leaned against the wall and tried to catch her breath. She'd never felt like such an idiot—not even during her sight-reading exams at the Conservatorium, or her first professional gig with Miss Molly's Sunshine Orchestra. Even her bandleader at the Trocadero had led her to believe that she was something of a musical prodigy, but now she suspected that he'd been humouring her because she was a girl, or that she was only what her father liked to call *a big fish in a little pool*.

The band finished playing "Bugle Call Rag" and she could hear a purr of applause from inside the dance hall. She shivered and rubbed her arms, feeling stupid for having left her alto behind; she couldn't go home without walking back inside to fetch it. Perhaps Martin would bring her sax out to her, or she could ask the woman at the desk to collect it—but then the man who'd been playing the wild solo suddenly appeared beside her, holding out her case.

Up close, he was about half a foot taller than she was, and she had to tilt her head back to look him in the face. Standing in the light pooling out from the hallway, his skin didn't seem as light as it had in the dance hall—more like the colour of wet sand. His teeth gleamed white as he smiled, and she noticed he had beautiful, unnaturally long lashes framing a pair of grey-blue eyes.

"Sunshine," he announced, "you play a mean axe!" His accent—all melodious, curly diphthongs—was straight from the American South.

She reached for the sax, but he grabbed hold of her wrist with his free hand.

"Bad reed," he told her. "Happens to the best."

She wasn't sure if he was joking or not, but she nodded.

He put down her saxophone, pulled out a pack of cigarettes and held it out to her.

She hesitated. She didn't smoke but, looking up into his eyes again, she felt a stab of excitement. Wanting to feel grown up and worldly, she pulled one from the pack and placed it between her lips.

He struck a match and lit first her cigarette and then his own. For a few moments they stood facing each other, Pearl taking shallow, tentative drags.

"Where'd you learn to play like that?" Smoke leaked from her nostrils, and she began to cough.

"Blow it out through your mouth," he suggested, smiling. "Otherwise you'll choke."

She snorted and took another short drag.

"Where I come from," he said, glancing over the wet lawn, "everyone plays. Ain't nothing else much to do."

She deliberately tapped on her cigarette, even though it didn't need ashing. "And where's that?" she asked.

"Looozy-anna!" he drawled, then leaned in closer to her and whispered, "Home of the devil's music." He flared his nostrils and widened his eyes, and she began to laugh.

"New Orleans?"

He shook his head. "Close. Grew up on a farm near the Mississippi border. But I been to New Orleans plenty of times. First time when I was seven. Went with my cousin. That was when I first heard King Oliver play."

At the sound of those magic words, "King Oliver," Pearl almost stopped breathing. She'd only ever heard the great cornettist on her bandleader's old records.

"You heard *the* King Oliver?"

He nodded. "On a riverboat."

"The bloke who taught Louis Armstrong?"

"The one and only."

The cigarette smouldered in her hand, forgotten. "What did he sound like?"

"Good," he said simply. "He'd turn a tune upside down, inside out, slap it against the wall, and then bounce it off the ceiling."

He flicked his butt into a nearby metal tray and Pearl copied him but missed, and had to chase her butt as it rolled across the veranda.

Embarrassed, she glanced at the musician who, she could see, was trying not to laugh.

"Sunshine," he said, "what's your name?"

"Pearl."

"Pearl, my name is James." He held out his hand and she

noticed how big it was, and that his palm was not the same colour as his fingers, more a musky pink, like the underside of a tongue. "James Washington."

When she shook his hand it felt like a big, warm mitten around hers. "How long've you been in Sydney, James?"

"Nearly a week. But they've had me stuck in camp till tonight and I ain't seen no sights or nothing." He leaned in and tucked a lock of hair behind her ear. "'Cept you, of course. You're a pretty good sight."

Pearl felt her face growing hot.

"And you sound great, too," he added. "You really wail on that alto."

She didn't really believe him but appreciated the praise. Smiling to herself, she glimpsed a shadowy couple near the hedge, kissing.

Pearl started to mumble, "Thanks," when James cut her off.

"Hey, Sunshine," he said, "what are you doing tomorrow night? What's say you and me go out?"

She was so surprised she didn't know what to say. If her mother found out she were planning to date a black American she'd probably have a stroke. She picked up her sax case and, stalling for time, gazed into the garden. With a start, she recognised the embracing couple. It was her brother, and his hands had disappeared under Roma's dress.

It struck her that her twin was behaving exactly as he wished, without worrying what their mother or anyone else thought. Besides, Pearl had never felt so curious about another person before. Maybe it was his accent or the way he looked into her eyes when he spoke. The way he blew his sax.

"Do you like fish and chips?" she asked.

He tilted his head to one side and said, "I like 'em if you do."

"Do you know where Circular Quay is?"

"Seen it on the map. Right by the harbour."

From the corner of her eye she saw Martin pressing Roma against the trunk of a tree. "Let's meet at wharf five," she said. "Say, six o'clock?"

"Make it six-thirty," he replied. "And don't be late."

And then he leaned down and kissed her briefly on the top of her head. Her scalp tingled at the touch of his lips.

2

"So what's with the girl?" asked Pearl, as she and her brother walked home.

It was after 1 AM and the rain had stopped. The streets were quiet except for the distant barking of a dog.

"Girl?" asked Martin, swinging his sax case as they crossed Bourke Street and headed toward Taylor Square. "What girl?"

Pearl thumped him on the arm.

"I can't help it if women find me irresistible," he declared, performing a little twirling dance just ahead of her, his free arm rising and falling like a wing. A gust of wind swept up the street, causing his coat to billow. He spun around again and clicked his heels together.

"I'm going out with that sax player tomorrow night," she said casually. "*He* asked *me*."

Martin dropped back to his regular walking pace. "Well, I'm going out with Roma. To the pictures."

They rounded the corner into Oxford Street.

"James is from the South. Near New Orleans."

"Yeah? Well, Roma's from the bush," he said. "A mission out Dubbo way. Lives with her aunty now in Redfern."

"James reckons I'm pretty."

"Roma reckons I should be in the movies," Martin countered.

"What as—Tarzan's ape?"

Martin swung an arm at her, but she ducked and ran across the street, laughing.

It was nearly two when they reached the Victorian terrace in Potts Point where they lived with their parents and grandmother. Their mother, Clara, and father, Aubrey, had lived in the house overlooking Sydney Harbour since 1920, which they'd bought in order to raise a family. (Clara was a drummer who also doubled as a singer/dancer in a half-man, half-woman routine; Aub was a tenor saxophonist and ukulele player who also wrote and sang his own songs.) Clara fell pregnant three years later, and Aub established a taxidermy business that he operated from the basement to bring in extra money. The house was also a haven for what Aubrey had dubbed "Clara's strays." Currently there was an old ventriloquist, Mr. Bones, who'd come to dinner three years before and had never left. He now slept in the attic, along with his doll, and often helped Clara with the housework. Another stray was Mikey Michaels, a kid about four years old whose widowed mother, a neighbour, had to work nights at a factory to support him. Mikey spent most of his time in the Willises' kitchen and slept on a canvas cot in the parlour.

The Willis home was a crammed museum of antique furniture and ornaments, relics from every bush town and foreign country in which Clara and Aub had performed: Persian carpets, a cedar dining table, oversized velvet chairs, gloomy oil paintings, an upright walnut piano. The main room of the house—the front parlour—boasted a large marble fireplace and stained-glass windows. An avid card player, Clara had a bridge table set up in one corner. And, of course, there were many examples of their father's obsession with taxidermy: a stuffed six-foot emu stood frozen in the foyer like some weird, feathered bellhop; a kookaburra with a foot-long wingspan was suspended by fishing line above the piano; and in the corner a Tasmanian tiger with large glassy eyes sat hunched, baring his sharp white teeth.

Once in bed, Pearl found it hard to sleep, despite the late hour. Had she made a mistake in agreeing to go out with James? He was a wonderful musician, and certainly was friendly—but maybe those were the very reasons she was feeling confused. Why was he so interested in going out with her: a girl wearing what looked like a wet bird's nest on her head and who couldn't get through a chorus of "Bugle Call Rag"? A girl who didn't even know how to smoke a cigarette? Maybe he was lonely, she reasoned. She remembered the way he'd kissed the top of her head, and her scalp began to tingle again. She was turning eighteen the following week and had never been kissed by a man on the lips—not unless you counted an Indian steward on an ocean liner who'd stuck his tongue into her mouth when she was eleven. As she drifted off to sleep she decided that even though she barely knew Private James Washington, she was determined to meet up with him.

*   *   *

The next morning, when the twins appeared in the kitchen for breakfast, Clara was shelling peas into a bowl. Mr. Bones was curled up and snoring on the chaise longue in the parlour while little Mikey Michaels kneeled beside him stroking the old man's shiny shoes.

"So what the dickens were you two up to last night?" Clara asked, not glancing up from the bowl.

Pearl and Martin only had to flash each other a look over the kitchen table to agree that they should lie. Clara didn't approve of Pearl "gallivanting all over town," as she put it, with her brother. It didn't look right—a girl her age. Her own mother, Lulu, had chaperoned her—Clara—throughout all her teenage performances and tours until she was officially engaged to Aubrey and had a ring on her finger.

"Pearl was over at Nora's place," said Martin automatically. Nora Barnes, the drummer of the Trocadero's girls' band, was Pearl's best friend and confidante, and lived nearby in Darlinghurst.

"Martin was showing a Negro soldier around the Cross," said Pearl.

Clara frowned and fixed them with a hard stare. She was a plump woman in her early fifties. Her chubby face was framed by short curls the colour of rust, but which the Miracle Hair Dye Company called Temptation Red. "Then why did I hear you come in together?"

Pearl and Martin locked eyes again. "The black soldier and I picked up Pearl from Nora's place," explained Martin. "So I could walk her home."

Clara turned her back to open the icebox, and Martin winked at Pearl.

"And the Negro met Nora," added Pearl. "They got on really well." She glanced into the parlour and saw that Mikey was tying the laces of Mr. Bones's shoes together.

Martin sipped his tea. "Actually, they're going out on a date tonight."

Pearl pulled a face at Martin. "And they asked us to come along."

Mr. Bones stirred and rubbed his eyes.

Clara pulled some butter from the fridge and put it on the table. "Why would they want you two along on their date?"

"The Negro plays bridge," Martin explained, causing Pearl to choke on a laugh. "We'll be playing doubles."

At that moment Mr. Bones stood up and, as Mikey ducked to one side, took one small step and fell to the floor. Clara rushed to his side. By the time she'd chastised Mikey, helped Mr. Bones to his feet, and mixed him a hot toddy to calm his nerves, the twins' tall tale was forgotten.

Pearl still felt embarrassed about her sloppy playing at the Booker T. Washington Club the night before and so she spent the afternoon in her bedroom, practising "Bugle Call Rag" over and over again. Later, Martin joined her and they played a few duets. By the time they noticed the sun was going down, it was after six o'clock and they were both running late.

Within minutes, she and Martin were rushing out of the house and, once they were out of eyeshot of their mother, they parted ways. Martin, who was meeting Roma at the William Street tram stop, ran up Victoria Street. Pearl leaped down the stairs from Potts Point to the dockside slums of Woolloomooloo, and on into the Botanic Gardens, which ran down to Circular Quay. But when she reached the gates at the western end of the park, they were already locked.

The thin bars looked like a series of upturned spears, with razor-sharp points. Desperate, she scaled them and hoisted her leg over the top, only to slip. Her dress snagged on an iron spike, tearing the skirt, and the stockings she'd sewn from an old lace curtain ripped. She felt a stab of pain as she fell and landed on the concrete path on the other side. There was now an L-shaped wound carved into her shin, beaded with blood and dirt.

When she reached wharf five she was late; the only people there were a man sitting on the ground, facing the harbour, with a scrawny, bald cockatoo on a leash, an old woman feeding bread to a screeching flock of seagulls, and a pinched-faced boy grimly holding on to a length of fishing line that had been cast over the side of the wharf. She waited five minutes . . . ten . . . The woman ran out of bread and the seagulls flew away. The boy gave up and wound in his line. The man on the ground began muttering to the cockatoo, which crawled up and perched on his knee, squawking, "*Shut up! Shut up!*"

Pearl felt disappointment well up. It was her first real date and she'd ruined it. Panicking, she turned in a circle, willing James to appear from behind a pylon or to step out of a taxi. She realised she had no idea how to find him again. Her upswept hairstyle was falling down in a mess of bobby pins. Her dress and stockings were ruined and her left leg was throbbing. A drunk lurched up and propositioned her, so she crossed the street and, feeling hungry and sorry for herself, headed toward the Emperor, the fish-and-chip shop where she'd planned to take James. She walked through the door and into the tart smell of vinegar and frying batter. She gazed up at the blackboard above the oil vats, where the menu and prices were chalked. She was trying to decide whether she wanted potato scallops or a battered sausage when she glanced down the back of the shop and noticed James sitting at one of the Laminex tables, a teapot and cup in front of him. He was wearing his uniform and cap, the brass buttons glowing like Christmas globes, his grey eyes fixed on her.

Pearl's heart hammered hard as she approached him. He was as handsome as she remembered him, and under the electric light he seemed as calm and dignified as a statue of a saint. Before she could blurt out an apology, he rocked back in his chair, smiling, and surveyed her torn dress.

She tensed, feeling ridiculous. "Sorry," she said. "I tried to take a short cut and got locked in the gardens."

He took a serviette from the table and, with a nod at her leg, said, "Looks like a long cut to me." He licked the serviette and dabbed the gash on her shin.

The gesture further embarrassed her. To change the subject she said, "I was going to introduce you to fish and chips. Do you still want some?"

He tried to look serious, but she could see that he was amused. "Yes, ma'am."

Pearl backed away from him, leaving him holding the white serviette speckled with blood. "Two fish and chips with salt and vinegar, please," she called to the Chinese man behind the counter.

Within minutes their dinners arrived, wrapped with an inner lining of butcher's paper and then pages of old newspaper. Pearl tore a hole in the top of the package. James did the same and steam escaped from inside. He reached into the parcel. "Chips, huh?" he said. "At home we call these fries."

They left the shop, carrying the fish and chips, and strolled down to the quay. A ferry blasted its horn, and on the spur of the moment Pearl said, "Let's catch it!" They bought tickets and sat on the deck, watching seagulls dip and glide across the harbour as they ate their food. To the east they could see the lights strung above troop ships docked at Garden Island. The ferry creaked and rocked. Suddenly a wave lurched over the deck, and they laughed as they were sprayed with water.

"Maybe we should've done this during the day," she said, "so you could've seen more of the city."

"I can see you all right," he said. "That's the main thing."

The ferry began turning to the left, heading toward the Harbour Bridge. James put his package of chips to one side and rubbed his hands, then leaned back and gazed at the lights glancing off the harbour. "Right now, in the States, it's the middle of the day. Actually, it's the middle of yesterday. Funny, huh?"

She sensed he was probably homesick and touched his sleeve. "Well, they're just living in the past."

He put his hand on hers. "That's right, Sunshine. Now, we're in the month of May, ain't we?"

She nodded.

"And right now it's fall—I mean autumn—right?"

"Soon it'll be winter."

"And back home, it'll be summer," he said, shivering. "Lightning bugs. Town parades. Sleeping on the back porch to catch a breeze from the river."

When Pearl had been eleven she'd sailed to Ceylon with her mother in an all girls' band. It was the depths of the Depression—1935—and for a year the band was the family's only source of income. The travel had taught her that there were several time zones around the world, but she'd never contemplated the idea of opposite seasons. It was odd to think that, at this very moment, in America, people were eating lunch and probably fanning themselves against the afternoon heat.

"Here summer means the beach, cricket, and lots of cold beer." She squeezed his hand. "You'll love it."

As the ferry chugged on toward the Milsons Point wharf, the gate of Luna Park amusement park loomed ahead, a giant grinning clown's face flanked by towers. The facade was as tall as a seven-storey building and had once pulsed with neon lights, but since the Japanese had bombed Darwin in February, the bulbous eyes no longer flashed and the eyebrows never moved. From where they were sitting, Pearl could see the sprawling wooden skeleton of the Big Dipper roller coaster with its wide, feminine curves, and the Arabian minaret on top of the fun house, draped in a necklace of muted yellow electric bulbs.

"How long does it take to sail to Australia?"

James groaned and crossed his legs. "Put it this way," he replied, "when I left San Francisco I was still in kindergarten."

She nudged him playfully. "No, seriously. How long?"

He pursed his lips. "Little over five weeks. Like sailing to the moon. 'Cept when you get off the boat all the moon people speak English in a funny accent and drink lots of tea."

The ferry slowed down and bobbed against the wharf. Pearl jumped to her feet. "Well, we moon people like to have fun, too!" She led James down the ferry plank and they walked over to the gate of Luna Park, entering beneath the clown's upper denture made from plaster of Paris. It was growing late but there were still a lot of people milling about, mostly American servicemen and local girls. A big structure called Noah's Ark creaked from side to side.

James smiled and said that the park reminded him of Coney Island, in Brooklyn. After he'd moved to New York, he'd go out there almost every weekend. Pearl told him that her mother and father had once performed at Coney Island, when they'd toured the States, before she and her brother were born. According to family legend, her mother had gone into labour with the twins while she was playing percussion in the pit orchestra of the Tivoli Theatre in Sydney. By the end of the first act of "The Flying Dutchman" Pearl was bursting out into the world, feet first, between the bass drum and the upright piano, three weeks premature. The stage manager cut the cord with a pair of scissors, and then Pearl, apparently, did the strangest thing: She didn't scream or cry with her first inhalation. Instead, she opened her mouth and laughed. The second act was postponed until Martin arrived ten minutes later, head first in the normal way.

By the time she'd finished the story, James was laughing so hard he was doubled over. "You're kidding me, moon girl. You're making that up."

"I'm not!" she insisted. "You can ask my mother."

"Sunshine, you planning on taking me home?"

"Only if you're good," she joked. She led him into the midway, which was decorated with Chinese lanterns and coloured flags. He paused to watch a fire-eater swallow a neon tube. When a sidekick flicked a switch, the tube lit up and they could see a silvery X-ray of the man's ribs and the permutations of his upper intestine.

"Damn," he murmured to Pearl, "you wouldn't want to see what's inside me!"

Pearl patted his flat stomach. "Fish and chips!"

At the shooting gallery, the lines of waddling ducks had been replaced with the heads of Japanese soldiers, made out of tin and painted yellow, already pockmarked with dents and holes. James pointed the rifle and fired, and within moments he'd won Pearl a glittery Kewpie doll on a cane. In the penny arcade they came across a machine that gave electric shocks. Pearl grabbed James's hand, dropped a sixpence into the slot, and with her free hand took hold of the metal handle. A bolt zigzagged through her limbs and out through her fingers and on into James and they were now conjoined and vibrating together and the sensation was so euphoric that they erupted with a kind of stuttering laughter.

As she glanced at her reflection in the door of the Mirror Maze she noticed her ripped clothing, the torn lace stockings, and when they came upon a fairy floss stand she ducked behind it, where no one could see her, and kicked off her shoes. James, curious, followed her. Winking at him, she stuck her hand up under the skirt of her dress, then unrolled the stockings and pulled them from her feet.

"A souvenir from Sydney," she said, pushing the balled-up pieces of lace into his hands.

He paused for a moment and regarded the gift, shaking his head, then slipped the stockings into his trouser pocket. She linked her arm through his but when a pimple-faced man selling fairy floss glared at them James pulled away from her.

They boarded the ghost train, climbing into the last carriage. The seat was so small that when they sat down their thighs rubbed against each other. Pearl's breathing grew shallow. The train roared into the tunnel, and an enormous mechanical bat swooped overhead, causing her to duck and cower against James. Eerie groans leaked through walls. A skeleton appeared out of nowhere and rattled its rickety joints. The gruesome faces, the surreal, wailing voices, and the banging of coffin lids made Pearl's heart hammer. In the green light shining from a werewolf's mouth, James suddenly turned and put his lips against hers, and then her tongue found his and James's hands began to follow the lines of her body. The citrus smell of his hair cream was in her throat. A vampire with bloody fangs leaped in front of them and disappeared when the carriage took a hairpin turn. James pressed his face against her breasts, traced her collarbone and neck with his fingers. His touch felt as light as breath, as sunshine.

The carriage plunged through a set of swinging exit doors and they pulled away from each other. As the train slowed Pearl was dizzy and flushed. She'd sensed there was something special about James but she hadn't expected her body to respond to him so quickly. It was as if her very being had made a decision before consulting her emotions—or maybe they were the same thing and she just hadn't realised it before. All she knew for sure was that the feeling was filling her legs, her hips, travelling up her spine—and whatever it was, she wanted more.

"Hey, buddy!" James called to the attendant. "We'll have another go!" As the other passengers clambered from the train James tossed him a sixpence.

The man narrowed his eyes and regarded them both, smirking. "Sorry, mate." He shook his head. "We're shutting down for the night."

Pearl could see the fun house had already closed and couples were strolling arm in arm toward the gates.

"He's been in New Guinea for a year," she lied. "Coral Sea. It's his first day of R and R."

The attendant sighed, glancing about.

James riffled in his pocket. He pulled out Pearl's stockings, then extracted a pound note and slipped it into the man's hand.

The attendant's eyes bulged. He glanced at James and back at the note then cranked the metal control lever. Within moments James and Pearl were once more gliding into the funereal darkness. Again they pressed against one another. His mouth on hers was warm and wet. Pearl lost herself in the noise of ghosts and dying werewolves. The cries echoing through the tunnel increased her restlessness, causing her to crave James more. She could have spent the entire night endlessly circling through the haunted tunnel, allowing his hands to grow familiar with her body, enjoying the shivers that shimmered through her like light. But when the carriage took the hairpin turn this time, above the screams of banshees, a siren began howling through the tunnel.

James shuddered and looked about. The piercing noise rose into a crescendo before dropping for what seemed like a breath and then rising again. Skeletons and werewolves sprang from the walls. The train continued to bang and crash through the tunnel while the siren howled louder. Pearl was too breathless even to cry out. The carriage plunged through the swinging doors and back into the open air, where they saw people yelling and running for cover. The train was supposed to slow down and stop, but the attendant had already abandoned his post and it continued to barrel along the rails, faster and faster. The siren rose in waves as the train hurtled back into the tunnel to repeat its race through the house of horror, crashing through swinging doors, rushing past gaunt, waxy faces dripping with blood. Pearl felt James's arms around her, holding her tight. The ghosts and monsters seemed sinister now, threatening.

"We're going to have to jump!" he shouted over the din.

He stood up and pulled her up with him. When the train barrelled through the exit doors for the third time, he wrapped his arms around her and yelled, "*Now!*" and before she had time to hesitate they were leaping from the carriage and sailing through the air. They hit the ground, but he took the brunt of the fall with his shoulder, and when she rolled off him the only pain she felt was from grazes on her elbow and knee.

The lights of the park had been extinguished, and almost everyone had disappeared. In their absence the sound of the siren was even louder and more foreboding. Pearl grabbed James's hand and, half running, half limping, led him around the brick wall that enclosed the ghost train ride.

The siren reached a fever pitch, and searchlights began sweeping the sky. They scooted back around the building, to the centre of the park, looking frantically for shelter. For all the talk around Sydney about an impending Japanese invasion,

Pearl had never imagined this, the awful whorl of dread in her stomach, being so far away from her family. She imagined enemy warships lurking in the darkness, guns angled toward the coast, scores of invading soldiers marching through the city, the hum of a distant aeroplane about to drop a fatal bomb. She thought of crawling back into the ghost train, but at that moment something exploded across the harbour, so loud and close it sounded as if the Harbour Bridge itself were being bombed.

She screamed and staggered backward, almost losing her footing. James grabbed her by the arm and pushed her up into a tub-shaped carriage of a ride called the Tumblebug. He crawled in after her and they huddled together on a seat shaped like a crescent moon. The carriage was suspended at the end of one of the eight metal arms that craned out from the centre of the ride. When it was operating, the arms moved up and down, circling out over the water and back, while the carriages spun in crazy circles; now, however, the carriage rocked gently in the breeze. Another explosion thundered across the harbour; a flare forked the sky like lightning, and a sob began deep in Pearl's throat. James drew her to him and held her tenderly, as if she might break, murmuring words she could barely hear over the deafening blasts.

The air-raid siren continued to wail. All sorts of sounds were carried across the water: shouts, car horns, barking dogs. She felt sure she would never see her family again, her friends, the house she had been raised in. She would die without ever having felt the sensation of a man inside her, without her body ever knowing what it was like to make love.

Gunfire stuttered.

"Don't worry," James murmured. "We're gonna be all right."

She suddenly turned and pressed her lips against his again. She found herself pulling at the buttons of his uniform, touching the bulge between his legs, but he grasped her wrist and pulled her hand away. She was bawling now, not caring anymore. She clambered onto his lap and sat facing him, one knee on either side of his hips, their bellies touching.

Another explosion boomed across the harbour, and then the coughing fit of a machine gun, closer now.

She dropped to her knees on the floor of the carriage and, squeezing herself between his thighs, pushed her face into his chest, like a child. James was trembling now, his hands on her hair, her shoulders. She found the zipper at her side and pulled at it. A moment later the dress was over her head and flung onto the ground below. She took his hands and cupped them against the lace of her brassiere. She was so dizzy for a moment she thought she might pass out. It was the same sensation that bled through her when she was about to go onstage—the warmth between her legs rising into her belly like dye seeping through a bolt of cloth. He eased his fingers inside her bra and held her right breast. As the howl of the siren rose and fell she could sense his short, sharp gasps. She went to unbuckle his belt but again he stopped her. Instead, he guided her down onto the floor of the carriage. In the flicker of a passing searchlight she saw him unzip his fly. Then he slipped off the seat and lowered himself on top of her.

For months, for years, she'd wondered what this would be like: the weight of a man against her, his mouth on her breast. She was shaking with fear and excitement. When she looked up she could see the ink-coloured sky with stars that looked like tiny hands. Another explosion thundered through the city and their carriage shook. He didn't remove her knickers, but merely grabbed the gusset and yanked the crotch to one side. When he nudged himself into her, it hurt a little, like a menstrual cramp widening through her groin. He must have sensed her tensing, for he slowed down then and moved into her gradually, in such small and gentle increments that she relaxed and found her breath again, and it wasn't long before her body was moving in a gentle undulation with his and something close to pleasure tingled up through her, radiating into her stomach, her breasts. The carriage began to sway back and forth until it was swinging in half-circles to the rhythm of their hips.

A soft, velvet hush enveloped the harbour. Pearl could hear water lapping against the nearby pontoon and the flutter of seagulls. The searchlights were gone, the sirens had faded, and the city was now cloaked in darkness. Still lying on the floor of the carriage, beneath the warmth of his jacket, Pearl folded into James and they dozed for a while, occasionally shifting against one another. When she awakened fully sometime close to dawn, she was surprised to realise that not only were they both unharmed, but she felt more alive than ever.

James kissed the base of her throat.

"Now that we're not dead," he murmured, "I've got something to tell you."

She tensed, wary of the note of warning in his voice. He pulled away from her and sat up on the seat of the carriage, helping her to sit up beside him. She could see the outline of his face in the moonlight and the bright whites of his eyes and teeth. She thought she knew what was coming: He was being shipped out tomorrow or maybe he had a girlfriend back in the States, or even a wife. Children, perhaps. She was preparing herself for the worst, yet she now felt closer to this near-stranger than anyone else in the world, including her brother.

"This is all new for me," he said finally. She wondered what he was referring to—the bombs? The sex? Being in Sydney?

He took her hand and held it as he gazed across the water. "And I guess it's new for you, too." He bit his lip, still not looking at her. "So let's keep this to ourselves, okay? At least until we know each other better."

She swallowed, trying to find the right words. She wasn't as self-conscious about their lovemaking as he obviously was, which she found surprising. Was he embarrassed by her? Or even ashamed? She felt her face and neck reddening.

He must have sensed her distress because he rested a hand on her shoulder and gave it a squeeze. "Folks back home told me about Aussie girls, but I never thought I'd find myself one as gorgeous as you. Prettiest package I ever seen. And you got talent, too."

He rubbed the back of her neck, and she began to feel calmer. Across the water, below the steel struts of the bridge, she could see a sliver of light on the horizon, the dappled surfaces of the harbour luminous and green with the early rays of dawn.

She suddenly had a crazy idea and blurted it out before she could stop herself. "James, will you teach me? Teach me to play like you?"

He said nothing, as if further embarrassed by the predicament he now found himself in. He leaned over and picked up her brassiere from the floor of the carriage.

She remembered with shame her clumsy solo at the Booker T. Washington Club, the bum notes, the dragging tempo. She jumped from the carriage and looked around for her discarded dress. It was on the ground, over by the ride's generator. She slipped it on and began doing up the buttons, in spite of the fact that he still held her bra. One of her shoes was over by another carriage and she shoved her foot into it, then clumped around in the half-light looking for the other.

"If you want me to teach you," he called out to her finally, "we're gonna have to go back to basics. Break some of those bad habits."

She paused, hardly breathing, waiting for him to continue, but he didn't speak, just fumbled in the pocket of his trousers.

When he found what he was looking for he held it up. It was small and blond-coloured, wrapped in cellophane.

"You don't even know how to put a reed into your mouthpiece properly. Yours was too loose." He gave her the reed he was holding. "We'll start with that."

They walked back to the city across the Harbour Bridge. The buildings on the other side were wreathed in mist, but they all still seemed to be standing. Pearl could make out the grey dome of the Observatory on the Millers Point hill, the clock tower of the general post office, the spire of the Mariners' Church, and the wharfie pubs opposite Circular Quay.

She was still rattled by the bombings, could still hear explosions echoing in her ears, but as she strolled beside James she felt as if she were fuelled by some potent substance her body was manufacturing for the first time. It wasn't just the electric lunacy of love, or lust, but something more indefinable. James had agreed to give her lessons, whenever he could secure leave passes from the camp, and it was this, coupled with everything they'd shared a few hours before, that sent a thrill through her.

He'd been adamant about two things, though: first, that she had to practise what he taught her at least four hours a day; second, she needed a new saxophone. Her father's old vaudeville alto was in terrible condition; James had noticed at the Booker T. Club the tarnished metal, the worn pads, the two lower keys held in place with rubber bands.

"If you're serious, Pearl," he told her, "you gotta get yourself a good axe. Not some piece of shit your daddy used to play."

"Okay," she murmured, knowing that she'd never be able to afford one.

As they neared the south side of the bridge, they could hear orders being shouted from the decks of naval ships. Boats zigzagged across the harbour, leaving trails of silver foam. Pearl asked James about America, about the musicians he'd heard there. "Have you ever heard Artie Shaw?" she said. "He's my favourite bandleader." James replied that he'd not only met the famous clarinettist, he'd jammed with him once in upstate New York.

Pearl was speechless. He then told her in a nonchalant voice—oh, as casual as you like—that he'd also played with Count Basie's band in Kansas City, along with the great saxophonist Lester Young. He'd toured the South with Benny

Goodman. He'd met the great trombonist Jack Teagarden in New York and had got drunk with him in a bar in Harlem. And one day he literally ran into the famous hunchback drummer Chick Webb, who was walking with his head down through the foyer of the Apollo Theater.

She, in turn, told him about the first time she'd ever heard an American jazz band.

"Sonny Clay's Colored Idea," she recalled. "A ten-piece band, twenty-five singers and dancers."

Pearl and Martin were not even four years old when Aubrey took them to the Tivoli Theatre. Pearl had a distinct memory of the moment the theatre curtain began to rise and the big, irreverent sound of the band burst into the auditorium. And she was astonished to see the skin of all the musicians was almost as dark as the black keys on a piano. She sat holding on to the velvet armrests of her seat, mesmerised by the fast, whimsical beat of the music and the appearance of the men who made it.

"It was the first Negro jazz band ever to tour Australia," she added. "And I knew on that very afternoon what I wanted to be."

James smiled. "You wanted to be coloured?"

"No!" She elbowed him. "I knew I wanted to be a jazz musician."

A few years later, she and Martin and Charlie Styles, a little boy who lived up the road and played the cornet, would pretend that they had formed their own band and would walk single file through Kings Cross, banging pots and pans and taking turns blowing into the boy's horn.

It began to rain. Pearl and James ran down the concrete stairs and into a tunnel that sloped toward a street in The

Rocks. She stopped and pushed him against the tiled wall and kissed him. They were interrupted by the sound of footsteps and glimpsed a figure silhouetted against the other opening of the tunnel. James abruptly pushed her away. "Not here, baby," he murmured. "Not now."

She was surprised by his sudden change of mood.

"Where's the nearest train station?" he asked.

"Why?" she asked playfully. "You got a date with another girl?"

He clearly wasn't amused by the joke. "I got to get back to camp."

They crossed the street and rounded a corner pub.

"How about you meet me after my gig tomorrow night?" she suggested. He was walking slightly ahead of her and she had to stride to catch up. "I know a café in the Cross that lets black people in. Some of them even play in the band!"

As they passed a row of dirty brick terraces, James replied, "I'll try."

Pearl felt panicky now, wondering if she'd ever see him again. "Well, what about next Sunday?" she persisted. "It's my birthday. And my brother's. We're having a Sunday lunch."

James shoved his hands in his pockets. "Will your parents be there?"

"Of course," she replied. "And my grandmother, too."

He merely pursed his lips, still not looking at her. "We'll see," he said finally. "I'll see if I can get away."

3

It was around half past eight by the time she reached her street in Potts Point. She'd already led James to Town Hall Station, had handed him a note detailing her address and the time of her birthday lunch and the café where they were to meet the following night. They said good-bye with a handshake and, before he disappeared down the stairs to the platform, a brief wave. She desperately wanted to see him again but was still unsure about how he truly felt about her.

Even though it had begun to rain again, she noticed some of her neighbours were moving furniture out of their flats and houses and loading them onto trucks.

The rain grew heavier. Pearl dashed down the block, suddenly now wanting to be home with her family and in front of the fire.

When she walked through the front gate—her stockings gone, her clothes torn, wet, and sticking to her skin—Clara appeared in the open front doorway and cried, "Thank God you're alive!"

She rushed down the path and threw her arms around Pearl, then stepped back and looked with horror at the rip in her dress.

"Those mongrel Japs! They did this to you? I'll kill 'em. I'll kill the bastards!"

"No, Mum," said Pearl. "I'm all right. I'm just—"Clara bundled her up the stairs and onto the veranda. Aub came racing up from the basement and hugged her tightly. Martin followed him onto the veranda, an unlit cigarette between his lips. He, too, was soaking wet, and when he walked his damp shoes squelched.

"This one just got home now, too!" Clara nodded at Martin. "I've been worried sick."

Martin glanced at Pearl's dishevelled state and joked, "Been out wrestling Japs, Burly?"

"You don't know the half of it!" She blurted out about her time at Luna Park, the crushing noise of the bombs, the Tumblebug ride she'd sheltered in all night.

"I thought you two were playing bridge last night," said Clara sharply. "With Nora and that Negro bloke."

Pearl shot Martin a panicked look. She'd forgotten about the ruse she and Martin had cooked up.

"Well, we did," explained Martin. "For a while." He held out his cigarette to Aub, who lit it with a match. He took a couple of puffs while everyone—especially Pearl—waited for him to continue. "But the Negro got bored and wanted to go to the pictures—" He took another puff. "While Pearl and Nora wanted to go to Luna Park."

Pearl was so in awe of Martin's effortless fibbing, she had to stop herself from slapping him on the back and bursting into laughter.

"Oh?" said Clara. "And what movie did you see?"

"*Keep 'Em Flying*. Abbott and Costello," replied Martin automatically. "State Theatre. When the bombs started going off, the black guy and I thought they were part of the show. That's until the screen went black and the ushers herded everyone down to the basement." Martin casually flicked the ash from his cigarette and inhaled again. "We stayed there all night. Singing sea shanties."

He looked at Pearl pointedly and grinned. And she beamed back with gratitude. "And Nora and I," added Pearl, "we stayed in the Tumblebug all night. We were too scared to move until the sun came up."

Aub nodded and took Pearl's hand. "Good idea, love. At least you're safe."

Clara sighed and shook her head. "Well, let's get you two in front of the fire. Before you catch your death of cold." She bustled the twins and Aub through the front door and into the warmth of the parlour, where their grandmother, Lulu, was dozing in a rocking chair and Mikey Michaels was drawing a picture of a burning boat.

Aub turned on the radio for a news update. The reader's voice was low and grim as he read the latest report: Early the night before, three Japanese midget submarines had entered the harbour. They'd been able to escape detection by the magnetic indicator loop installed on the harbour floor. For several hours they'd cruised beneath the passing ferries. No precautions had been taken to black out the city because, at the time, there was no reason to assume that Sydney was under threat. Even the naval base, Garden Island, had sat like an open target, with hundreds of arc lamps flooding the harbour until they were finally extinguished. By then, however, it was too late, as Pearl so vividly remembered.

She realised that the Pacific war had never before edged so close to Australia's biggest city, but, as she digested the news, she felt oddly detached from the growing danger. Sure, it was a genuine threat on her city's doorstep, but that same threat had also brought James into her life, and she knew intuitively she would never have had one without the other.

The following day, as Pearl walked the wet streets of Kings Cross, she began to grow wary of the war again, especially when she heard the rumours that were spreading over shop counters, from open window to open window, over front gates and through paling fences. The story was that the surviving Japanese had escaped their submarines and were hiding in buildings at the lower end of Wylde Street, just around the corner from where she and her family lived. The enemy could attack at any moment.

"They'd bloody well better not!" she said to the fruit stall owner on Macleay Street who was rushing to pack up, throwing his produce into wooden crates. She certainly didn't want a bunch of invaders—or, indeed, anyone—interrupting her romance with Private James Washington.

She arrived home to find her street cluttered with trucks and vans. They were loaded with furniture and clothes from flats and bedsits. Sofas were strapped to the roofs of cars; chair legs poked out of windows; pots, pans, gramophones, side tables, and armoires were being thrown onto the backs of horse-drawn carts, in spite of the heavy rain. Everyone, it seemed, was intent on escaping the Japanese threat by moving to the Blue Mountains and beyond, to Lithgow, to Mudgee, even as far as Bourke.

Clara, instead of making arrangements to move, signed up for the local chapter of the Sydney People's Army, which gathered in the hall of Plunkett Street School, in Woolloomooloo. Around sunset, she returned home to boast that she'd learned how to make hand grenades out of jam tins, and how to bake eggless puddings. Aubrey, in the meantime, had begun drawing up plans for an air-raid shelter in the basement: an insulated, double-brick room that would include, eventually, foldout beds, plumbing, and a thick steel door.

The following day an air-raid warden appeared on the doorstep and demonstrated how to stick black tar paper to all their windows. Unfortunately Mikey Michaels got hold of a few spare strips when no one was looking and stuck his fingers to the upper register of the piano. Then two policemen knocked on the door and told Pearl they were preparing for a second invasion of the area.

"If you come in direct contact with the enemy, miss, you should simply smile and wave."

She was neither smiling nor waving late the following night as she waited in the Arabian Café for James to arrive. She was sitting with her best friend, Nora Barnes, at an open window overlooking Darlinghurst Road. Usually, the street would be alive with pulsing neon, car headlights, American soldiers, and good-time girls, but since the Japanese invasion, the revellers had vanished and the streetlamps had been dimmed with metal shields. Even the café, which was packed most nights, was only half full—mostly criminals and old-time locals who couldn't be bothered moving away despite a possible invasion, including the piano player with the wooden leg who was now thumping out "Beale Street Blues." It was a popular venue with the underworld because it served sly grog—usually red wine—in teacups.

Pearl had already told Nora about James—describing their

night in Luna Park, their morning stroll into the city, how tall and handsome he was—until Nora murmured that she'd like to meet him sometime.

Pearl then felt guilty for gushing about James. Her friend had enamel-smooth skin, shiny ginger hair, and slate-blue eyes that glistened when she laughed. She had an almost perverse sense of humour and was one of the most generous people Pearl had ever met. But she was the plumpest girl in the band—she was virtually bursting out of the uniform white lace gown—and that, combined with the fact that she played the drums, seemed to put off potential suitors. At the age of twenty-four, Nora had only been out on two dates in her life, and both had ended early and in tears. For a few months she'd been enjoying a flirtation with the Trocadero doorman, Pookie, but nothing had come of it yet.

"Well, you can meet him tonight!" Pearl had assured her. "After the gig, at the Arabian Café."

Now it was almost midnight and there was no sign of James or even Martin and Roma, who were supposed to be meeting them there, too. Nora sipped wine from a chipped cup and listened attentively to the piano player, who soon took a break and hobbled into the kitchen. Pearl was growing more edgy, not only because James was half an hour late but because she sensed that Nora was feeling sorry for her and had already written off James as one of those American cads who picked up and dropped local girls faster than they could order a double hamburger.

Finally, Martin appeared in the doorway, still wearing his tuxedo from the Trocadero, with Roma on his arm. In the candlelight, the girl's white, knee-length dress shimmered against her coppery skin. She had her hair swept up into a loose bun studded with lilies. She glanced around the café uncertainly, as if she wasn't sure that she was in the right place.

Martin walked her over to the table and introduced her to Nora. Roma nodded shyly and took a seat next to Martin. Up close, Pearl saw that Roma's skin was darker than she'd first thought, and she had a distinctive beauty spot to the side of her upper lip. For a moment, she felt a stab of jealousy—no girl had ever come between Martin and herself before—and yet she was acutely aware that, had James already arrived, she probably wouldn't be feeling this way.

Pearl made an effort to be welcoming, ordering them cups of wine. She asked Roma polite questions about her family and hometown, and learned that she was the daughter of a stockman, and had been harnessing horses from the age of five. This was her first trip to Sydney.

Pearl asked her what it was like to be a hostess at the Booker T. Washington Club, but before Roma could answer, Martin butted in, "You know, Pearl met her boyfriend there the other night—James, the sax player."

This was followed by an awkward silence. Pearl looked into her teacup and swilled the wine around in it, as if she might glimpse her future in the dregs. It was bad enough that James hadn't turned up, but seeing Roma and Martin so happy together made her even more miserable. The piano player began packing up his sheet music and the owner called for last drinks. Had she offended James somehow? Embarrassed him? She recalled how he had pulled away from her in the tunnel in The Rocks. Maybe he thought she was too forward.

Pearl raised her hand for the bill. Or maybe Nora's suspicion was right.

*　　*　　*

Since they only worked at night, Pearl and Martin spent their days helping their father build the air-raid shelter in the basement. As she helped Aub pour cement and lay bricks, Pearl mentioned that she wanted a new saxophone for her eighteenth birthday, but the request was met with a grunt and a long silence. Money was tight, she knew that, but she'd had to try at least once.

The days passed slowly, and she found James entering her thoughts repeatedly, like a recurring dream. It had been five nights since their evening at Luna Park, and still she hadn't heard from him. She'd tried ringing him at the Booker T. Washington Club from the one telephone at the Trocadero, but the receptionist always reported that he was unavailable. What if he didn't want to see her again? What if he'd been transferred to another state and hadn't bothered to let her know? What if he'd met another girl—someone black like him?

As she swept up dust and mixed cement, she yearned for a telegram boy to arrive with a message. Whenever she heard the doorbell's trill echoing through the house she dropped whatever she was holding and ran up the basement stairs, only to discover another inquisitive neighbour who'd heard about the shelter she and her family were building and had come to see it for themselves. She would just have to face the fact; it was over. And it had barely even begun.

4

By the morning of her birthday, Pearl still hadn't heard from him. When her father asked what time her guest was arriving, she just shrugged. Days before, she'd explained to her parents that their bridge-playing friend, James, had mentioned how lonely he was—being so far from home—and that she and Martin had invited him over for a home-cooked meal.

While Pearl's love affair had faltered, Martin's romance with Roma seemed to be progressing well, but Roma had made it clear that she was in no hurry to meet her beau's parents. She'd grown up in the bush, wary of white people. "It's not that I don't like them," she'd explained to Martin. "I just don't know how to act when I'm around them."

Pearl realised it was probably just as well. Their father wouldn't say much about his son dating an Aborigine—in fact, the man was so easygoing he probably wouldn't mind if Martin brought home Siamese twins and announced that he was in love with them both. Their mother, however, was a different matter: far more religious, and more conscious of the family's reputation in the local community. Clara wouldn't deliberately offend Roma, Pearl knew, but she'd probably embarrass the girl without even trying.

Toward lunchtime, the twins' favourite orchestra, Artie Shaw's Navy Band, was playing on the radio, and Pearl drifted in to join the others. Father Jim, an old family friend, was sitting in the parlour with Lulu, the twins' deaf grandmother. Mr. Bones was warming himself by the fire, while Mikey Michaels sat on the floor, playing with wooden blocks. When no one was looking Pearl took a half-bottle of brandy she kept stashed behind the bathroom cistern and added its contents to her mother's fruit punch. She downed two glasses in quick succession to quell her disappointment.

Martin was already sitting at the dining room table, drumming his fingers in time with Artie Shaw's "Airmail Special." A headache began to crawl up Pearl's left temple. She could smell the heavy aroma of overcooked meat. When her father handed her another glass of punch she downed it in one gulp. Surely she couldn't be that thirsty, said her mother.

"I'm not dying of thirst," Pearl replied. "I'm dying of sobriety."

Father Jim was on to his fourth glass of punch. His face was red and swollen, and the ash on his cigarette became a crooked grey finger pointing to the floor until it dropped without him noticing and landed on the bearskin rug.

As the smell of burning chicken filled the kitchen, Pearl pulled her father into the dining room.

"Serve the lunch, Dad," she said. "James must have been held up." She turned her attention to lighting the three candles in the centre of the table.

When they were all finally seated—the family, Mr. Bones, and Mikey—Father Jim said grace and thanked the Lord for the miracle that was Pearl and Martin. He also expressed his gratitude for the fine meal before them during these times of hardship, death, and destruction. Lastly, he prayed for peace and protection, and they all echoed his "Amen." Aubrey carved the chooks up. Martin passed the vegetables. The doorbell chimed.

Aubrey pushed back his chair, but Pearl leaped to her feet. "No, let me."

She forced herself to walk slowly through the dining room and into the parlour, between the scattered chairs, past the fire. For a moment she was giddy with anticipation, before telling herself it was probably a neighbour who'd run out of sugar or eggs. Turning into the hallway, she saw a tall figure on the other side of the door, silhouetted against its stained-glass window. She checked her appearance briefly in the mirror hanging on the wall, and turned the door handle.

James was on the doorstep wearing a clean and pressed military uniform. He smiled nervously, but couldn't look at her directly, and instead stared down at his polished black boots. "Sorry 'bout the other night," he murmured. "Captain put me on laundry duty."

He glanced up the street, as if he were lost and was now planning to retrace his steps along the footpath.

"Happy birthday," he said, proffering his gift. It was a square, thin package, obviously a record.

She smiled, and with her free hand took his arm and walked him through the foyer. When he bristled at the sight of the stuffed emu, Pearl laughed and said, "Don't worry, that's just Cedric," and led him toward the dining room. As they appeared in the doorway, everyone at the table paused in their serving and talking to stare at Martin and Pearl's new friend.

James gave a little salute. "Hi, folks." His Southern accent echoed through the dining room. Everyone was still staring as Pearl guided him toward the seat next to her own.

"Stone the crows!" exclaimed Clara finally, a spoonful of mashed potato suspended in the air. "Love, you didn't tell us he was so handsome!"

There was laughter then—a flutter of white serviettes—and, seventy minutes late, the birthday lunch finally began.

Clara passed James a plate of pumpkin so overcooked the pieces looked like a pile of black and orange rocks. "We understand you boys are starved for company and good food," she said. "And believe me, we certainly appreciate the fine job you're doing here."

Aub salted his food, picked up a single pea, and ate it, then shook more salt over his plate.

"I'm a song-and-dance girl!" Clara announced unexpectedly. Pearl realised her mother was swaying now. Clara rarely drank, and the punch must have gone straight to her head.

James glanced at Clara warily. His shoulders were taut as he leaned forward to spoon some cauliflower onto his plate.

"I also play the drums and cornet," she added.

James straightened in his chair and held his glass up to her. "A Renaissance woman," he said, his accent bending the vowels.

"No, I'm a Catholic!" she chirped. "Father Jim here baptised me. And the kids, too."

The priest gave a little self-deprecating shrug of his shoulders as he sawed away at his dry chicken leg.

"I just hope he lives long enough to marry them," Clara said. "Not to each other, of course."

Aub cleared his throat and asked James where he hailed from.

"The South!" Pearl volunteered eagerly.

"Not far from New Orleans," added James, pronouncing it *Noo Awlins*.

"Mother comes from New Orleans," chimed Clara.

Lulu smiled back serenely, as if she had heard every word. It was difficult to be sure how much she could still understand. Sometimes she nodded at a question or shook her head when she possibly disagreed with somebody's comment. However, the doctor believed the head movements were coincidental rather than genuine responses to auditory stimuli.

Soon the punch and the wine were having the desired effect: The chicken didn't taste so burnt, the cabbage was not so soggy, and the peas didn't seem as dry. The gramophone crackled with Aubrey's favourite records from the vaudeville days.

Everyone was more than tipsy by the time the table was cleared. While the women scraped plates and placed leftovers in the icebox, the men sat in the parlour, sampling the Javanese cigarettes that Martin had bought on the black market. The room was soon filled with aromatic plumes of smoke, redolent of cloves and other spices.

Pearl, feeling that James was ignoring her, sashayed unsteadily across the room and dropped onto his lap. Father Jim, staring at them, began coughing. Aubrey let out a long whistle, pretending to be shocked.

"Enough of that!" cried Clara.

James nudged Pearl off his lap, and she suddenly felt silly. She had been trying to act worldly and had looked childish instead.

James picked up his gift from the sideboard and handed it to her. She pulled on the blue ribbon and unwrapped the plain brown paper. Pearl knew, of course, that it would be a record, but when she saw the label she was so thrilled she wanted to throw her arms around him, but merely squeezed his arm. It was a phonograph recording of Sonny Clay's Colored Idea.

She turned to her father. "Remember when you took us to see Sonny Clay at the Tiv?"

Aub nodded.

Martin took the record from Pearl. "That was a hot band. I mean, really hot." He turned to James. "And Aub reckons that when they came onstage, Pearl burst into tears. She was terrified."

"Why?" asked James.

"It was the first time we'd ever seen Negroes," said Martin.

James shifted his gaze to Pearl, frowning.

"I was only a little kid," she said hurriedly. "Once they started playing, I stopped crying."

James shook his head briefly, but said nothing.

"They even had tap dancers in the troupe," she added, to no one in particular.

Martin slipped the record from its camel-coloured sleeve and dropped it on the turntable.

"For weeks after that," she added, "Martin, Charlie Styles, and I nailed bottle tops to the soles of our shoes and tried to imitate them. Remember?"

After winding up the gramophone, Martin lifted the needle

and dropped it onto the record's first grooves. The scratchy opening chorus of "Plantation Blues" filled the room.

A strumming banjo and the deep throb of a tuba, and what sounded like flutey clarinets, slightly out of tune, propelled the melody along.

Clara's red lipstick was now smudged against her teeth and bleeding into the small creases around her mouth. "But don't you remember?" she said. "The whole band was deported from Melbourne."

"What, for playing jazz?" asked James.

Clara shook her head. "Loose morals—the police raided their rooms one night and found six of them in bed—with six white girls." She sighed heavily. "All naked as the day they were born. *Nude*. Can you imagine?" She pursed her lips primly. "Or would you want to?"

James shifted in his chair and his eyes flickered.

"Well," said Pearl, trying to make light of the comment, "boys will be boys—no matter what colour they are."

Clara lurched across the parlour toward the punch bowl. "It didn't look good in the papers, young lady."

Pearl, standing by the fire, glanced at James and saw his eyes wandering toward the hallway that led to the front door. She wished her mother would shut up.

"Ruined the girls' reputations," added Clara. "Pity the poor parents. Who'd ever get over a thing like that?"

"'Nude girls in jazz orgy,' or something like that," Aub recalled. "I think they used the White Australia policy on that one."

The last strains of the song filled the room, the dying harmonies of a trumpet and clarinet.

James cleared his throat. "The White Australia policy?"

Aub waved a dismissive hand. "It was set up years ago."

"To keep coloureds out?"

Aub absently twirled the ginger hair sticking out of his nostrils, as if he were spit curling a moustache. "Only the Chinese, really. To keep 'em out of the goldfields. But I remember back in '08, when they let in that Negro boxer, Jack Johnson—*woohoo!*" Aub, grinning, leaped up and began weaving and shadowboxing around the room. "Pummelled that white bloke—what was his name?—pummelled the guts out of him." Aub ducked and punched his way out of the room and down the basement stairs to collect more wine.

James glanced at the clock.

Pearl, sensing that the mood of the party was going downhill at a cracking pace, asked her mother if there was any dessert.

But Clara was on a roll now and waved away Pearl's question, drunkenly declaring that the musicians from Sonny Clay's band had also been diagnosed with venereal diseases.

"Syphilis?" murmured James.

"It was there in the paper—in black and white."

James pulled on the cuffs of his sleeve and stood up. "I didn't realise how late it is," he said. "I've got to get back to the camp."

"No!" cried Pearl.

"Good Lord, son"—Clara waved her empty glass in the air—"we haven't even served the tea."

James looked pained; it was obvious he wanted to flee.

Aubrey suddenly burst into the parlour carrying a large rectangular box wrapped in gold paper, with a smaller one, covered in the same paper, balanced on top of it.

"You can't leave yet," he said, almost blocking James's way. "The twins haven't opened the rest of their presents!"

He handed the smaller gift to Martin, who opened it to find a hand-tailored tweed suit, with a double-breasted jacket and silk lining.

Aub handed the larger parcel to Pearl. "It's from Mum and me."

Pearl put the present on the floor, kneeled, and tore back the wrapping to reveal a large cardboard box. Inside was a big black case in the shape of a thick question mark. Her heart was doing a fast tap dance in her chest as she flipped back the silver catches and opened the lid. Resting in recesses of plush red velvet was a gleaming saxophone.

Her hands flew up to her face in shock. "It's mine?"

"Almost," said her father. "We took out a loan."

"Down payment of five quid," said Clara.

"Two bob a week," finished Aub, prodding the fire with an iron poker.

"Better not get the sack now," joked Martin, putting the recording of Sonny Clay back into its sleeve.

Pearl fitted the instrument together and held it out to James. "Here," she said, trying to cheer him up, to make him stay. "You get to play it first."

He waved her away. "It's your birthday, Pearl."

"Then play for me," she implored him, but he shook his head and stood up.

"Thank you for your hospitality," he said stiffly, looking at the carpet. "God bless." Then he strode down the hallway and out the front door.

Pearl put down the sax and ran after him.

About halfway up the block, she finally caught up and slapped him on the back. He stopped and turned to face her.

They glared at one another. The street was empty except for some neighbours sticking black tar paper against their front windows in preparation for the night ahead.

"Well?" she said.

He sighed and began walking again, cocking his head to indicate that she should walk with him. They strode up Victoria Street in silence. She could tell he was furious but she didn't know how to begin to talk about it. They crossed William Street and came to the tram stop.

"Hell, I don't care about your mama," he said finally, "or goddamn Sonny Clay."

"What is it then?" she asked, shivering in the wind.

James closed his eyes, as if she'd asked a stupid question.

At that moment a tram came clanging around the corner and pulled up. James jumped onto the running board and gave her a little salute. "Thursday morning. Ten o'clock," he ordered. "Botanic Gardens, by the roses." As the tram began rumbling down the hill, he shouted over the traffic, "And bring your sax."

5

Pearl was so busy curling her hair, wanting to pretty herself up for James, that she lost track of time. After glancing at the clock—nine forty-five—she threw on her clothes, realising her stockings were sagging. When she gathered her bag and arrangements, she noticed there was strawberry jam on one of her Goodman charts and then she couldn't find her mouthpiece, which she eventually discovered when she slipped her foot into one of her black suede shoes.

By the time she rushed up the path toward the rose garden, lugging her new saxophone, it was almost half past ten, and she was flustered and out of breath. From a distance of about twenty yards, Pearl saw James sitting cross-legged on the grass, hugging his knees. His eyes were closed and his face was tilted back to the sunshine, which highlighted the coppery colour of his skin. His hair seemed darker in the morning light. Catching her breath, Pearl stood watching him. Then, struck by a mischievous idea, she darted behind a weeping fig, opened her case, and quickly fitted her instrument together. Hiding behind the tree trunk, she began to play "Between the Devil and the Deep Blue Sea." She was trying to imitate the way she'd heard him play at the Booker T. Washington Club, but found the tempo she'd begun with was too fast. During the second chorus she struggled to maintain it, then slowed down, fraction by fraction, until it was eased back into a medium bounce.

She finished with a flourish, expecting him to applaud or whistle or perhaps even laugh, but when she peeked around the trunk she was surprised to see he'd vanished, and in his place on the lawn was a magpie. The magpie suddenly took wing, and for one crazy moment she imagined her solo had somehow transformed him into a bird and he'd flown away and out of her life forever. She looked across the rose garden to the iron gates, and back down a path that led to the water. There was no sign of him.

"Lesson number one," a voice boomed.

With a gasp, she looked up to see him directly above her, straddling a branch of the Moreton Bay fig. "Don't ever be late for a lesson." His face looked cross in the leafy play of light and shadow.

"Lesson number two: In order to play fast you gotta play slow. Real slow. Practise everything like it's a ballad."

She shielded her face from the sun with her hand, confused. "I hate ballads."

"Play the tune again," he ordered. "This tempo." He began clicking his fingers at a ridiculously slow pace, so slow she could hear the honking of ferry horns and chirps of birds between the beats.

*   *   *

After her first lesson with James, she was a bit shaky. She hadn't expected him to be so stern and exacting. It was as if he became a different man when he was teaching, one who was abrupt and impatient. Still, they parted on good terms, with a furtive kiss and a hug behind the fig.

Later that night, after playing at the Trocadero, she met up with him at the back of the Booker T. Washington Club and he smuggled her through the basement kitchen and up the stairs to the ground floor. He led Pearl into a walk-in linen press, where he turned on the light by pulling a string. He undressed her gently, sliding her woollen jacket off first, then undoing the mother-of-pearl buttons of her blouse one by one. He slipped down her brassiere straps, cupped her breasts and kissed them. She could smell the tart scent of starch and Sunlight soap, and everything inside the press was white, except James. He rubbed the small of her back gingerly, as if she were wounded there, then he slid his hand between the waistband of her skirt and garter belt. That night she wasn't wearing knickers—she hated the bite of elastic against her skin—and with time and a little probing his fingers found places that made her insides ripple. Everything was slow and rapturous, and her legs grew so weak she thought her knees would buckle. She could hear the faint laughter of men. The sound of approaching footsteps. Short gasps for air that she realised were her own until everything swooned through her in a rush, and she was biting into James's shoulder to keep from shouting.

Days later, James told Pearl that when he was out at the

Granville base, unloading trucks and sweeping out offices, the imprint of her teeth was still there on his shoulder. When he went to bed at night on his straw-filled mattress, when he was bawled out by his white sergeant, when he was put on latrine duty for the third time that month, when he felt anxious or bored or just plain frustrated with the army, he'd raise his hand and finger the oval-shaped branding and recall her salty taste.

But it wasn't all lust and longing between them. Sometimes, when he could secure a leave pass, they would catch the tram down to Bondi and picnic on the beach. James had never seen surf so big before, and the sight of the huge rolling waves left him wide-eyed and speechless. There was nothing so powerful in Louisiana, New Orleans, or even along New York's Rocka-way Beach. Pearl tried to get him to come into the sea so she could teach him how to body surf. She wasn't sure if he was afraid of the breakers or just plain modest about his own body, but the closest he came to swimming was allowing the water to lather around his bare brown feet. While she swam, he often played with small children on the shore, building castles and digging tunnels. Once, she emerged from the breakers to find that a group of kids had buried him in sand right up to his neck and had crowned his head with a wreath of seaweed. The children were laughing and so was he, laughing with complete abandon, and she realised she'd never seen him so happy.

Occasionally, they went to the movies, mostly musicals and comedies. His favourite films starred Laurel and Hardy, and the harder the two comedians hit one another, the clumsier the pratfall, the louder James laughed, until he looked as if he was doubled over in pain.

Gradually, she learned more about his life back in America. His father was a white guy named Floyd, who'd been a cornet player and gambler. He'd run out on James's mother when James had been only five. His mother picked soy beans on a farm to help make ends meet. Later, in grade school, at the suggestion of his teacher, he took up the tenor sax. It was a large instrument for a young boy, but he was the only kid in the class who was tall enough to hold it, let alone play it. By this time he was living with his mother's sister, Aunty Bee. For a few years, he studied with and performed in the school marching band. On Sundays, he played with an ensemble at the Bogalusa First Baptist Church. At night, he'd sneak out of his room and go and jam with the old blues guys down in the High Yella juke joint, which was just a boat shed standing on crooked stilts over the river, selling bootleg corn liquor and pickled pig's feet. After the juke joint was burned down by some white guys on the other side of the railway tracks, James kissed his aunt goodbye and hitchhiked with the drummer to New Orleans. There, he found a job on a riverboat. For nine months he played night after night on the stretch of the Mississippi River between New Orleans and Memphis. He could already sight-read, and knew a lot of tunes. An old clarinettist patiently corrected James's embouchure, and taught him intricate chord progressions. At fifteen, he hitchhiked to Kansas City and hung around the clubs there, sitting in with bands and jamming. Sometimes, he couldn't cut the tempo, and the older musicians laughed him off the stage, calling him White Boy and Yellow Butt.

Humiliated, he was determined to improve. He began listening to records of Lester Young and Chu Berry over and over, for hours each day, practising in his rented single room every run and lick that burst from the gramophone. He lingered in the doorways of clubs, trying to figure out how Buster Smith could double the time on any tune he was playing.

It was during those months that he felt a deep sense of urgency churning away inside him, as if he needed to double the tempo of the pace at which he lived; he drank black coffee with Benzedrine because it allowed him to keep playing, day and night, without sleep. His lips cracked and bled on hard new reeds; and his heart raced all the time now, a thunderstorm in his chest.

A season passed, and by the time he returned to the jam sessions he'd once been laughed out of, much thinner and looking older than his years, he'd developed a lightning technique and could glide through chord changes that even Buster Smith was unable to follow. One night in a club he was spotted by the clarinettist Benny Goodman and was invited to join his tour. James hadn't yet turned sixteen.

And thinking of all this, about everything he'd told her, Pearl daydreamed about forming a band with James, playing the latest American jazz styles. She imagined herself composing music that astonished crowds and had them begging for more. She saw herself and James harmonising with one another, attuning themselves to the rhythms of country roads. Of course, there was one small problem—the war—but she knew it couldn't go on forever. It had been nearly three years since Britain had declared war on Germany. She was giving it another six months; she could wait that long. Anyway, she figured she'd need that much time to absorb the material he was teaching her, to become as good as he was.

*   *   *

During the first few weeks of her apprenticeship, James had her practising only one thing: She had to play long tones on her instrument for four hours each day. This was to refine her breathing, pitch, and timbre. As the sun moved across the sky, as shadows inched their way over the footpath and garden, she'd stand on her bedroom balcony, blowing one sustained note over and over, until the barking of dogs turned to howls and neighbours complained and she was banished to the basement air-raid shelter by her mother.

By her sixth lesson in the gardens, when James thought she was ready, he asked her to play, in succession, all the major scales and their triads, which turned out to be a series of lurching rises and falls, a breathy ladder of awkward progressions. When she achieved the right tone, her fingering was inconsistent, and when the fingering was correct her embouchure faltered. The two techniques never seemed to unite, and she grew frustrated.

James instructed her again to merely practise minor, major, and blues scales, with corresponding triads, in slow, long tones. It was monotonous work and sometimes her mind would drift from the next chordal progression in the scale to thoughts about him, their conversations, to the stories he'd told her as they strolled beneath palm trees or sipped milkshakes down at Circular Quay.

There was one aspect of James that still perplexed her, however, and late one night, when they were playing cards in the Arabian Café, she decided to broach the subject.

"How come, when we're out, you don't—you never . . . " She was trying to sound casual but her voice came out all high and nervous. She took a deep breath. "How come you've stopped touching me? Not—not even my hand?"

James frowned and rearranged his cards. The pianist was playing "My Blue Heaven" with lots of flourishes and cadenzas, his wooden leg thumping in time against the floor.

"Well?" she prompted.

James sighed and put his cards facedown on the table. He fixed his eyes on her. His gaze was steady but his right eyebrow was twitching.

"Honey, where I come from, no white girl'd invite a guy like me to her home—'specially not to meet her parents."

"Why not?" she asked. "Why not just as a friend?"

James's eyes suddenly flared. "You know, my granddaddy got hanged from a tree in the Bogalusa city park?"

She was shocked into silence. He began balling and releasing one fist against the table, as if he were warming up for a boxing match.

Finally she asked him, "Why?"

A drunk lurched out of the toilet and steadied himself against the piano.

James sighed. He leaned across the table. "Because he whistled at a white girl who passed him on the street."

Pearl gaped at him. What he had just told her seemed impossible. What about the justice system? What about the police?

James had a sour look on his face, as if he had just swallowed something bitter. He took a sip of water, then held the glass with two hands and gazed into it intently. "Last time I toured the South," he said, "I was with Benny Goodman's band. Me and the bass player, Herschel Evans, we were the only Negroes in the group. And every restaurant the band stopped at, me and Herschel always had to eat in the kitchen."

Pearl picked up her teacup and gulped at her wine. James's voice remained low, but angry, almost menacing.

"And forget about hotel rooms. No niggers allowed. Sometimes me and Herschel'd doss down with a local black family. A couple of times—in Georgia—we even slept backstage after the gig. And some nights, when the band pulled into a new town and the club owner realised there were two niggers in the band, they'd cancel the booking but wouldn't pay us."

She started to say something, to express her outrage and dismay, but he cut her off.

"But the worst time," he continued, "was when the sheriff of some two-bit Texas town ran us offstage with a shotgun. We had to fight our way out of the hall and back to the railway station before he put a bullet in us both." His eyelids were half closed now, as if he were trying to shut out a flood of bad memories.

Pearl hung her head, blushing at her own naivety. James had experienced more misery and fear in his life than she could have ever imagined, let alone endured. Losing his grandfather like that, and having been threatened so often himself . . . And she'd been thinking only about herself, about why he wouldn't walk arm in arm with her down a city street, why he refused to kiss her in public.

She reached across the table and rested her hand on his. "Sorry," she murmured. "I'm so sorry, James."

He didn't reply, just slid his hand away and rummaged in his pocket. He pulled out a crumpled pound note and threw it on the table. "C'mon," he muttered. "Let's get out of here."

Pearl never broached the subject again. He was a complicated man with the kind of history she'd never understand completely. Instead, they talked about music: mixolydian scales and perfect fourths.

These lessons excited her more than a roller-coaster ride, especially when James put his arms around her from behind, placed his hands on hers, and applied pressure to her fingers against the saxophone keys, demonstrating some particular technique, which turned into a kind of musical foreplay. Then they'd creep off to an isolated part of the gardens and make love behind a curtain of jasmine vines or on a bed of dewy ferns. And as his fingers traced paths around and inside her, all his talk about harmonics and embellishments and scales united into the one tingling sensation and coursed through her in a flood.

Sometimes they played imported records in Palings Music Store, and he explained why the string section of a certain band was arranged in such a way, or showed her how Ben Webster achieved his breathy, fluffy tone on the tenor sax. He told her about how Glenn Miller stole the riff to "In the Mood" from an old Fletcher Henderson tune, and how Charlie Barnet arranged "Cherokee" in a car on the way to a recording studio.

He tried to teach her how to play conventional melodies against a Latin rhythm structure. Sometimes she found it hard to follow the intricate flights of his instructions and she simply sat back on the grass and marvelled at how his face and limbs grew light and animated as he lectured. Once, while he was demonstrating a passage of "St. Louis Blues," passing children took one another in their arms and cavorted across the buffalo grass, while grown-ups stood at a distance, shading their eyes with their hands and swaying in time with the music. Another time, for a lark, they went busking down at Circular Quay and, after three hours, they'd earned over seven pounds, a bottle of beer, a handful of walnuts, and a scattering of religious leaflets.

They tried as often as possible to meet on Pearl's two nights off from the Trocadero. Usually, they ended up having supper in the Arabian Café in Kings Cross, where James would jump up and jam with the one-legged pianist, playing melody with his right hand while the pianist played stride chords on the lower register.

One night, they left the café at closing time and strolled along the footpath, he with his hands wedged into his trouser pockets, she with hers tucked inside the cuffs of her coat to keep them warm. The wind rustling through the plane trees sounded like car tyres against a wet road. The streetlights had been dimmed to a series of cloudy moons vanishing into the darkness ahead. A couple of white GIs lurched out of the Californian Café across the road, dragging with them two women, who were waving fox fur stoles above their heads. One almost tripped over before the men bundled them into a waiting taxi, which promptly took off and turned left into Springfield Avenue.

Pearl and James continued down the block, the electric light-ing gradually disappearing. All the clubs and cafés had closed,

and, as they crossed Elizabeth Bay Road and rounded the corner into Macleay Street, the world quickly faded to black. Pearl
blinked for a few minutes. She could see nothing at first, though
she knew that an old mansion stood just ahead to her right, but
it was several seconds before her eyes adjusted and she could
make out the silhouette of a turret against the stars.

Emboldened by the darkness she slipped her arm around
James's waist and dipped her hand into his trouser pocket.
Now, with her fingers cupping the curve of his hipbone, it was
as if they were a regular couple in a normal world, no longer
concerned about the possible reactions of other people—the
smirks, the frowns, the possible hostility. It felt so warm being
in his arms—so quietly thrilling—that she wanted the sensation to last forever.

As they passed the Victorian mansion a daring idea occurred
to her.

Pushing open the creaking iron gate, Pearl led James up the
path. He didn't protest or make a sound, but merely followed
her. The house belonged to five elderly spinster sisters who, after
the Japanese invasion of Sydney Harbour, had fled with their
clutch of cats and canaries. They hadn't been seen for months;
the windows were boarded up and the once-manicured garden
was a jungle of overgrown grass and dandelions. The front door
was locked, of course, so she walked along the veranda, around
the right wing, to the backyard. She tried to open a window,
then the service entrance, but they, too, were bolted shut. It
wasn't until she pulled on an iron ring attached to the cellar
door that she gained entrance to the grand old manor.

She expected James to object to her breaking into the house, but as she felt her way down the steps, along the stone walls of the basement, and up the wooden staircase that led to the ground floor, the only sounds she could hear were his footsteps padding behind her. Once they were inside, James lit a match and slowly a woodstove, a fireplace, and a row of cupboards emerged from the gloom, only to disappear again as the match burned down. He lit another and Pearl glimpsed a candlestick on a sideboard. She picked it up and James lit the wick. Holding the candle, she led him through to a dining room, where a huge oval table set for eight sat covered in a thick layer of dust, as if the sisters had been about to sit down for a formal lunch the moment they'd decided to flee.

Upstairs, there was an open book on a table, dead flowers in vases, a half-finished painting of a country landscape standing on an easel. The wardrobes and armoires were still filled with long dark dresses, fur coats, and stoles. In one of the bedrooms at the end of the hallway, a radio still played softly some classical music she didn't recognise. The atmosphere was both eerie and exhilarating, as if she and James were two ghosts haunting the abandoned mansion.

Pearl put down the candle, pulled on one of the musty fur coats, and began dancing around the room, pretending she was waltzing with an imaginary partner. When she glided past James, he grabbed hold of her and pushed her down onto the mattress of the four-poster bed. There they made love, on the satin quilt, until the early hours of the morning.

And so the mansion became their beloved home, the place where they could behave like an ordinary couple. The larder was still stocked with preserves and condiments; the cellar was filled with dusty bottles of wine; the gramophone still worked, and a wooden cabinet contained an impressive collection of classical 78s: Beethoven, Brahms, Bach, and even Stravinsky.

They became so attached to the deteriorating home that when the roof began to leak James crawled into the attic and repaired the damage. When Pearl noticed mould slowly crawling across the kitchen wall, she scrubbed it off with vinegar and baking soda. James fixed a damaged copper pipe in the laundry. Together, they dusted the antiques, brushed away cobwebs, and hung mothballs in the musty wardrobes. They even retrieved the mail accumulating in the letterbox by the front gate and left it in a neat pile on a side table in the foyer.

Late at night, they ate food from porcelain plates, drank Merlot from crystal glasses, and played cards in the back parlour, all within the gentle glow of candlelight. In the bathroom, they soaked top to tail in the big old tub, massaging one another's feet. And each time they visited the mansion they slept in a different bedroom, from the one on the ground floor in the servants' quarters to the eighth bedroom on the third floor, in the turret. Pearl explained her overnight absences to her mother by saying that she was staying with Nora Barnes.

One night, as they lazed in a small, high bed in the turret, sipping wine and gazing through the window at the clear night sky, Pearl pointed at Venus and the Southern Cross and outlined with her finger the constellation of Sagittarius. James grew quiet as he stared at the stars—so quiet, in fact, that when she asked him some insignificant question, all she heard in reply was a kind of hiccup.

When she shifted and caught a glimpse of his face in the

candlelight, she realised he was struggling to hold back tears. Fearing he was in some kind of pain, she put down her glass and moved to hold him, but he flinched and she went no further. They sat in awkward silence for a few minutes, still looking at the stars, James occasionally wiping his eyes. He went to the bathroom, and she heard a tap running. At last, after what seemed like a long time, he returned, eyes swollen, and poured them each another glass of wine. Then he sat down beside her.

"You all right?" she asked.

The rim of the glass clinked against his bottom teeth as he took another swig of his drink. "My momma used to do the same thing. Every single night."

She wasn't quite sure what he was talking about. The wine? Some Southern ritual he would soon explain to her?

"Yeah, every night," he added. "There on the front porch. She'd show me Mars. Sirius . . . the North Star."

He paused and sipped his drink again, still staring out the window at the stars. She wanted to ask him a hundred questions but sensed she should keep quiet.

"One night," he continued, "she stood up and started drawing the outline of the Big Dipper with her finger. Right when she reached the top of the curve she began kinda choking and doubled over."

Pearl could hear his breath faltering again. She put one hand on his. "Hell, I ran to the neighbour's house," he choked, "but by the time the doctor came—"

He bowed his head and took a deep breath. She squeezed his hand and realised that she, too, was blinking back tears. "How old?"

She felt a shudder move through him. "Heart attack," he murmured. "Thirty-eight. Goddamn heart attack."

He put his glass on the floor and lay down, turning his back to her. At once, Pearl wanted to hold him tightly, to rinse away his grief, but since she'd never experienced the death of any-one—let alone a parent—she was unsure about how to comfort James or if, indeed, he wanted sympathy at all.

Eventually, he slid down and fell asleep against the pillows, still dressed in his uniform. She rested beside him, gazing at his long eyelashes, his childlike pout, the silver trace of a tear on his cheek, the rise and fall of his chest. All at once she could see in him the grief-stricken young boy still pining for his mother, the tough yet vulnerable teenager, and the determined, almost hardened musician who would not let anything or anyone get in his way. And as she watched him sleep, she realised she'd fallen in love, hopelessly in love, with a man she adored but did not know.

6

One Saturday night, during their last break at the Trocadero, before the final set of the evening, Pearl—flushed with love—confided in Nora Barnes. They were standing in front of the soda fountain, watching the eighteen-piece men's band playing on stage, when Pearl, sipping from a flask of brandy, and feeling a little tipsy, declared, "I love him more than anything. Or anyone." She passed the flask to Nora. "I just don't know if we've got a future together."

Nora swigged from the flask. "But he loves you, too. Doesn't he?" She passed back the flask and Pearl, contemplating her answer, took another gulp.

"He loves living together at night," she said. "In the mansion. For sure." Her head was spinning and the music suddenly seemed louder and closer. "But out in public—I don't know—he seems like another person. Quieter, you know? He kind of pretends we're not together."

"Ahh, come on, Pearly," said Nora. "He's in a strange country. With strange customs." Nora seized the flask, and drained it.

"And he's going out with a strange Australian girl—with an even stranger best friend!" Nora let out a loud burp and Pearl, in spite of herself, burst into laughter.

Her brother, though, was not so warm and sympathetic. Roma had suddenly packed her bags and fled back to Dubbo, leaving behind a depressed and increasingly drunk Martin, who refused to discuss her sudden departure with anyone. According to James, the rumour going around the Booker T. Washington Club was that Roma had fallen pregnant, but when Pearl asked Martin about it he was adamant that the stories were all bullshit.

As if this weren't enough for him to deal with, the week before, Martin had received government papers instructing him to register for a daytime Manpower job. Now he was working in a factory forty hours a week while still playing at the Trocadero every night.

While they lingered by the soda fountain waiting to play their last set, a busboy rushed up and handed Pearl a note. She unfolded it: *Front doors. Emergency!*

Nora stuffed the flask back into her cleavage, and they both strode through the crowd, weaving between tables, to the foyer. Nora, quite tipsy by now, was a little unsteady on her feet. They had to hurry because the men were playing their last tune for the set—"Airmail Special"—and soon the stage would begin to revolve. As the men slowly slid away to the right, the girls' band would circle into the ballroom from the left, as if they were all on some musical carousel. Lionel Bogwald, the English conductor, was a strict taskmaster, and any band member—man or woman—who was not in their seat backstage by the time the stage began its revolution would be sacked immediately.

On the front steps they discovered Pookie, the doorman, arguing with a tall American soldier. "I'm sorry, mate," he was saying, "but those are the rules." He was a rotund man in his thirties, slightly balding, wearing a scarlet uniform and a gold-braided cap.

Pearl, still holding the message, brushed against the tall American from behind and, when she looked up, was startled to see a frowning James, who rested one hand on her shoulder and declared, "See? I'm with her."

Pookie stared at Pearl with a mixture of puzzlement and horror. Pearl sighed. She and James had arranged to meet a little later, after her last set.

She nodded at Pookie. "It's true," she said. "He's with me."

Pookie glanced between the two of them and shrugged. "Nothing to do with me. All I know is that we're not allowed to let coloured folks in. That's the law."

"Ooooh, come on, Pookie!" said Nora. She pulled the flask from her cleavage, flipped the cap, and offered him a drink. The doorman's eyes lit up and he looked nervously from side to side. He clearly wanted a sip from Nora's flask, but that, too, was against the rules. He shook his head.

"He can sit in a corner." Nora grabbed his coat sleeve and tugged on it playfully. "No one'll see him."

The doorman was blushing by now and found it hard to look at Nora directly. Instead, he addressed Pearl. "If I let him in, I'll get the sack."

James shrugged and murmured something about leaving, but Nora was drunk and determined. Throwing her arms around the doorman she kissed him so deeply he nearly fell backward. When they finally pulled away from one another, the doorman's face was as red and swollen as a boiled beetroot. But then a smile spread across his face and he declared, "Your mate still can't get in, but whaddya say I buy youse all a drink after the show?"

Pearl hardly ever bathed anymore; she liked walking around with the smell of James on her skin. Love-struck Nora had given her the idea: She and Pookie had quickly fallen for one another and now Nora was turning up for work smelling of her beau's spicy aftershave. To Pearl's surprise, mere weeks after Nora and Pookie had started dating, Nora announced that the two of them were resigning from the Trocadero. It turned out that Pookie, whose father had died recently, had just inherited a large property in the Blue Mountains, and the two of them were moving up there to live.

When Pearl wasn't playing at the Troc or sneaking about with James, she stayed down in the basement, practising what he'd taught her. Swing rhythms rose through the house like a tide, and the constant repetition of the same phrases over and over drove her mother and father wild with frustration. It would have driven Martin mad, too, but these days he was rarely home.

Gradually, her tone improved and, after weeks of her pestering him, James agreed to teach her about harmonics and improvisation.

"But we need a piano," he said.

There was a piano at her house, but Pearl knew he'd refuse to go back there again. She thought for a few moments, then led him out of their usual spot near the rose garden, through the gates, and into the Conservatorium of Music, where she'd studied as a child. They prowled the corridors until they found an empty rehearsal room on the second floor. James sat at the piano and began playing a set of chord changes on a tune that she recognised as "Cherokee." When he told her to play along, she lifted the alto to her lips and joined in. She'd played this tune many times at the Troc, and when he nodded at her to take a solo, she blew the melody with the minor ornaments and embellishments she'd memorised, note for note, from a Johnny Hodges record. At the end of the chorus he waved at her to stop.

She asked him if her tone was too thin, but he merely frowned. Had her tempo been dragging then? He snorted and shook his head.

"Pitch is off?"

James sighed and swung himself around on the stool to face the piano. "Okay, just listen to this."

He began playing the tune again. She stood by the piano and watched the ballet of fingers across the keys. After the second chorus, with every chord, his right hand began improvising up and down the piano in a way that seemed as if he were constantly veering away from the key of B-flat, but somehow remaining just within it. Occasionally, she recognised phrases and arpeggios repeating or inverting themselves in slightly different keys until, just when the whole harmonic scaffolding threatened to collapse beneath his fingers, he miraculously slipped back into the chorus without playing a bum note or missing a beat.

"How'd you do that?" She laid one hand on his shoulder, as if the answer could be transmitted magically through his skin, his army shirt, and into her.

James explained that every time she played a solo, she played it exactly the same way.

She frowned, not comprehending what he was getting at.

"You gotta learn how to improvise," he said. "Take risks. Ain't no risk playing the same lines over and over every time with a few embellishments. You remind me of some old guy who gets up every day and walks exactly the same way to work that he's been walking for forty years, head down, never seeing or hearing anything new. You wanna be like that all your life?"

Pearl, embarrassed, insisted that she tried new things all the time.

He fixed her with a hard stare. "Like what?"

"Like . . . like *you*."

"I ain't a melody, Pearl."

"No, but you're a risk."

He slid around on the stool. "What kind of risk?"

She paced the length of the room and turned. "Well, if I'm some bloke walking the same old path to work every morning, what do you make of a man who can't even hold his girlfriend's hand as they walk down the street? You talk about taking risks. About being adventurous . . . " She knew she was going too far, but she couldn't stop herself.

"Girl, I'm trying to teach you how to solo."

"If you think I'm so boring . . . "

"I don't think you're boring," he said. "Your playing is."

It was as if he'd speared her with a fire poker. She gripped the neck of the saxophone, wanting to throw it down on the floor and flee.

"What's all this about, anyway?" he said angrily. "You wanna parade me in front of your parents? Is that what it is? So they can be all horrified and spit in my face?"

"I want to know where—" She paused, to search for the right words. "I want to know what this all . . . I mean, do you think you and I, after the war . . . " She swallowed, not knowing how to complete the sentence.

He sighed, and turned his face to her. "Honey, in America, what you and me are doing is illegal in thirty-three states."

"But what if we got married?"

"Girl, ain't you been listening to anything I been telling you? We'd be thrown in jail before we even got out of the church. Uncle Sam's happy to fight fascism—long as it's the German kind."

"But we're in Australia."

"I'll end up like one of them niggers your mama talked about. Caught in bed with a white girl, out on the next boat."

As the significance of what he was saying dawned upon her, something broke inside her. She bolted from the room and ran.

At home, Pearl went straight to her room and locked the door. She lay on her stomach and bawled into her pillow, choking on her own snot and hyperventilating. Was James trying to break up with her for good, or was he merely trying to slow things down a little, to reduce the tempo at which their relationship was now playing? Everything seemed hopeless and beyond repair: her future with James, her saxophone playing, the seemingly endless bloody war.

Suddenly, she heard the sound of smashing glass. She got up and hurried downstairs just as Clara came stomping up from the basement and Aubrey shot through the back door, covered in sawdust. In the parlour, the three of them discovered broken glass scattered across the floorboards and a strong smell of whisky. Lulu sat in her chair, gazing at the mess as if it were a thing to be admired. And there was Martin, his face ruddy, holding on to the back of a chair and swaying. In his free hand he held a second bottle that looked as if it hadn't been opened. He bowed, stumbled, and then lurched backward. But the biggest surprise of all was his hair: He was now sporting a severe crew cut. He looked like a convict, Pearl thought, or an inmate from an asylum.

He was lurching toward Clara when the other bottle slipped out of his hand and smashed at his feet.

Pearl stared at her brother. When she'd seen him early that morning, he'd seemed quite normal, dressed in his blue overalls and a worn tweed cap as he headed off to the factory. Now it was four o'clock in the afternoon and he was roaring drunk.

Martin looked surprised that the second bottle was no longer in his hand, as if it had somehow smashed itself.

"Guess what?" he announced, grinning.

No one dared say anything.

"Next week I'll be gone!" Martin saluted his family and began marching around the room, a big childish grin on his face. "I've joined up."

At first, as she watched him stumble in circles, Pearl didn't believe him. Martin abhorred the idea of war, of any kind of combat. Maybe it was just the booze talking, or an unfunny practical joke.

But as Clara went to make some tea for her son, she said to Pearl that it wouldn't surprise her if he had, indeed, signed up for duty. "Lately he's been edgier than a butcher's knife."

Pearl had been so preoccupied with James and her saxophone that she'd paid scant attention to what Clara dubbed "Martin's monster moods." According to the twins' mother, he'd been irritable, not eating, suffering from insomnia. And as Pearl watched him staggering about the parlour, she realised just how much weight he had lost.

She sat on the arm of the couch and studied his uneven crew cut. Was he still upset about Roma? she wondered. Had he loved her that much—as much as she loved James? She felt a pang of guilt for not having noticed how much her brother was suffering, followed swiftly by a stab of trepidation as she remembered what James had tried to tell her: that he couldn't see a future for the two of them.

The next day, as they quietly sipped beers in Martin's bedroom, he explained everything. He was nursing a hangover, but was still excited by the fact that he'd volunteered for service.

His misery had begun when he'd received the papers instructing him to register for a Manpower job in a Redfern factory that manufactured and canned corned beef for the U.S. and Australian armies. The huge iron shed in which he worked always stank of stale blood and intestines, a smell that came to represent the aroma of desperation and despair. Like most musicians at the Trocadero who had been conscripted into Manpower, he was supposed to leave the ballroom as soon as his last set was finished, while the girls' band was still playing, and go straight home to grab five hours' sleep before rising at dawn to go to the factory. No sleeping in, no more jam sessions at the

Booker T. Washington Club, just vats of meat, endless queues of cans, and the rattle of machines. Most mornings he found himself half hoping for a Japanese invasion: Anything would be better than this awful purgatory.

Pearl cocked her head. "So this sudden decision to join up hasn't got anything to do with Roma then?"

Martin bristled. "It's got to do with Merv Sent, dingbat!"

It was Merv from the Booker T. Club who finally came up with a way to avoid being conscripted into combat while still getting out of working at the factory. On 10 August, Martin would join Merv Sent's 41st Division Entertainment Unit and embark on a national tour of Australian army camps. He'd already passed his medical exam and now had to go through six weeks of basic training at a Victorian base before he could join the concert party.

According to Martin, it wouldn't be all that different from the usual touring circuit that most musicians travelled. "The only difference," he boasted, "is that the food's all free and I get paid every fortnight on the dot. No wrangling with nightclub managers." He sounded almost happy, Pearl thought. But Pearl wasn't happy at all. She and her brother had been inseparable throughout their childhoods—together they had skipped school, contracted illnesses, formed bands. They'd shared beds, clothes, shoes, instruments, and even, as kids, swapped identities for an entire day. It was as if Martin were part of her and she of him.

As Pearl gazed at his shorn head she was keenly aware of how much she would miss him. Indeed, she sensed that he was already gone, travelling along bush roads, over distant bridges, vanishing into valleys, away from punch clocks, the factory, and the draft— disappearing in a cloud of dust down a highway, away from her.

7

The morning that Martin was due to leave, Pearl woke before dawn, feeling nauseous. When the time came, she hugged him good-bye so tightly she could feel his rib cage through his jacket. This would be only the second time they'd been separated in their lives, the first being when Pearl and Clara had toured Ceylon years earlier.

Before he walked down the front steps she gave him one of the superior saxophone reeds James had given her. "Thanks, Burly," he said, bowing and kissing her on the hand. "Every time I play it, I'll think of you."

She tried to think of some witty comeback, but she was too upset, and instead watched in silence as he shouldered his backpack, stopped at the gate to salute his family, and marched up the street as if he were already a soldier.

Later, still wearing her pajamas, she retired to the basement with her saxophone to practise. She was already missing Martin. Nora was gone. And so that morning she was experiencing a double dose of loss and she dealt with it the only way she knew how: by blowing it all into her horn.

She hadn't heard from James since their argument at the Conservatorium, but their regular weekly lesson in the rose garden was due to take place at ten o'clock that morning. She assumed he would turn up as usual. She felt foolish now for running off the way she had. She just hoped he'd understood.

After forty-five minutes or so of practising scales she began the second exercise in the sequence James had suggested. She would play "Cherokee" in every key signature—all twelve of them—and in the coming weeks and months she was supposed to rehearse every song she knew in this way, until her body was so intimate with each nuance of any piece of music that her embouchure and fingers, ears and lungs could interpret it effortlessly.

She heard the doorbell ring but didn't stop playing. Moments later, Aub came clumping down the stairs with a telegram. She ripped it open and read it with a sinking heart. NO LESSON TODAY. NO PASS. JAMES.

"Bad news?" asked Aub.

"No," she said, trying to hide her disappointment, wondering with a feeling of dread if James was giving her the brushoff. She needed to see him—that day. To wait another week would be agony.

An hour later she was boarding a train at Central station, carrying her saxophone case. She'd heard of the camp where he was stationed, about fifteen miles out of the city centre in Granville. She knew it was a reckless thing to do—to just turn up at the camp like a lovesick girl—but the missed saxophone lesson gave her an excuse. Hadn't he himself done crazy, wonderful things for the sake of his music? Coffee and Benzedrine for months on end. Hitchhiking to Kansas City and then on to New York. Working as a dishwasher at the Savoy Ballroom for a year just so he could hear Art Tatum play the piano every night.

At Granville station, she asked directions from the ticket collector who pointed down a road toward a cluster of huts that stood in perfect rows, behind which were a baseball pitch and a swimming hole. The passages between the huts were lined with ferns and daisies. A unit of American GIs, shouldering rifles, was being marched around the outskirts of the camp, under the command of a drill sergeant who was shouting orders. She suddenly felt ridiculous, peering through the fence at an army post, wearing her primrose-print dress, holding her saxophone case, planning to invent a flagrant lie just so she could have a brief glimpse of her lover.

A uniformed man popped his head around the doorjamb. "You lookin' for someone, lady?" He was wearing spectacles and chewing gum.

She told him she was looking for Private James Washington.

The soldier thought for a moment. "You mean Ernest."

Pearl put down her case. "No. James. James Washington."

The man chomped on his gum. "I'm the company clerk, lady. Type up the rosters every week. Ain't got no James Washington on my books."

She squinted against the morning light, watching the unit marching back toward the camp, and could see them all clearly now, their faces covered in sweat.

She told him that her Washington was in the Quartermaster Corps.

The man looked her up and down. "What's a nice dame like you want with a coloured boy?"

She picked up her case. "Do you know where I can find him?"

The clerk shrugged and shook his head. "We keep 'em over there." He nodded across the dirt road at a group of tents huddled against a scrubby rise. "We call that there the zoo." She began backing away.

"Hey," he called after her. "You a charity moll?"

Pearl kicked a stone toward him. He ducked out of the way, and it skittered off into a flowerbed. "I'm a musician," she replied testily.

She walked down a path toward the tents. Now that she was so close, she felt anxious and unsure. What if James didn't want to see her? The stubby grass died away and she found herself slogging through a bog of mud indented with thick tyre marks and boot prints. The stench of raw sewage blowing on the westerly wind made her breakfast flip in her stomach. She could see now that the camp was enclosed by a chain-link fence crowned with razor wire, and the sight of it almost defeated her: Not only would he be unable to get out; there was no way she'd be able to slip in undetected.

The fence, however, was ringed by bush, and as she circled the settlement she was camouflaged by trees and scrub. Unlike the camp across the road, with its straight avenues of wooden huts roofed with corrugated iron, its rows of daisies, its swimming hole and baseball pitch, its air of middle-class military civility, this camp looked like a shantytown. The company seemed to be housed in a series of large, sagging tents, and when she glanced through the open flap of one she could see there were no cots inside, and no flooring, just rows of bedrolls lying on the ground. And the mess was right out in the open, beneath a canopy of canvas stretched between four gum trees. Two black men were cooking something in a huge steel drum over an open fire. In the distance, on the other side of the camp, she noticed a group of tiny figures bobbing against the ground, performing push-ups. Behind them was what looked like a huge warehouse rising out of a cluster of ironbark trees. Leaves and twigs whipped her face as she traced the length of the fence. She saw many black soldiers as she passed—fixing trucks, washing jeeps, cutting trees—but not one of them was James. When the fence veered off at a ninety-degree angle, she continued to follow it.

After about five minutes, she saw the head of a man level with the ground, as if he were buried alive from the neck down, but as she got closer she realised he was standing in a ditch, shovelling dirt, and that there was a second man in the trench with him, also digging. When she was upon them, she hid behind the trunk of an ash gum and, after peering at the two bobbing heads for a few moments, she finally recognised the second man and had to stop herself from throwing down her saxophone case and scaling the fence.

She hadn't planned what she would do in the event that she actually found him, and for a while she just stood there, heart pounding, wondering if she should retrace her steps before he realised she was there. She found it hard to reconcile her proud, dignified James with this man standing in a ditch, sweating profusely and shovelling dirt. It was like seeing a sultan scrubbing a floor, or a prince cleaning a toilet. She couldn't believe the man who'd played with Count Basie and Benny Goodman had been reduced to digging trenches.

He was only about ten yards away from her. She tried to draw his attention by hissing, but he just went on with his work, oblivious. It wasn't until he and his mate took a break for a cigarette that she mustered the courage to whistle the melody of "Cherokee." His head jerked around, trying to find the source. She emerged from behind the tree and pressed herself against the fence, and with a grin he jumped up to join her. His friend, Tyrone, kept watch for the sergeant, while James kissed her through a gap in the wire. "Oh, baby," he murmured. "I'm sorry." And between kisses she stammered her apologies, too, until he hushed her by kissing her deeply again.

"I've got something to tell you," he whispered, glancing over his shoulder. "I been thinking about what we talked about last week." He gripped the fence with his fingers. "Yesterday, I put in for a request."

"A request—what?" She swallowed hard. "For a transfer?"

He shook his head. "For permission"—he glanced over his shoulder again—"for permission to marry."

"Who?"

"*Who?*" he asked. "Who do you think? My buddy Tyrone?"

Her pulse was racing as she asked, "Are you proposing to me?"

"We'll have to get my CO's permission first. And wait two months from the day the request was lodged, but . . . " He looked at the ground, suddenly shy. "Course we'll have to deal with your parents. But Tyrone here, he found out there ain't no law in Australia stopping you and me being together. And I got to thinkin', well, maybe this country ain't so bad."

So many words winged through her mind, but she was too overwhelmed to utter a sound. She laced her fingers through his. Their lips found each other, and they kissed again through the wire and the taste of him made her feel as if she were levitating and falling at the same time.

When they finally pulled away from each other, he smiled and licked his lips. "Your embouchure's improved," he said, grinning.

Tyrone suddenly called that the sergeant was coming. Pearl pulled away from the fence and fled back into the bushes.

The next week passed in a fast, delirious rapture. She floated through rehearsals, the sets at the Trocadero, her household chores, and her daily four-hour music practice. She was dying to tell someone about the proposal, especially Martin, but he was on the road now, heading west across the country.

When Nora Barnes telephoned Pearl at the Trocadero and told her that she was now engaged to Pookie, who was converting his property into a peacock farm, Pearl could no longer contain herself. In a rush she told Nora about her own impending marriage. Nora, far from being shocked that Pearl was to marry a black man, was so happy for them both that she insisted they come up and visit. The four of them could go bushwalking together, and at night they could dine at the Carrington Hotel. Nora would be Pearl's bridesmaid and Pearl would be Nora's. Perhaps they could even have a double wedding, suggested Nora. "A double white wedding—with one black groom!" The two of them laughed until the line went dead.

Pearl could hardly wait for her weekly meeting in the rose garden with James, but on the Thursday morning another telegram arrived with exactly the same message as the week before: NO LESSON TODAY. NO PASS. JAMES.

"Looks like your teacher's been misbehaving," said Aub, glancing over Pearl's shoulder at the message.

"What do you mean?"

"Denied passes two weeks in a row. Must've done something really bad."

Her hand began to tremble as she pocketed the telegram. She knew her father was only teasing, but it worried her nonetheless. She hated being denied James, so suddenly, without warning, and wondered whether the same wording in the telegram was a covert invitation for her to seek him out at the camp once more.

This time, she left her saxophone behind, and caught the train out to Granville with a ham sandwich in her handbag. She skirted the camp again, half expecting him to be standing in the same trench as the week before, waiting for her to appear. But when she came upon it, no one was there. The stench, though, was overpowering, and she realised that the camp had no proper sanitation; what James and Tyrone had been digging the week before was a defecation pit. She hurried away and continued to circle the camp. When she caught no sight of him, she sat beneath a blue gum and ate her lunch. Finally, as she was brushing crumbs from her skirt, she saw Tyrone, about twenty yards away, carrying some tools toward the warehouse south of the camp. She picked up a stone and lobbed it over the fence, trying to get his attention. It wasn't until her third attempt, when a rock the size of her fist landed at his feet, that he looked over and saw her.

She had to wait almost another hour before James could get away from the warehouse. As he strode toward her, she could see his eyes were glassy, a deep frown set in his face.

"God, you look gorgeous," he murmured, and kissed her through the fence. His hands were covered in grease, but she clutched at them anyway—wanting any part of him that she could have—and asked him what had gone wrong.

He pulled away a little, staring at the ground. "CO's got it in for me, baby. It don't look good." She tried to remain calm, but felt her queasy insides flipping. James sighed. "CO's denied me permission to marry you."

"What?" she gasped. "What's he got to do with it?"

"I told you, everyone has to get permission."

"But I thought that was just a formality. Just paperwork."

James snorted and pressed his forehead against the fence. He looked exhausted, as if he hadn't slept for days. "CO has the right to deny permission if he figures a marriage ain't in the soldier's best interests. My CO, he's from Georgia, and he ain't happy 'bout the likes of you and me gettin' married."

"But you said it's legal here."

"It is, but—"

"So what's to stop you walking out of camp and us getting married anyway? We don't even need permission from my parents."

"Honey, why you think he's had me locked up in here, on extra duties every day, for the last two weeks?"

"He'll have to let you out on leave sometime."

"Here's the kicker, baby," he said, gripping her fingers. "Now I don't want you to get upset. We'll find a way around it."

"What?"

A nerve in James's right cheek began to twitch. She could tell he was bracing himself to deliver more bad news.

"He's having me transferred."

Things were falling apart so fast she could hardly digest the news.

"Where?"

"Queensland. Next week. Friday, I reckon."

"I'll come with you," she said automatically, as if it were as easy as following him across a city street.

"You can't do that."

"Why not?"

"With the war on, you ain't even allowed to cross a state line without getting permission from the cops."

She hadn't thought of that. Deflated, she, too, rested her forehead against the fence, racking her brains for a solution. Everything felt taut and intense and urgent, as if it were all happening at twice the tempo it should, and just as she felt she was about to be swept up in a current of panic, Nora Barnes and her generous invitation popped into her head.

They arranged to meet the following Saturday night, in the back lane behind the Trocadero, after she'd finished her last set and collected her pay. James knew he wouldn't be able to get a leave pass, but Tyrone was on duty that weekend, driving a supply truck between the Granville camp and the White Bay wharves, and he was confident he could smuggle James out. Then it was just a matter of catching the last train to the Blue Mountains, where they would hide out at Nora and Pookie's farm until the war ended. When Pearl had proposed the idea to Nora during a subsequent phone conversation, Nora was thrilled by the idea of harbouring fugitives. She and Pookie could do with the company, she said. "As long as it's *bad*."

With Martin gone, the thought of running away was easier. The house seemed empty and lifeless without him. Her parents moved in the same, boring rhythms; Lulu sat mute by the fire all day. Of course, she'd miss playing at the Trocadero at night, but in her romantic daydreams she imagined that she and James would eventually perform on bigger stages after the war, ones that could accommodate the two of them together without prejudice or fuss. What they were about to do was against the law, but to Pearl it was probably the most virtuous step she had ever considered taking.

Each night that week, when she left for work, she sneaked out a small instalment of clothes and personal items, which she stored in her locker backstage at the Troc. The transfer of belongings from her bedroom to the ballroom was so gradual and subtle that neither of her parents suspected she was planning an escape. She stockpiled two skirts, three dresses, stockings, four pairs of shoes, five changes of underwear, her favourite records, photos of her family, cosmetics, her address book, musical arrangements, and the twenty-three pounds she'd stashed in a hole in her mattress. She bought a new pair of pumps to match the new life she was about to embark upon. By Saturday night, the suitcase was bulging so much she had to tie it shut with a piece of rope. She'd already written a letter to her par-

ents—an explanation, an apology, urging them not to worry—
and would post it before they boarded the train to Katoomba.

All through Saturday night, she was intensely conscious of
the fact that this would be the last time she would play in the
Trocadero Ballroom: the last time she'd blow second alto on the
revolving stage, the last time she'd solo there on "Take the 'A'
Train,'" the last time she'd hear the bandleader, Lionel Bogwald,
announce the prize for the best dancers as coloured streamers
fell from the ceiling. It was the only time she felt any misgiv-
ings for everything she was giving up.

The winter wind cut through her overcoat as she waited in
the back lane. Midnight came and went; now it was almost half
past twelve and he still hadn't appeared. He'd told her not to
worry if he ran late, but she couldn't help herself: Maybe the
truck had broken down; maybe his sergeant had caught him
trying to escape; perhaps Tyrone had been assigned a different detail and hadn't been allowed to drive the supply truck.
The Trocadero had closed up. She pulled her coat more tightly
around her, knowing that if he didn't turn up soon they'd miss
the last train and would have to try to book into a hotel, which
would probably be impossible. What made it all worse was that
she needed desperately to pee and her anxiety was now exac-
erbating the urge. She sat on the suitcase and crossed her legs.

After what seemed like hours a hunched figure slipped
around the corner and walked down the lane, his footsteps a
staccato rhythm against the pavement. She jumped up and ran
toward him: Her whole life was about to hurtle off into an entirely new direction—she was *improvising,* she told herself; she
was taking risks.

But as soon as she threw herself into his arms she knew that something was terribly wrong. It wasn't his smell, his touch, his voice encompassing her, but the scent of wet newspaper, a gruff squeeze of the arm, someone muttering, "I'm sorry, Pearl," in a low, unfamiliar voice.

"He ain't coming," said Tyrone. "He asked me to give you this." And as she took the envelope he held out, as the shock of what was happening slammed her, she felt something inside give way, and a stream of hot liquid began running down her thighs and splattering her new leather shoes.

Dear Pearl,

I'm not much of a writer—wish I could play this on my sax instead. Baby, this is the hardest decision I've ever had to make. I love and admire you more than anyone I've known. Always believe that. You deserve everything. I don't want you to throw away your life on me, give up your family and your job. What it gets down to in the end is that I want what's best for you, and a life with me, no matter what country we live in, won't be able to give that to you. But I do want you to know that I've never felt so loved by anyone in the world. You've changed me in ways I can't describe. And I know that because of you I'll never be the same again.

All my love,

James X

For days after, Pearl was overcome by a suffocating kind of panic. Her heart raced constantly and she couldn't sleep or eat. She went over and over in her mind every moment she could remember that she and James had shared, trying to fathom some other reason for his breaking off their engagement. Had she come on too strong? Or not strong enough? Had he really loved her or had he just been stringing her along? Would he replace her with another woman once he'd resettled in Queensland? Most days she'd weep herself into exhaustion by midafternoon, then she'd draw a bath and soak in it with the lights off until it was time to go to work.

She grew more and more absentminded, walking into traffic, arriving late most nights at the Trocadero, forgetting that her period had arrived and wandering about the house in soiled pyjama pants. She half expected to receive a second letter from James, recanting his first one and summoning her to some secret location, but no such letter arrived.

As the weeks passed, she tried to quell her grief and frustration by blowing it into her saxophone. But struggling through her musical exercises each day became a chore as mind-numbing as starching petticoats or polishing the kitchen floor. She couldn't concentrate. She had no appetite. And even though the muscles around her mouth throbbed from practice, the soft sinuous tone that James had assured her would emerge still evaded her.

Martin wrote to her every few days, always beginning the letter with *My dearest Burly* . . . He described the purple mountains of the Great Dividing Range, rural towns choked with the frost of late winter, travelling west across the country in the back of a cattle truck. His company was made up of a six-piece jazz band, a ventriloquist who also doubled as a female impersonator, a baritone, a tap-dancing comedian, a magician, and a compere who also performed a juggling routine. They took their meals in the mess halls of army camps and slept on military bedrolls. They performed beneath the stars each night on a portable stage built of floorboards and balanced on forty-four-gallon drums. When they weren't working or rehearsing, Martin and the others lazed around the beaches of the Indian Ocean, on the other side of the country, chatting up the WAAC girls, eating local crayfish, and drinking beer.

Martin's letters provided brief respites from her overwhelming grief. She often yearned to trade places with her brother so she could be the one who travelled country roads, performed in bush clearings, who slept beneath a waxing moon. Instead, she played by rote through her sets at the Trocadero, stayed away from the other girls in the band during breaks, packed up her sax at the end of the last set, and fled home on the tram. She continued to wait for another letter from James, and the longer she waited the thinner she grew.

Her parents seemed oblivious to her distress; they were engaged in constant arguments over the petty details of the air-raid shelter: the plumbing, the food stocks, how much water should be stored at any one time. Now that the Japanese were almost upon Australia, Clara insisted that they should have a telephone installed, even though they couldn't afford it.

"When the bombs start falling," said Aub, "who're you going to ring?"

Nevertheless, one morning in late spring three men in overalls arrived and spent the day laying wires along the skirting boards of the hallway and parlour. The next day, Pearl woke to the telephone's pretty trill echoing through the house. The telephone was the colour of ebony, the same texture as the black keys of a piano, with letters as well as numbers printed under the dial, and it sat on its own, against a white lace doily, on a side table in the parlour.

Surprisingly, Clara's intuition proved to be correct: Within forty-eight hours of the telephone being installed, it saved the family from tragedy.

On 27 November 1942, Pearl mixed up a cocktail of her father's taxidermy fluids—formaldehyde, ammonia, arsenic, and borax. She drank it down in six or seven gulps, lay down on one of the mattresses in the air-raid shelter, and waited for it all to end.

8

The Master of Lunacy had a part in the middle of his straight, ash-coloured hair. When he leaned forward to take Pearl's pulse, she noticed the pale translucent line of his scalp. He wore round silver spectacles on the bridge of his nose and he looked younger than he probably was because his face was untanned and unlined, as if he'd spent his entire life indoors. He was wearing a tweed suit and a brown velvet bow tie that sat at a crooked angle against his neck. His real name was Hector Best, but the official title of the doctor who presided over Sydney's mentally ill was the Master of Lunacy. He had two offices: one at a Darlinghurst treatment centre and the other on the grounds of the Callan Park insane asylum.

After Aub had discovered Pearl unconscious in the air-raid shelter, he made the first call on the new telephone. She was spirited off in an ambulance to St. Vincent's Hospital, where two doctors pumped her stomach and hooked her up to a drip. Pearl spent eighteen hours in intensive care before she came out of her coma. When she opened her eyes she didn't smile with relief; she stared at the ceiling, opened her mouth, and screamed—not because she was scared, mind you, but because she was still alive. The staff, unable to control her, sedated her with morphine, aspirin, and cold towels against her forehead.

A couple of hours later, once she'd calmed down, the Master of Lunacy appeared in her ward and sat on the edge of her bed. He took her wrist and made a bracelet around it with his thumb and forefinger, the last joints of which overlapped. He then examined her tongue and checked her reflexes. He questioned her about how much she ate each day, and Clara answered for her that Pearl ate next to nothing, like a bird, a sparrow.

"Are you scared of dying, Miss Willis?"

Pearl brushed the hair out of her eyes, shook her head, and replied, "No, I'm scared of living."

The Master frowned and took her temperature. He took out a stethoscope and pressed its cold metal disc against her heart. His fingers were long and smooth, with short, clean, manicured nails, and his hands were so soft they were like satin gloves against her rib cage. He shone a torch into each of her eyes and then gazed down her throat as if he might discover something valuable. He measured the circumference of her head and wrote down the results in a lined notebook.

After the Master had finished examining her, Aub and Clara asked him if he knew what was wrong with their daughter. The Master replied, as if Pearl wasn't there, that she was suffering from an acute nervous condition brought on by the war. He'd seen a lot of it lately, particularly among girls and the elderly. It was their great fear of dying.

"Even in matters of lunacy, Mrs. Willis," he said, "men and women are separate species." He touched his velvet bow tie, as if he were checking that it hadn't disappeared. "Men go on the attack, women worry and fall apart."

"She's always been a bit different," said Clara, glancing at Pearl, "but she's never wanted to do anything like this before."

The Master prescribed twelve weeks' total rest and three doses a day of quinine sulphate. He referred her for further treatment to Reception House, which was his clinic in nearby Darlinghurst.

In order to expedite the benefits of Pearl's treatment, the Master of Lunacy advised Clara and Aub to discourage any extreme behaviour or activity: no late nights, no alcohol, no contact with any of her rowdy musician friends. Of course, she could forget about her job at the Trocadero. She needed rest, food, peace, and quiet.

Pearl needn't have worried about resigning from the Trocadero. By the time she was released from hospital, after three days of observation, Lionel Bogwald had already replaced her with a woman from Melbourne.

Still tired and depressed, she was picked up by her parents in a taxi and driven home. After lunch, a boy from the chemist on Darlinghurst Road delivered a large brown bottle of quinine sulphate, the crystals that had to be dissolved in port wine. At 2 PM, Aub abandoned the silky terrier he was stuffing, washed his hands, and accompanied his daughter to Reception House for her first session. It took almost a quarter of an hour to walk up Victoria Street and into Darlinghurst, and all the way Pearl clung to her father's arm. She was convinced the people they passed were stopping to whisper to each other, while others pointed at her from a distance. The faces of neighbours appeared from behind the curtains of parlours, and she was sure they were staring at her, sure she could hear their snorts of laughter and clicking tongues: "Crazy Pearl Willis, Crazy Pearl Willis." And when a mouldy orange fell from the window of a terrace on Macleay Street and landed at her feet, she was certain it had been aimed at her.

The Reception House waiting room was drab and the walls were stained with tobacco smoke. The Master of Lunacy appeared in the doorway, a white coat buttoned up over his dark suit. He glanced at Pearl shyly, his eyes barely meeting hers.

Aub stood up, but the Master waved him back to his seat. "Just the girl. We'll be finished in an hour."

Pearl followed the Master's white coat down a hallway and into a small room with a dusty windowpane. The Master drew the curtains and handed her a robe. His face reddened as, with his eyes averted, he told her to undress.

When he left, Pearl unbuttoned her dress and kicked off her shoes, resigning herself to whatever treatment lay ahead. Soon a nurse entered and led Pearl to an adjoining room, where a narrow wooden cabinet stood in one corner. It was about six feet long and three feet wide. It looked to Pearl like an upright coffin.

The nurse opened the door of the cabinet and clouds of steam billowed into the room. She removed Pearl's robe, and Pearl stepped inside. There was a tiny bench that she was told to sit on. When the door slammed shut and she heard the click of the lock she felt as if she were being buried alive.

Each day from then on, she would be confined to a steam

cabinet, would have cold water poured onto her head, followed by wet packs and douches and enemas prepared from herbal teas. It was as if the doctors were trying to flush from her the very essence of her being.

Now that she'd lost her job at the Trocadero, she was listless and bored. Only her bickering parents, her deaf grandmother, the radio, her daily therapy, and the postal service now defined her life. But her lowest point was when Clara returned her saxophone to Palings to help pay off the debt her parents now owed—not only on the remaining balance on the bank loan they had taken out to buy the instrument, but also on the mounting bills of the new telephone that had saved Pearl's life the month before. As the sax was packed away in its case and carried out the door, she felt her entire face go numb and she began to itch all over. After that, she stayed in bed for most of the day, staring at the embossed roses woven around the borders of the pressed metal ceiling of her room.

The only things that could lift her mood were the postcards she received from seaside villages and gold-mining towns, with pictures on the front and arrows drawn over them, pointing to a riverbank or hillside where Martin's unit had been performing. And early in the new year, she received a letter from Nora Barnes in the Blue Mountains. Pookie's peacocks were bringing in truckloads of money, she wrote; his plumes were now feathering the hats of all the girls in Sydney. She also confessed that she and Pookie had eloped to Lithgow for a quickie marriage, because she was already two months pregnant and wanted to avoid a scandal within her circle of family and friends.

Twice a week, after her treatment in the steam cabinet, she'd be summoned by the Master of Lunacy to his office in Reception House. It had deep leather chairs and a wide bay window. He'd take her pulse and check her blood pressure, put a stethoscope against the left side of her chest. And while he examined her, he asked her seemingly irrelevant questions, like what her favourite flower was, and if she liked to wear perfume.

She made an effort to eat more, and whatever she couldn't she hid in her pockets, later flushing it down the toilet or throwing it over the back fence when no one was looking.

One afternoon in late May, after the Master of Lunacy had checked her heart, pulse, and weight, he asked her to sit in one of the big leather chairs and offered her a glass of lemonade. He disappeared for a minute and returned with two filled glasses, handing her one before settling into his chair and picking up her file. Staring at his notes, he asked her how she was feeling.

Pearl shifted, wondering if it were a trick question. She sipped her drink. "My little finger's sore," she said, waggling it. "I accidentally cut the nail down to the quick."

The Master smiled briefly and shook his head. How did she feel *inside* herself? he wanted to know. How did she feel *generally*?

She still didn't know how to answer and so remained silent, her hands folded on her lap.

"Are you feeling better than you did, say, in December? When we first began?"

"Oh, yes." Pearl nodded. "I'm sleeping more."

"Well, you're certainly eating more. Eight pounds in five months. Do you feel any happier, any more at ease?"

Pearl thought for a moment, watching the ice cubes bob in her glass. She began to blush, terrified that she would burst into tears in front of the doctor and tell him how lonely she was, how she'd ruined her career and how there was nothing in the world she looked forward to anymore and she had no idea what she'd do with the rest of her life.

Instead, she drew in a deep breath, lifted her chin, and flashed the doctor a smile. "Your therapy has worked wonders, Doctor. I feel like a woman reborn."

She wondered why she'd told such a brazen lie, and could only attribute it to the fact that she'd sensed the doctor had very much needed to hear it. And her intuition was confirmed when his hunched shoulders relaxed, his legs uncrossed. He sipped his drink, a nervous smile playing on his lips.

"Well, Miss Willis, I've been reviewing you, I mean your file, and uh, well"—he glanced at the papers in his lap—"you've made such good progress, such excellent progress. Don't you think?"

Again, Pearl wasn't sure how to answer: It was as if her true feelings were the subject of an examination for which she hadn't studied. She still felt like a husk of her former self but—it was true—she was improving. She suspected, however, that this was due more to the monotony of her life than to any particular treatment. Finally, she nodded.

"Good!" said the Master. "I think it's time we terminated your treatment here at Reception House. I'd like to refer you to your local GP, Dr. Vincent Ward, whom you should visit once a month." He glanced at her file again. "Keep taking the quinine sulphate, but halve the dosage from now on."

The Master's eyes narrowed as he read something on the chart.

"It's almost your birthday," he observed. "Are you doing anything special?"

Pearl shrugged. "Mum and Dad want to take me to an afternoon tea at the Coogee Bay Hotel."

"Ah, lovely," he said, turning one foot in a semicircle, as if he had a stiff ankle.

"I wish my brother were here." Pearl ran her finger around the rim of the glass. "It's our first birthday apart."

The Master of Lunacy nodded sagely. "It's all part of growing up, Pearl." And then the Master did something highly unusual: He leaned across and touched her hair briefly, as if he were blessing her.

As soon as Clara learned that Pearl had officially recovered from her illness, she began to talk about packing her off to typing school, or the possibility of her getting a job in one of the local shops, or perhaps joining the Women's Army. But Pearl didn't want to do anything but play music. She yearned only for her saxophone, her lover, and her brother.

In any case, Clara's ideas came to naught; within two weeks of her recovery, Pearl received a letter from the government telling her to register for a Manpower job and begin work for the war effort immediately.

In some ways, the letter was a gift, as it relieved her from having to make any decision herself. The work was compulsory, like her treatment at Reception House had been, and would get her out of the house and away from her nagging mother.

At her interview at the local Masonic Hall, she was given a choice between a job at Armstrong Steel, a clerical position at the Rationing Commission, or a place at A. Jordan & Company, sewing army shirts for the Allies. She had no desire to make steel wool or keep books in an office, so she opted for the third choice, and within days was surrounded by bolts of material, buttons, and the hum of machinery. Her job was to sew the front pockets of khaki shirts. To relieve the boredom of the job she often wrote notes to the soldiers and slipped them inside: *Thanks for the great job you're doing. . . . Are you far from home? . . . I used to be a jazz musician.* One day, she received a letter back from an Australian stationed in New Guinea: *I have to get out of this shithole. I don't know why I'm here anymore.* His name was Private Jack Stanley. They wrote to each other twice more. Six weeks later, a brief, matter-of-fact note arrived from Stanley's best army mate, informing her that Stanley had been killed in the New Guinea jungle.

The day of her nineteenth birthday was unusually warm, with light clouds scudding across the sky and a breeze that carried the scent of salt and seaweed. From the roof of the Coogee Bay Hotel, she could hear the gentle rhythm of waves breaking on the shore across the road. The musicians were seated on a dais at one end of the roof, tuning their instruments, framed by an arbour of flowering vines.

Clara and Aubrey had told her she could invite a friend. Pearl had written to Nora Barnes, asking her to visit Sydney for her birthday weekend, but Nora was now heavily pregnant and did not wish to travel alone. Instead, as a gift, she sent Pearl a bunch of long feathers from one of Pookie's finest peacocks.

And so Pearl sat alone with her parents, quietly sipping tea as the band finally struck up and couples rushed to the diamond-shaped dance floor. The roof was decorated with ceramic pots holding tall ferns and window boxes of flowering geraniums; the tables were covered with heavy linen cloths fringed with lace. It was a kind and thoughtful birthday treat, but Pearl couldn't stop comparing it to her birthday of the year before, when James had been with her and she'd unwrapped her saxophone and all her dreams had seemed within her grasp.

She nibbled at a sandwich as the band played their first number. It had been months since she had played any music herself, but still she recognised that the band wasn't very good: The trombonist's tone was painfully thin, the trumpet was out of tune, and the tempo kept speeding up during the chorus. She abandoned the sandwich and stood up, weaving her way between tables, trying to find the ladies' powder room. When she found it, she bludged a cigarette off one of the waitresses and sat smoking it on one of the stools, staring at her sad twin in the mirror.

After pinning wisps of hair back into her pompadour bun, she returned to the rooftop. As she made her way back to the table she gazed at the slate-coloured ocean and swooping seagulls and then something to her right caught her eye—a ship on the horizon—and before she knew it she was walking straight into one of the potted palms. She reeled back, spun on the ball of one foot, and fell into the lap of a man, knocking over his ice bucket and bottle of champagne.

"I'm so sorry!" she exclaimed, springing to her feet.

The man was dressed in a black suit and wore a charcoal-grey hat that shaded his face. He was pale and clean-shaven, with a spot of blood on his left cheek where he'd cut himself shaving. He still wore his glasses but in the sleek black suit and white tie he looked curiously transformed, more debonair. He stood up, and she took the hand he held out to her.

"Miss Willis," he said, peering into her eyes. "You're looking so much better." He crooked his arm and held it out to her. "Would you care to join me on the dance floor?"

The band was into the second chorus of "Tea for Two." She didn't know how to dance but for the first time in her life she didn't care. She hooked her arm through his and allowed the Master of Lunacy to lead her onto the polished wood, to take her into his loose embrace. As she rested her cheek on the lapel of his jacket, Pearl glimpsed her mother beaming at her as if she'd performed some heroic deed or miracle. Her father, how-ever, was stony-faced.

During the winter of 1943, at Clara's invitation, Hector Best visited the house twice a week. He joined the family for their traditional Sunday roast, and on Saturdays escorted Pearl to whatever recreation or amusement she desired. Her health was gradually improving, and the Master of Lunacy was an atten-tive companion who tried very hard to please Pearl. Sometimes he seemed more like a close, adoring uncle than a beau, and to be sure, he was no longer the young sportsman who had once thrown javelins and discuses in state competitions. He was still tall and slim but his limbs had grown stiff over the years, and now his only daily exercise was walking from his home in Millers Point to his Office of Lunacy at Hyde Park Barracks, or from the Barracks to Reception House. He wore expensive tailored suits and crisp starched shirts with grandfather collars and neckties the colour of dishwater. His skin was so pale he often looked as if he were recovering from an illness himself. His eyes were the Master's most attractive feature—wide and gentle, the colour of honey. He was almost thirty-six and had never been married.

Aubrey did nothing to encourage the relationship, believing that Hector was taking advantage of Pearl, particularly since she hadn't fully recovered. Clara, however, was thrilled that a professional man, especially a doctor, was romancing her— even if he was nearly twice her age. The Master was a refreshing change from all the vaudevillians and musicians in the family. Clara told Pearl that he was the type who would always have a good and regular salary, and in the delicate way he guided Pearl down a flight of stairs or wrapped his coat around her shivering shoulders, Clara recognised a man who would take care of the girl, who would always cherish her.

The companionship that the Master provided each week was a welcome diversion from the monotony of sewing shirt pockets in the factory. Each Saturday, he brought her bouquets of lilies or dewy violets cultivated in a small greenhouse that he'd built in his backyard. They often strolled through Hyde Park, and he would point to plants and flowers, reciting their various popular names and then the Latin monikers. Sometimes they walked as far as Circular Quay and caught a ferry across to Manly, where they picnicked in an area of the beach that wasn't sectioned off by fencing and barbed wire. If Pearl wished to see a particular film, they both saw it immediately. If she had a craving for sausages, the Master promptly found a café or restaurant that served them.

Hector was intimate with all Pearl's weaknesses, yet they didn't seem to deter him; if anything, they seemed to make him care for her even more, as if her flaws were something to be admired. They occasionally enjoyed a chaste kiss now and then, but the doctor had never ventured further.

To please him, she pressed and dried the flowers he picked, mounted them on white cardboard, and framed them behind glass. She loved to see his face brighten when she presented him with a gift. Even though his name was Hector Best, Pearl preferred to call him the Master or, when she was in a whimsical mood, Mr. Lunatic, which always made him smile with embarrassment. His hands were gentle and warm, and when he traced the curve of her jaw or dusted her hair with his fingers, she often felt more relaxed and secure than after drinking the quinine sulphate or undergoing her hydrotherapy.

One day in early August, Clara announced that she could hear the telephone ringing and suddenly left the parlour. Before Pearl could say she couldn't hear a thing, the Master fell to his knees and, with a magician's deft sleight of hand, suddenly produced a ruby-studded ring. Pearl had sensed this would happen eventually, but she hadn't been expecting it so soon after her illness. She was uncertain of her feelings for Hector. She didn't know whether she felt affection or love or something else that she couldn't name. Perhaps it was merely gratitude—

gratitude for his friendship, his tenderness. All she knew for sure was that she wasn't obsessed with Hector as she had been, and still was, with James. She took the ring between her thumb and forefinger and turned it in the sunlight. She then placed the ring over her right eye and looked through it, as if it were a tiny monocle. "It's pretty, Mr. Lunatic."

Hector chewed on his bottom lip. "Will you, Pearl?"

Stalling for time, she tried to slip the ring onto the third finger of her left hand, but it was too small and she couldn't push it over her second knuckle.

Hector's face dropped. "I'll get it enlarged."

Pearl turned the band of gold around the first knuckle of her finger. She was desperate not to hurt his feelings.

"You think I'm too old," he said.

"No, I don't." Her reply came a little too fast, and he wilted a little before lowering himself from his kneeling position to sit directly on the floor. "I was your doctor once. Does that make a difference?"

She considered lying, agreeing with the suggestion and letting him down easily, when she noticed Hector had begun to tremble. She reached out and touched his shoulder, but he whimpered like a young boy. And she realised that she no longer felt like that carefree young girl who had frequented the sly grog joints in the Cross and made love in a fairground, in the Botanic Gardens, in an abandoned mansion. She had thought of herself as a woman of the world, but now her younger self seemed immature and childish, never thinking about the consequences of her actions, or how many people she hurt. Perhaps marriage would mature her, would make her more responsible.

9

Her engagement to a doctor redeemed Pearl's reputation in the neighbourhood. The Willis girl was now no longer considered a reckless teenager, but a beautiful young woman who was about to be married. Of course, there were still a few cynics who thought it was entirely appropriate that someone as mad as Pearl should wed a psychiatrist. For the most part, however, friends of the family were happy for the couple and began dropping off gifts for her glory box.

There were invitation lists to draw up, bouquets to design. Nora Barnes, who had given birth to a baby boy, was to be the one and only bridesmaid. Aubrey's five-year-old great-niece, Lavinia, would be the flower girl (Clara decided the girl could wear her polio brace at the wedding, but not her thick round glasses). Hector didn't have any close friends so his father was appointed to be the best man, which made a good joke when anyone asked about it—the best man really *was* a Best man: Hector Best, Senior.

War rations made it difficult to find any decent materials for a wedding dress, and after weeks of scouring the tables of department stores, Pearl had to settle for one of her mother's old theatre gowns made from ivory magnolia satin. Clara would alter the dress, while Lulu would stitch the pattern of teardrop crystals around the bodice. They decided on a net veil crowned with a garland of fresh camellias.

On the weekends Hector brought her bouquets of tiger lilies from his greenhouse. And it was this behaviour that continued to draw Pearl to Hector—his thoughtfulness and generosity—when many men as accomplished as he was would find it easy to be narrow-minded and demanding. These qualities didn't make her want to rip the buttons off his shirt or tongue his ear all night; theirs was a quieter, gentler connection. She was fairly certain she wasn't in love with him, but she knew now that she'd never hear from James again, and she couldn't bear to hurt Hector and cause him unhappiness. And even if she did have the occasional reservation about spending the rest of her life with him, she figured that her feelings were a normal response to such a serious commitment—and anyway, they were engaged now and it was too late to change her mind. She was also aware that she would never lose Hector to the war effort, as his position as Master of Lunacy was a protected occupation. Marrying him was the right thing to do.

One bright Saturday morning in September, a fortnight before their wedding day, Hector and Pearl bought matching gold bands from a jeweller on King Street, the same one who'd enlarged her engagement ring. Hector's fingers were so long and

narrow his ring was only a half-size bigger than Pearl's, and she
joked that if she ever lost hers, she could always borrow his.
They walked back to Potts Point arm in arm through the Botanic Gardens. As they strolled through the shadows of tall trees,
beneath a colony of dozing fruit bats, Pearl was struck by the
fact that she and James used to walk exactly the same paths
during the days of their courtship—though never arm in arm,
of course. For a moment she found herself fantasising that the
arm crooked around hers was James's, that it was his citrus aftershave she could smell above the loamy odour of the duck pond.
She smiled guiltily at Hector for her momentary betrayal before
they walked through the gates and down the staircase that led to
the wharves of Woolloomooloo. Sagging streamers and shrink-
ing balloons still hung from awnings of milk bars and grocery
stores, remnants from the post-election parties the week before,
when Prime Minister Curtin had been voted back in.

Pearl had insisted on wearing her wedding ring until she
arrived home; only then would she return it to its velvet box
and give it back to Hector. Now she lifted her hand and saw
the sunlight glint off the band, and stopped in the middle of
the footpath to kiss Hector on the lips while the barefoot kids
playing in the street whistled lewdly.

She was laughing at the whistling children when a man
swept out of a pub and bumped into her.

"Sorry, love!" he apologised, breathing cheap whisky fumes
over her. She was about to brush him off when she recognised
the thinning, slicked-back hair and pencil moustache: It was
Lionel Bogwald, her former bandleader from the Trocadero. He
recognised her at the same time, and suddenly he was throwing

his arms around her and kissing her on the cheek. "How I've missed you, dear girl! We all have!" Then he held her at arm's length. "My, you're looking well."

Pearl was laughing self-consciously. "Well, I've missed you, too."

"It hasn't been the same since you and Martin left," he added. "No practical jokes. No fun anymore!" He opened a silver case and offered her a cigarette, which she accepted, took one for himself, and lit both with a lighter. As she was exhaling Pearl realised she'd forgotten to introduce her fiancé. He was standing beside her, frowning.

"Oh, I'm so sorry!" she said. "Hector, this is Lionel Bogwald, my old bandleader. Lionel, this is Hector."

Bogwald uttered some pleasantries and offered him a cigarette, but Hector shook his head. The bandleader asked Pearl about Martin and the rest of her family and then reminisced about the night the twins had tied a dead fish to his trombone slide. When he'd picked up his instrument to play his solo, the cod flopped and swung about wildly until the string snapped and the fish went flying through the air and ended up in the lap of the Lord Mayor's wife.

Pearl and Bogwald laughed at the memory of it, but Hector barely cracked a smile. She'd never seen him so serious and withdrawn, not even when he'd been her doctor.

She and Bogwald threw down their butts and stepped on them. They bade an affectionate good-bye, and the bandleader shook Hector's hand again, even remembering his name.

"And don't forget," Bogwald added, as he headed off toward the Domain, "don't be a stranger at the Troc, my dear girl. You come down and sit in with us any night you like."

"I will," she promised, waving.

"Fancy running into him," she remarked, as she and Hector crossed the road. "He's a great bandleader, you know—the best. He trained in England, with the London Philharmonic."

Hector said nothing until, after what seemed like a long while, he cleared his throat and said, "I didn't know you smoked."

Pearl shrugged. "Just now and again."

Hector pursed his lips and looked away. She was expecting him to say that women shouldn't smoke, especially in public, or that it wasn't good for her health, but after a minute or so he asked, "So how long have you known this chap?"

"Who, Lionel?" She thought for a moment. "Well, I auditioned for the Troc when I was seventeen, so I guess that'd be a couple of years."

Hector kept his eyes fixed on the aircraft carrier to their left. "And how often did you go out with him?"

Pearl was so startled by the question she wasn't sure if she'd heard him correctly. "He was my bandleader, Hector. My boss."

"Never your boyfriend?"

Pearl assured him that she and Lionel Bogwald were just friends—no, not even friends, merely former colleagues. She couldn't think of anything more ridiculous than a romance with Lionel Bogwald: His breath often smelled of gin and, when it rained, black hair dye ran down the side of his face. Hector was silent as they began to climb the steep McElhone Stairs to her house. She wasn't sure if she'd convinced him about the bandleader, but he asked no more questions.

When they arrived home, Pearl's unease about Hector's behaviour was forgotten when they walked into the parlour to find Lulu lying on the floor gasping for air. Her eyes were rolled back and she was shaking as if a thousand watts of electricity were bolting through her system. Clara was on her knees, crying, "Mum! Oh my God. I'm here!" The wedding dress Lulu had been beading was coiled around her body and, remarkably, she still had the needle between her thumb and forefinger, as if she intended to keep sewing once her seizure had passed. Hector fell to his knees, stuck his fingers in her mouth, and removed her false teeth.

By the time the ambulance arrived the spasms had receded and she'd fallen into a limp semi-consciousness. Clara rode with her in the back of the ambulance, while Aub, Pearl, and Hector hurried up Victoria Street on foot, through the Kings Cross intersection and on into Darlinghurst to the emergency ward of St. Vincent's Hospital. A team of doctors was now examining Lulu to determine what had happened. Aubrey took his distraught wife into his arms and rocked her, kissed her eyelids, and in a soft voice called her "Pigeon."

After an hour or so Lulu was breathing regularly again and her heart rate had finally steadied. But she was still unconscious and was transferred to a bed in Intensive Care. The doctors believed she'd suffered a stroke, and warned the family that Lulu's chances of regaining consciousness were slim, especially since she was eighty-three years old. They suggested that any family or close friends should be summoned at once.

A vigil formed around her bed. Pearl, Hector, Aubrey, and Clara took it in turns to talk to Lulu's impassive face. When Father Jim arrived he sprinkled her with holy water and uttered the last rites in a soft, faltering voice. Aubrey sent a telegram to Martin through the main army headquarters in Brisbane, urging him to return home immediately. Clara decided that the wedding should be postponed. Lulu could die at any time and no one wanted grief to taint a celebration. And then there was nothing left to do but pray.

Two days later, Pearl was returning from the ladies' room when she saw a tall, suntanned man in uniform walking down the corridor toward her, weaving between a tea trolley, two nuns, a man on crutches, and an empty wheelchair. His blond hair was cropped short. He had a bounce in his step, and she caught herself thinking that he was rather handsome.

Then the man cried out, "Burly!" He broke into a run and she was suddenly swept up into his arms and swung about in circles.

"You're too skinny," he chided, his big hands spanning her waist. "Didn't they feed you in the madhouse?"

Pearl was teary and laughing at the same time. "Just Mum's cooking," she said. "That's enough to drive you crazy."

He seemed taller, bigger somehow; the skin on his nose was peeling; his hair was sun-bleached; lines had formed above his eyebrows. He slung his arm around her and they walked down the hall together toward Lulu's ward.

Later, as Martin and Pearl strolled home from the hospital, Martin teased, "So you're almost an old married lady now? Can't wait to meet the bloke who's pulled that off."

Hector arrived in the early evening, wearing a dark suit

and bow tie. His light brown eyes seemed at once small and averted. Over dinner, he began to speak of Pearl in an unusually possessive way. "Pearl shouldn't drink, you know," he told Martin. "It's not good for her complexion. . . . Pearl doesn't miss playing the saxophone at all—it was just a phase she was going through. . . . Pearl's not really clumsy—it's just a lack of focus. We're trying to train her to concentrate more."

Pearl became increasingly irritated. Hector had only known her for a year or so while Martin had known her his whole life.

Hector left soon after the meal, giving Pearl a brief peck on the cheek and telling her to get some rest. In fact, the entire family was so exhausted that they all retired to their beds straight after the nine o'clock news. Near midnight, the phone rang; Lulu had taken a bad turn and might not make it through the night. They pulled their coats on over their pyjamas and made the pilgrimage on foot back through the darkness to St. Vincent's.

Throughout the following day she seemed to waver between this world and the next, and no one could predict to which one she'd commit herself. Clara had by now planned and cancelled Lulu's funeral twice. It was hard to know what to do and when to do it. Merv Sent called Martin, wanting to know when he was returning to the band, but Martin told him he couldn't leave just yet and suggested he find a temporary replacement.

Eleven days after her initial stroke, Lulu suffered another seizure and fell into a deep sleep. The family linked hands, formed a circle around the bed, and prayed. Sometimes the rise and fall of LuLu's chest would slow. Sometimes it stopped altogether. And those around the bed would lean over her and stop breathing, too, in anticipation of her death.

The night passed in this way, but as dawn broke next morning, she unexpectedly opened her eyes. She blinked a few times, as if she didn't recognise the people around her. She swallowed; her lips began to quiver. And then, after years of sustained and utter silence, Lulu made a distinctive sound.

"T—" she said.

Clara exchanged looks with Aub. Pearl raced into the hallway to find a nurse, who bustled up to the bed and checked Lulu's pulse.

"T-ti—" she said again. The nurse took her blood pressure as Lulu repeated the same syllable over and over.

"You wanna cup of tea?" Clara asked finally.

Lulu's eyes brightened, and she smiled.

Father Jim and Clara were convinced it was a miracle, a gift from God for their patience and prayers. But later on, when the doctors examined her, they were told the restored hearing and limited speech was a consequence of the second stroke, which had positively affected the damaged neurones in her brain. Apparently, sometimes this could happen through the electrical impulses of the stroke.

Lulu's condition was monitored for four days. The doctors were surprised to find she'd suffered no permanent physical damage, except limited mobility in two fingers of her left hand. She was released from hospital with a prescription for pills to regulate her blood pressure and returned to the house on Victoria Street in better condition than when she'd left it.

10

It was as if the family had a new baby in their midst, one who was starting to utter sounds and words that gradually formed into phrases and made sense. Lulu began to say things like "Pretty" and "Happy day" and "I like." The twins encouraged the return of Lulu's hearing and speech by telling her stories. They'd sit around her bed at night, or huddle with her in front of the parlour fire, as she had done with them when they'd been little.

Martin was the one with the best stories. He told them his unit had travelled through mining towns and forests all over Western Australia, playing in camps, in hospitals, on riverbanks and banana plantations. They even performed for an Aboriginal leper colony on a remote island.

After they'd travelled to Alice Springs the unit's bus was stolen. They'd done two gigs in the afternoon, and afterward the CO pulled over at a pub for a quiet beer that turned into five or six rounds. Then the magician began making cigarettes disappear up his nose. The local drinkers were enthralled. By the time the entertainers had staggered out onto the street, the bus had vanished. The next day the owner of the pub drove Merv Sent and Martin out of town and along the dry bed of the Todd River until they spotted it. There was a dent in the side, and one of the rearview mirrors had been broken off. Inside the bus they found four black kids: Two were asleep on the seats, and another two sprawled in the aisle. One girl was wearing the magician's tuxedo, a boy was dressed in the impersonator's fishnet stockings, a third was in the tap dancer's tramp outfit, and the fourth wore some oversized clown pants. There were broken biscuits and lolly wrappers strewn all over the bus. And then they spotted the empty bottles from the stash that Merv always kept below the fourth seat on the left; the kids had managed to drink three pints of whisky and a quart of rum. There was a large puddle of vomit on the top step of the bus.

When Pearl heard this for the first time, she laughed so much she got the hiccups, and it seemed to her that for the first time in a year she felt young again.

Now that Lulu was on the mend, Martin contacted the entertainment unit in Pagewood to arrange his return to Merv Sent's band, but the position had been filled by another saxophonist and arranger. So while Martin waited for a transfer to another unit, he and Pearl spent hours talking and listening to music, and soon regained their old closeness.

Hector never really objected to all the time Pearl was spending with Martin, but whenever she drank more than a single glass of wine at the dinner table or laughed loudly at one of Martin's jokes, he grew quiet and edgy, and this caused Pearl to fall quiet, too. She would take Hector's hand and hold it, trying to reassure him that she was still his entirely.

But when Hector wasn't around, the twins soon fell into their old routines: playing records in Martin's room, sneaking bottles of their father's beer up from the basement, listening to jazz pianists in the Arabian, and drinking coffee so strong it made them twitch. And with Martin's return came all the music that had left Pearl's life. His tenor saxophone in her arms was like the return of a former lover, and as she tongued the reed and blew into the mouthpiece she felt herself melting into the sounds it made.

One night, Martin suggested that they go down to the Trocadero and catch up with their old friends. Pearl remembered Lionel Bogwald's invitation to sit in with the band any time she wished and ran to get her coat.

The twins jostled through the kitchen, Martin calling out to Clara, "We're off to the Troc! Don't wait up!" Pearl, carrying Martin's saxophone case, rushed into the parlour to find her hat. Clara was sitting by the fire with Lulu—and so was Hector.

Wide-eyed, Hector glanced at the sax, then back at Pearl, as if she were carrying a bomb.

"I brought over some brochures." He reached into his inside pocket. "Of Melbourne. For the honeymoon."

Martin walked into the parlour. "You ready, Burl?"

Pearl gazed at the pictures of Flinders Street railway station, the tram lines on Collins Street, the Exhibition Gardens, and shuddered. She'd only been to Melbourne once, when she was eleven, touring with her family's band, and had hated every moment of it: The city was cold, wet—even the clouds had been oppressive.

"I was going to take you to the Mayfair for supper tonight."

Hector fiddled with one silver cufflink, turning it around and around. "It was going to be a surprise." He glanced at Martin. "But, of course, if you have other plans . . . "

"No, no," Pearl found herself saying. "We didn't really plan anything." Reluctantly, she passed the sax back to her brother. "It was just something to do. To fill in time."

She forced a smile and took Hector's hand, and was startled to realise he was trembling—just as he had been on the day he'd proposed.

The following morning Pearl woke Martin up by jumping up and down on the edge of his bed. He'd gone to the Troc without her the night before, and she'd heard him come in sometime after midnight. She, however, had been in bed by ten o'clock.

"Get up!" She bounced toward the pillow and back again. She had a rolled copy of the *Sydney Morning Herald* in one hand, and was waving it about.

"Look," she said, batting him on the head with it. "This is fantastic!"

Martin rubbed the sleep from his eyes and sat up, glancing at the clock. It was a little after six. "I'm going to get you for this!"

He grabbed a pillow and socked her in the stomach, and she belted him back with the paper. He snatched it from her and unrolled it. Pearl pointed to a small column on the right-hand side of the page with the headline ARTIE LANDS ON OUR SHAWS. Artie Shaw's Navy Band, led by the famous American clarinet-tist, was flying into Sydney from the Solomon Islands in two days' time to play a single concert at the Trocadero.

"They're only the greatest big band in the world!" Pearl crowed.

"Just one problem, Burly," said Martin. "It says here only Yanks are allowed. And only military."

Pearl sat up and crossed her legs. "You must know some soldiers who could smuggle us in."

Martin rolled his eyes. "How? In their kit bags?"

"Can't you borrow some uniforms or something?"

Martin threw a pillow at her head. "Even if I could, *you* still wouldn't get past the MPs."

The day Shaw's band was due to perform, Pearl pretended she had the flu and didn't go to work at the factory.

In the late afternoon, Clara dragged Aub off to a meeting of the local civilian army. Pearl had been instructed to heat the stew and serve tea in Clara's absence.

The twins lazed about in the parlour, drinking beer and playing records. Pearl was still determined to bluff her way into the Trocadero, but Martin was pessimistic.

"White Yankee soldiers only, Burl," he repeated for the hundredth time. "Not even your precious James would be able to get in—assuming he did get back to Sydney in time."

Pearl frowned. "What do you mean?"

But Martin avoided her eyes, shaking his head.

Sensing that there was something more to his casual comment than he was willing to let on, she asked him again, but he remained evasive.

"I bloody well know you're hiding something, Mart. Come on, out with it."

Martin sighed and gazed at the ceiling. Finally, he rose, and picked up his tobacco pouch and matches. "Not here," he said. "In my room."

He closed the bedroom door behind him, his face serious.

"We were in Queensland, in the middle of nowhere," he began, "miles from the next camp, when the clutch of the bus gave out."

Pearl sat on the bed, hugging herself, waiting for him to continue.

"The only way we could drive the bus was to put it into reverse. Nine and a half hours of driving backward through the bush. Can you imagine?"

It was near dark before they reached their destination, a base camp with two narrow airstrips cut into a forest. They were supposed to have performed a lunchtime show but were half a day overdue. There were six or seven corrugated-iron sheds along one side of the airstrip and the olive-green peaks of dozens of canvas tents. On the other side of the strip was a band of men cutting down trees and clearing bush.

Their next concert was scheduled for lunchtime the next day, at a camp just outside of Mackay, almost two hundred miles away, and they'd need to be on the road by seven. So while the company performed on the stage that folded out from the back of the bus, two mechanics lay beneath the engine at the front, trying to fix the clutch. Sometimes their tools could be heard clanging between the beats. Torches were lit during the second half of the show and the GIs joined in on some of the new American swing songs Martin had arranged and added to the repertoire.

After the show, Martin noticed one of the GIs was still working on the clutch, his army boots sticking out from beneath the bus. The beam of a flashlight flickered now and then, and Martin heard a voice saying, "Come on, dammit. Come on!"

"Problems?" Martin asked.

"Yeah, man," the mechanic called back. "MacArthur lost the Philippines. Tojo's still holding Lae. And your bus is some kind o' mama, man." Martin heard the man drop a tool and pick up something else. "Your music was good though."

"You're into music then?" he asked.

"Sure. Ain't heard much since I left Sydney though. Hey, you ever heard that guy Fogwald? I heard he plays a pretty mean 'bone."

Martin drained his beer. "Lionel Bogwald? I used to work for him."

"No, shit! What, at that joint with the stage that turns 'round and all those gorgeous dames?"

"Yep," said Martin. "In fact, my sister's one of those gorgeous dames."

"She play tenor, too?"

"Alto. Well, she used to. She's getting married next week." Martin took out a cigarette, and as he struck a match he saw the mechanic emerge from beneath the bus. He stood up briskly and dusted down his uniform. His flashlight was wedged into his left trouser pocket, and in the small disc of light it cast Martin found himself gazing into a familiar face.

"It was James?" Pearl breathed, not daring to move.

Martin drew nervously on his rollie. "He's just as good at fixing buses as he is playing his sax."

Pearl had a thousand questions jostling in her mind.

"Well, what happened then?" she demanded. "Did he ask after me?"

"I told him you were fine." The doorbell chimed.

"You've known all this time and you didn't tell me?" Pearl could hear her voice rising.

The bell rang again—one, two, three times.

Martin let out an exasperated sigh and skirted around his desk, heading for the bedroom door. "This is exactly why I didn't tell you. I knew you'd carry on like—"

"Like what?"

Martin paused, his hand on the doorknob, and Pearl threw her empty beer bottle across the room. It bounced off the desk and fell to the floor.

"God, you're a selfish bastard," she raged. "Is this about Roma? Has she had the baby yet?"

"For God's sake," said Martin. "You're about to marry someone else!" He flung open the bedroom door only to find Lulu standing in the hallway.

"Boy," she announced, waving an envelope in her hand. "Give me."

Pearl could see it was an army telegram.

"Great!" cried Martin. "My movement orders."

He grabbed the envelope and ripped it open, but instead of exclaiming in excitement about his next tour, as Pearl expected, his face paled and his hands began to shake.

"Christ—" he murmured, still staring at the telegram. "They're sending me to New Guinea."

11

Martin lay on the bed, his face tight. Pearl, who had been down to the basement for more beer, filled his glass.

"Maybe it's not as bad as you think," she said.

"George Franklin up the road was shot in Wau," her brother replied bitterly. "The Weaver brothers were grenaded."

"You'll just be playing in camps and hospitals again."

"Yeah," muttered Martin. "Camps right at the front. I met this one bloke in Brisbane, his piano was blown up in an air raid in Buna before he even got a chance to play it. He's lucky to have three fingers left."

"MacArthur reckons all the big battles are over now. Kokoda. Milne Bay." She took a swig from the bottle. "The Japs are retreating north."

Martin was holding his glass so tightly his knuckles were white, and Pearl feared it would shatter in his hand. "I couldn't kill anyone," he murmured, staring into his glass. "Not even myself."

"Request a transfer," she suggested. "Another tour of Australia."

Martin snorted, rubbing his finger around the wet rim of

the glass. "I was bloody lucky to get the furlough when Lulu was sick."

A rattle of dinner plates sounded from the kitchen as Lulu set the table.

"You're still coming to hear Artie, aren't you?"

He finished his beer in a single gulp.

"Come on," she said. "We have to give it a go."

Martin put the glass down on his bedside table. "You'll never get in, Pearl. Forget it." He turned over and pulled the bedclothes over his head.

"Well, if you're not coming, you still have to help *me* get in." She picked up the blankets and wrenched them back off him. "Come on, Mart. Don't be such a coward."

When that failed to sway him she lowered her voice. "You saw James weeks ago and never told me. Come on, you owe me one."

Pearl leaned against the table and folded her arms.

Martin groaned and punched his pillow. Then he crawled out of bed, opened his wardrobe, and pulled a pair of military trousers from a hanger. Pearl stripped off her dress and drew the trousers on. The length was fine, but the waistband sagged around her hips. She tightened the belt to the very last hole in the leather, then Martin handed her the khaki shirt. She slipped into the bathroom, pulled off her blouse and brassiere, and grabbed a roll of bandages, which she wrapped around her chest until it was almost flat. Then she pulled on the shirt and did up the buttons. The gaiters and boots were almost her size, once she tightened the laces. She popped his hat on her head, and gazed at herself in the mirror. A tall, long-haired soldier stared back at her warily.

"We're going to have to do something about your hair," said Martin. "Don't know why you're bothering, but. You'll never get in."

Pearl gathered her hair and pinned it close to her scalp, then jammed the hat back down on her head so that there was no trace of her blond locks. Pleased with her own transformation, she strutted proudly around the room, swinging her arms and saluting.

"You've gotta be joking," said Martin. "Men don't prance around like that." And then he demonstrated his own loose-limbed swagger. He showed her how to sit like a bloke—one ankle crooked against the knee of the other leg, how to salute smartly, how to flick away the burning butt of a cigarette with her thumb and middle finger.

"And don't forget," he added, "men swear a lot."

"Bugger!" she cried. "Bugger! Bastard! Shit!"

"They also piss standing up."

Pearl snorted. "I'll need to work on that."

Before she left she begged him to change his mind and go with her, but he shook his head and crawled back into bed. He wanted to stay there as long as he could before he was shipped out in less than thirty-six hours.

As she walked out the door, she heard Martin murmur, "By the way . . . "

She paused, still holding on to the doorknob.

He was staring up at the ceiling, as if he were mesmerised by the plasterwork. "I heard on the bush telegraph that Roma had the baby. A boy. Blue eyes. Everyone says he looks like me."

Startled, Pearl opened her mouth to congratulate him, but

the look on his face stopped her. "Well, I'll see you later then," she said.

She stuck a note reading DO NOT DISTURB to her bedroom door so her parents wouldn't check on her when they returned. She snuck past Lulu and out into the back lane, carrying Martin's saxophone case.

Hiding behind a van on the opposite side of the street, she re- alised she'd forgotten how elegant the Trocadero building was: the sandstone tower that rose from the roof, silhouetted by the set- ting sun; the black-and-green stainless steel strips of the awning; the gleaming glass doors, through which she glimpsed again the marble floor of the vestibule and the polished granite walls.

Martin's tenor case was wedged between her feet as she stood across the road, watching the queue of uniformed Ameri- cans edge along the block, up the stairs, and into the crowded foyer. Instead of the redcoats who usually manned the doors, six American MPs stood at the entrance, admitting the soldiers one by one. Already, she'd witnessed a couple of scuffles. Two civilian men dressed in suits had tried to bluff their way past the MPs, as had a pretty young woman in an evening dress on the arm of a barrel-shaped GI. When the civilians refused to leave they were wrestled down to a police truck parked farther down the block; the American soldier promptly abandoned the pretty woman when the MPs wouldn't let her in.

She practised speaking in Martin's voice, which had the same cadence as her own, but was two tones deeper and a little more resonant. The line across the road grew shorter; four of the

MPs walked inside, leaving only two patrolling the entrance. And this, she quickly realised, was the time to make her move. She swallowed and breathed deeply, pulled back her shoulders, and flexed her buttock muscles. She picked up Martin's saxophone case and, as if she were about to start playing the sax, counted herself in—*one, two, three, four* . . . And suddenly she was bolting across George Street, darting between taxis and automobiles, past the GIs still standing in line, up the stairs, not even glancing at the MPs as she made for the door.

"Hey, buddy!" One of the MPs grabbed her by the arm. For a split second she feared her disguise was a failure and it was blatantly obvious she was a girl in a man's uniform. But the word *buddy* was still echoing in her ears and she realised no one had ever called her that before.

"I'm making a delivery," she said, trying to make her voice sound gruff.

The MP swung her around. "No Aussies allowed."

"You don't understand." She pulled away from him. "We got a call. From Artie."

"Sure, Mac." He was now bundling her down the steps. "Artie Shaw rang you up and personally invited you to the show."

She struggled free of him. "His sax player—Sam Donahue— his horn got stolen at the air base. My captain sent me. Castigan. I'm from the concert party headquarters in Pagewood."

The MP narrowed his eyes and looked her up and down. "What'd you say his name was?"

"Castigan."

"No, the horn player."

"Donahue. Sam Donahue."

He fixed her with a hard stare, lips pursed, hand on the holster of his gun.

"If he doesn't get this"—she held up the black case—"Artie'll have your stripes, mate. Donahue's his best muso."

"Don't tell me what to do." The MP gave her a shove. "I was listening to Donahue back in Chicago before you even knew how to wipe your own ass."

"Well, you won't be listening to a damn thing tonight if you don't let me through."

The MP snorted. He muttered something under his breath and shoved her back up the stairs, past the men in line, and pushed her through the open doorway.

She found herself inhaling the familiar scent of lilies, fresh bunches of which always stood in vases in the foyer, and she glimpsed, through the throng of soldiers, the scarlet carpet, the murals on the wall, the cream velvet chairs, and felt a rush of relief—not only to be able to hear Artie's band live for the first time, but to be back inside the ballroom, the place that had once brought her so much pleasure.

She pushed her way through the groups of soldiers, around the circular lounge, but she hadn't even made it as far as the refreshment bar when she felt a hand on her shoulder. Suddenly the same grimacing MP was spinning her around. There was a man at his side dressed in a white sailor's suit and cap, who was carrying, she could see now, a black tenor saxophone case.

"Okay, wise guy. Out!" The MP grabbed her sleeve and rammed her through the crowd, out the double doors, and back down the stairs to the street. She stumbled across the footpath, fell over, and landed on top of Martin's case.

She lay there for a moment, trying to catch her breath. She could hear jeers and whistles from some of the Americans in the queue. Her right palm was stinging from where she'd skinned it while trying to break her own fall. Her timing, unfortunately, had been no less than disastrous, and she cursed her lousy luck. What were the odds that the real Sam Donahue would turn up at the Trocadero, saxophone in hand, only moments after she'd bluffed her way in?

She leaned on her elbow and went to get up, when a pain forked through her right knee and up her thigh and she inadvertently let out a girlish cry that sent the nearby GIs into greater peals of laughter. "Little Aussie's gonna cry!" they mocked.

Suddenly, she felt two arms engulf her from behind and pull her to her feet as the soldiers began booing and hissing.

"Convicts and niggers stick together."

"Crims and gollywogs!"

They were now throwing orange peels and matchboxes. An apple core hit her straight between the eyes. As she ducked, she glimpsed the man who had helped her up and, when she did, it felt as if fifty butterflies were swarming through her stomach and her head might explode. His skin was darker than she'd remembered it from the year before, and he certainly looked older—reddened eyes, sunken cheeks, a triangular scar to the right of his chin—but it was him.

"Jesus, Martin," cried James. "Where's Pearl?"

He'd mistaken her for her brother. She let out a cry and— just to make sure he was actually real—abruptly embraced him, pressing her face into his chest.

James reeled away and stared at her in shock. All at once, the anger drained from his face, and he stood gazing at her with such disbelief that for a moment she was sure he was unhappy to see her.

"Go back to the cotton field," cried a man with a Southern accent.

James ducked as several lollies came flying toward him. "Go fuck your mama!" he yelled back.

Two GIs lunged toward him, one with a Coke bottle in his hand, screaming, "Take this up your ass, Sambo!" and before Pearl could think she found herself smashing one of them in the face with the saxophone case, while James was ducking and weaving and landing blows on the other. The crowd was roaring; the MPs were yelling and trying to pull everyone apart. She pummelled the same man again and again with the case, staggered back, spitting blood, and then a paddy wagon pulled up and two civilian cops leaped out and wrenched them both away.

James struggled against the copper who was cuffing his hands together. "What the hell are you doing?"

"Easy now, son." The metal lock clicked into place. "Don't make things any harder for yourself."

"They attacked me!"

"They did!" echoed Pearl.

"Niggers aren't allowed in," snarled one man. Pearl clenched her fist and landed a blow against his stomach. He doubled over and made a strange sound, like a whining dog. She went to hit him again but one of the cops grabbed her by the arms to restrain her and, before she knew what was happening, both she and James were being marched across the footpath and pushed into a paddy wagon. The soldiers on the street cheered and applauded and shouted for an encore.

The doors slammed behind them.

"Jesus, girl," James breathed. "Where've you been? I've been trying to track you down for days."

"Me?" She rested against the battered sax case. "Where've *you* been? I had my bags packed, for God's sake. I waited for you, but you never came."

The engine kicked over and the wagon began rumbling down the street.

"Didn't Martin tell you?" he said sharply. "I told him to tell you!"

"Why? Because you didn't have the guts to tell me yourself?"

"No, dammit. Up in Queensland."

"What d'you mean?"

"Hell, I fixed his damn bus for him. Told him he could return the favour by telling you I was on my way. Couldn't get down here any sooner, sweetheart. I've been hanging 'round outside the Troc since Friday, trying to catch you."

He was speaking so quickly she was having trouble taking in all the information. "Didn't you get my letters?" he asked.

"No!"

"I posted 'em to the Ballroom."

"You sent me letters?"

"Three."

The paddy wagon slowed down and turned left.

"I don't work there anymore. I . . . " She drew her knees up to her chest. The chain of his handcuffs rattled, and suddenly she felt his fingers on her hair and a warm tingle spiderwebbed across her scalp.

"I would've sent 'em to your house," he said, "but I didn't think your folks'd approve. Now you're engaged and all."

The wagon swerved right, and a car horn sounded. She heard a man cry out, "Paper! Paper!" and felt a sob begin in her belly. She grasped James around the waist and slipped her head and shoulders through the circle of his cuffed arms, pressing herself against him.

"Baby," he crooned. "It wasn't anything to do with you." He flexed his biceps, squeezing her. "You know we couldn't make it together—not forever."

The paddy wagon slowed down again and came to a stop. Two car doors slammed, and then there were footsteps.

"But what about in Australia? We could've—"

"I get shipped out tomorrow." James's voice was low, almost a whisper. "New Guinea."

Pearl heard a jangle of keys and the muted voices of the policemen and suddenly she wanted to stay locked inside the wagon with James, his arms cuffed around her, forever.

"I don't blame you for marrying what's-his-name, but I want you to know"—she felt his lips against hers—"no one's ever gonna love you as much as I do."

And as she tasted the blood from his split lip she knew that no one could ever love James as much as she did, either; that nothing could now break the mysterious force that bound them.

12

At the police station, Pearl and James were separated and charged. Pearl was put in the city lockup with what looked like several prostitutes while she waited for her parents to come and bail her out. The basement cells were narrow and smelled of mould and stale tobacco. It was well after midnight, but she could still hear the chatter of other prisoners through the metal bars. She dozed off and on, and, just after dawn, she heard footsteps echoing through the passage and cringed when she saw her parents and a policeman walking toward her. Her bail had been set at ten quid, and she had no idea how they'd raised the cash. She imagined the sergeant had already explained to them in detail why she'd been thrown in jail: assault, resisting arrest. When Clara noticed that she was dressed in an army uniform, her hair a mess of tangles and knots, she barked, "Get up off the ground! You look like the lunatic everyone says you are."

"Mum, you don't understand—"

"We'll discuss this when we get home."

The guard unlocked the gate, and Pearl walked behind her

parents between the two rows of cells. She glanced at the other prisoners, hoping to catch a glimpse of James, to say good-bye. She peered at the gallery of faces—a man with a mango-shaped head, another with a handlebar moustache, a bone-thin man with not one hair on his head—but James was not among them.

Her parents took her home in a taxi. Later, in the kitchen, Pearl stared sullenly at the worn grain of the wooden tabletop. Aub sat quietly, drumming his fingers against a cutting board, while Clara paced the room and fired a series of questions.

A door slammed shut, and they could hear Martin's footsteps. Clara raised her voice and summoned him down to the kitchen. When he appeared, he was still wearing his pyjamas.

"Were you in on this?" she demanded.

Martin yawned. "What?"

Clara gestured at Pearl, who was still wearing her brother's army uniform.

He glanced at her, expressionless. "I've got bigger things to worry about than Pearl playing dress-up." He opened the icebox and pulled out a bottle of milk.

"Do you know anything about this—this *coloured* chap of Pearl's?"

His face tensed slightly. "Coloured?" he said. "Like how?"

"Like black!" said Clara. "Like the man the pair of you invited to your birthday last year."

Martin swallowed and fingered a button on his pyjama top.

"I know you know what I'm talking about!"

Martin shrugged. "Has he been lying in the sun too long?"

"This is serious, young man," said Clara. "You two have always been thick as thieves."

"Mum, I've been home since I got the telegram last night."

"And what about when Hector finds out?" Clara continued, turning to glare at Pearl. "Have you thought about that?"

"The only way Hector'll find out is if one of us tells him."

"What about the court case next month?"

"Two GIs attacked us."

"You were seen lying on top of him in the police wagon, doing God only knows what."

Pearl, exasperated, placed her palms against the table and looked directly into her mother's eyes. "I love him."

Clara blanched and leaned against the sink. "And there I was thinking you were having some kind of mental breakdown— but now I realise you're just a silly, ungrateful slut who'd . . . who'd run off with the devil if he showed you a good time."

"At least I'd know how to."

Clara lunged toward her, and before Pearl could duck she felt a hard slap against her cheek that sent her reeling back in her chair.

The room fell silent.

"That's enough, Clara," said Aub. "Everyone calm down. Jesus, this isn't the end of the world."

Pearl raised a hand and pressed it against her stinging face. It felt as if she'd been scalded with boiling water. But she refused to cry, to allow her mother to see her in any way diminished.

The memory of James stayed with Pearl throughout the day and long into the night, like a perfume that had stolen into her clothes, her hair, the corners of her pillowcase. Even though her brother had withheld a secret from her for the first time, and even though she'd been in a brawl and had been thrown in jail, her brief reunion with James saturated her thoughts to the exclusion of anything else. She had no doubt now that her fate was entwined with his. This knowledge eased the welt on her cheek, calmed her anxiety, relaxed the knot of muscles against her spine.

When she awoke her mouth was dry and it was still dark outside. She could see stars framed by the window and a crescent moon. For a moment she thought she'd dreamed it all— her chance encounter with James, the arrest, the fight with her mother. And then it all came foaming around her like a breaker at the beach: his handcuffed arms encircling her in the back of the police van, the music they'd once played together thrumming in her ears, the fingerprints she imagined he'd left inside her, at her core. But she was startled out of her reverie when she remembered that it was Martin's last night in Sydney and she'd already slept through most of it.

Downstairs, all the rooms were dark. She flipped on the kitchen light and could see that tea had already been eaten. The washing-up was standing in the rack on the sink. Through the door she could see the outline of Mikey asleep on his cot in the dining room. The clock above the stove told her it was eleven minutes past ten. She must have slept for almost nine hours straight. She was starving.

Martin was due to leave the house at four the next morning and his breakfast sat covered with a dinner plate on the table. Pearl lifted it and found four cut sandwiches filled with cold meatloaf and boiled eggs. She picked up one and ate it, noticing that Clara had wrapped fruitcake and biscuits and had left them for Martin on the kitchen counter, as if he were going on a school excursion.

Next to them were other little extras: Clarke's Blood Mixture, DeWitt's Antacid Powder, Woods' Great Peppermint Cure for Coughs & Colds.

Seeing all the efforts Clara had made for Martin caused Pearl to wonder if her mother even liked her anymore. Was it possible that all the therapy, the quinine and other medications, the saxophone being returned to Palings, the wedding plans were designed by Clara to make Pearl burn less brightly, to limit her? Suddenly, reckless ideas were careening through her head: She'd pack a bag and hitchhike to another state, to a place where no one knew her. She could assume a false identity, style her hair differently, beg, borrow, or steal a saxophone and get gigs under a pseudonym. Maybe when the war ended she and James would find each other again, discover a place and a culture that welcomed them equally.

Through the candlelight she could see her wedding dress hanging from a hook on the wall next to the upright ironing board: extra darts in the bodice, layers of fine netting, crystal beads glinting in the half-light, the sweetheart neckline. Now, after seeing James again, and realising that he still loved her as much as she loved him, she could hardly imagine herself wearing the dress, let alone standing next to Hector in the local church, taking her wedding vows. Her brother might be dreading his posting, but she envied him—the adventures he would have, the music he would play in the highlands of New Guinea—while she'd be entombed in Hector Best's Millers Point terrace, starching shirts and polishing furniture. Hector's widowed father would come to lunch every Sunday after church. Hector would forbid her to play music professionally. And she would never see James again.

On the hook next to the wedding dress hung Martin's army

uniform—washed and pressed since she'd taken it off that afternoon: the khaki shirt, trousers made of herringbone twill,
the bush hat. The canvas gaiters and boots sat beneath them on
the floor, next to his bulging rucksack.

The two outfits reminded her of a prank she and Martin
had pulled when they were kids. One day they had turned
up to school wearing each other's uniforms: Pearl in Martin's
blazer and long pants and he in her blouse and navy-blue tunic.
They took their places side by side in the classroom. At first
the teacher, Miss Winthrop, didn't notice, and merely asked
the class to open their readers. Pearl, unused to itchy woollen
trousers, kept scratching at her crotch. Miss Winthrop turned
her back and began writing on the blackboard, while Martin
lifted the hem of his skirt and flashed his knickers at the other
kids. A boy sitting directly behind him couldn't control his
excited fits of giggles, which became infectious. When Miss
Winthrop heard the children laughing she swung around and
saw everyone pointing at the twins and, recognising the ruse,
she laughed, too. She allowed the twins to impersonate each
other for the rest of the day, and whenever she addressed them
she good-naturedly reversed their names.

Pearl glanced at the wedding dress, then back to the army
uniform, and a crazy, impossible idea flared in her mind.

Intermission

"The idea was so outrageous," Pearl says on tape number twelve, "that for a moment I thought I'd gone crazy. Crazy with love. Crazy with grief. Crazy with the whole damn—" She pauses and I can hear ice tinkling in a glass as she slurps on a drink. "All I knew for sure was that I had to see him again. And I really didn't care what—" Her voice cracks. A police siren sounds in the background. "I didn't even care if I—not even if I—"

I'm on the edge of my seat now, waiting for her to get to the point. I hear a little static, like a badly tuned TV station. Then the speakers emit a sound like crumpling paper, followed by a squeal, and I look down in horror to see the wheels of the cassette slowing down and chewing up the remains of the tape.

I hit the Stop button and then press Eject, and the cassette drops forward in its slot. Fortunately, the tape hasn't broken but is tangled up in the machine like a glossy brown ribbon. I go to the bathroom to find some tweezers. My heart's racing and my fingers are trembling as I rummage through the cabinet. Never in my life have I felt such a strong sense of urgency, not even when I began writing my detective series. It's not just the responsibility of writing Pearl's biography—or her version of it; I'm hooked on what will happen next, how the story of Pearl and Martin will resolve itself. Will she find James again? Will they reunite? And what about Martin and Roma?

No one talked much about my mother when I was growing up. All I knew for sure was that she was a teenager when she fell pregnant and that Martin had hardly known her when he got her up the duff. She died of pneumonia shortly after my birth. I've never seen a photo of her but my father always told me she was unusually beautiful, with cascading black hair and wide amber eyes. She was also a fabulous dancer and used to do impersonations of Jimmy Cagney in *Yankee Doodle Dandy,* a film I've watched over and over again, just to imagine her in the role.

My own son has never had to resort to such lengths in order to know me. Even though his mother and I broke up after about a year, we shared custody of Arnhem, who's now twenty-four. He mainly grew up with his mother's people, the Bundjalung of northern New South Wales, but would always spend school holidays with me.

In fact, I last saw him only a few nights ago, at the Deadly Awards at the Opera House. It was the first time a father and son had been honoured at the same ceremony: me for services to Indigenous literature; Arnhem for his choreography with Bangarra Dance Company. We had a great night together with all our old mob and ended up at the Iguana Bar doing tequila shots and dancing to Barry White.

Where the fuck are those tweezers? The phone starts to ring, and I let the machine pick it up. It's bloody Brian Jackson again, asking me if I've found the tapes of the live recordings yet. Since I started listening to the cassettes a few weeks ago, I've been avoiding him. I can't bring myself to hand over any of this material until I know how the story ends, until I complete the job.

I start going through the bathroom drawers, which I really must get around to cleaning out. I find a set of my father's old dentures, a twisted tube of menthol ointment, Pearl's grey pumice stone, a bottle of bubble bath still containing the dregs of some rude yellow liquid, and plastic prescription containers—some still half full—that date as far back as 1989.

I haven't smoked a cigarette for nine years but I'm suddenly dying for one. I dump everything on the floor and claw my way through miniature bottles of hotel shampoo, spools of dental floss, bobby pins, and emery boards. I search the next drawer, and then the next, packed with shower caps, razor blades, Band-Aids, and foot powder. I'm just about to break, to race up the street to buy a pack of Marlboro and a set of tweezers—in that order— when I remember Pearl often used to sit at an antique mirrored vanity that had once belonged to her grandmother, and which now stands in a corner of Clara and Aub's former bedroom.

The room—on the second floor—hasn't been touched since Pearl died, and when I open the door I inhale the tart sting of mothballs. It's a large room, full of heavy wooden furniture and a canopy-covered bed.

I rush over to the mahogany vanity with the oval mirror. The drawers are tiny, as if made for elves. The first drawer: white face powder and puff and a metal hip flask still smelling of whisky. The second: three tubes of lipstick and a faded coupon for half-priced false eyelashes. The third: six plastic hair rollers and an old packet of pipe tobacco. The fourth: a nail file, clippers, a few false fingernails, a safety pin and, at the very back, behind a jar of Tiger Balm ointment, a pair of tweezers.

Back at my desk, I stuff one of my grandfather's old pipes with the stale tobacco, light it and inhale. Suddenly, I'm both dizzy and slightly delirious, the tension draining away from me like dirty dishwater down a sink. After a few more puffs, I put the pipe down and pick up the tweezers. I lower them to the coiled tape, pinch one edge, and begin, very gently, to pull.

12 (cont)

As Pearl headed through the predawn darkness of Kings Cross and into Darlinghurst, she was relieved to be wearing Martin's uniform again, to feel the rub of twill between her thighs, to hear the steady clump of his boots against the footpath. As she walked, she chanted Martin's serial number over and over to memorise it like a piece of music, or the telephone number of someone she'd recently met and whom she longed to see again. She wished she could move faster along the footpath, but the weight of the army pack, along with her brother's tenor sax case, slowed her down.

As she approached the sandstone walls of Victoria Barracks, she felt at once terrified and intensely alive. She was moving toward everything she now knew she couldn't live without: the adventures she longed to have, the jazz she yearned to play, the only man she'd ever love. As she passed through the gates, it was as if she'd stepped over some invisible line that divided her past from her future, separated one fate from another, and no matter what painful death or glorious reward was ahead, there was no turning back now.

*   *   *

It hadn't been easy to convince Martin that her plan would work. When she'd burst into his room six hours before and shook him awake, she'd already called Nora Barnes and had only a short time to put her scheme into action.

"Mart," she hissed.

He stirred and glanced at the clock. "I just got to sleep, Pearl."

"Do you still want to get out of going to Moresby?"

He rubbed his eyes. "What?"

"The army," she said, hardly able to contain herself. From the parlour she heard the grandfather clock chime ten-thirty. "Get up, we haven't got much time."

"What the fuck?" he groaned.

She quickly outlined her idea: He would dress in her clothes and assume her identity.

Martin rolled his eyes and lit a cigarette. "You think Mum and Dad aren't going to notice that I'm not you? And have you thought about Hector?"

Ah, Hector. It was thinking about Hector that had precipitated the whole idea. Pearl explained that she'd called Nora Barnes to confide that she was having serious doubts about her marriage, but was terrified of how her mother would react if she called off the wedding; she'd probably kick her out of the house or—even worse—have her locked up in Hector's asylum. Nora suggested that she could hide out on their farm if she wanted to disappear for a while. Now that Nora had a baby they could do with a hand.

Martin listened to Pearl's so-called solution, frowning with confusion. "That all sounds fine," he said. "But how's it going to get me out of New Guinea?"

Pearl slapped her hand on the mattress. "Don't you get it? I'll dress in your army uniform and take your place!"

Martin considered this for a moment then shook his head. "There's no way you'd pull it off."

"I fooled a whole bunch of people yesterday," Pearl reminded him. "Including some American MPs—even James thought I was you at first."

Martin paced the room, trailing cigarette ash across the carpet. "You know bugger all about the army," he pointed out.

"Neither do you!" she retorted. "All you've been doing the last year is travelling around, playing in bands, and having a good time."

"Not in New Guinea, for Christ's sake." He stubbed out his cigarette. "Why the hell would you want to go there anyway?"

Pearl felt a blush creep up her neck. "James," she said. "He's being shipped out there, too. Mart, I have to find him—I'm in love with him! We have to be together."

There was a long silence between them. Pearl could hear the grandfather clock ticking in the parlour, counting down the few remaining hours until Martin had to report to Victoria Barracks.

"It's not like I'd be the first woman ever to do it. What about those women last century who dressed up as men so they could travel with their sailor husbands? And you know there are Aboriginal girls in the outback who cut their hair short and wear men's clothes to work as drover's boys. And don't forget the big Boxing Day fight down in White City."

That particular story was legendary in the Willis family. In 1908, world heavyweight boxing champion, Tommy Burns, was considered unbeatable, until a match was scheduled in Sydney between him and the black American boxer, Jack Johnson. At the time, White City was the biggest stadium in Australia. It could seat over ten thousand spectators, and every ticket was sold out weeks in advance. One of these tickets was purchased by their father, Aub. The event was such an anticipated international spectacle that the *New York Herald* commissioned the American novelist Jack London to report on the bout; he happened to be in Australia at the time, accompanied by his wife, Charmian. She was as much a sporting enthusiast as her husband, and was outraged when she found out that women were barred from attending the fight. So she dressed in one of her husband's suits, pulled a man's felt hat onto her head, and bluffed her way past the ticket collectors. The reason Pearl and Martin knew this story so well was that Charmian happened to be sitting next to Aub in the stadium, and on her other side was London himself, scribbling madly in a notebook as Johnson pummelled Burns onto the floor of the ring during the fourteenth round.

"It was the hands that gave her away," Aub had always said. "White, smooth, and manicured. No man except a surgeon or a nancy looks after his fingernails so well."

Pearl grinned at Martin, picked up a pair of scissors from the sideboard, and began clipping at the air.

After about a quarter of an hour, she looked in the mirror. The crew cut she now sported looked like a pale yellow cap against her head.

Martin then instructed her in how to perform drill, to obey commands, how to turn. She memorised the markers, looking down at her feet: "Check, T, L, V, Away!" Using a broom as a prop, she learned how to shoulder a rifle, then how to salute, raising her hand slowly and abruptly bringing it down. At first it felt awkward, as if she were dancing some stiff-limbed quadrille with the broom in her arms as a wordless partner. But as she marched and saluted around the room, it seemed more and more like a music rehearsal, and she found her body gradually absorbing this strange new choreography.

Pearl gave Martin a slap on the back. "Now all we have to do is work on you."

Martin did a double take. "What d'you mean?"

"Well, I've turned into you; now you have to turn into me."

Martin bristled. "No way. I'll just look like a poofter—or a lunatic."

"You won't look like a lunatic," Pearl argued. "You'll look like me."

Martin gave her a withering glare.

"Christ, Mart, I just cut off all my hair! You can't back out now. You'll only have to wear a dress and hat for a few hours, until you get to Pookie's farm." She softened her voice. "In lots of ways, it's better if you have to become a woman. Otherwise someone's sure to recognise you."

Martin sighed heavily. "You don't know squat about the military."

She was growing frustrated with his pessimism. "Look, I won't be at the front, fighting the Japanese. I'll be in a bloody jazz band, playing the saxophone!"

When he buried his face in his hands and didn't respond she finally lost her temper.

"Fine then," she said. "Fucking go off to New Guinea. Fucking get killed for all I care." She stormed out of his room and up the stairs.

It wasn't until she was closing her bedroom door that he caught up with her and hissed, "All right. You've got the bloody swearing down pat. Let's go."

After she and Martin had traded identity cards and clothes, she sat down to do the hardest thing of all, which was to write a letter to her parents and Hector, detailing why she was running away. In many ways the explanation she gave was true—she wanted desperately to play music professionally again, and she knew she couldn't do it while still living in the house of her parents or in the home of her husband-to-be. Other things she wrote were also true: that she cared deeply for the three of them; that she hoped they could one day forgive her. She also left a fair bit out, like where exactly she was running away to, and under what guise, and the fact that she was in love with another man.

Once she was through the gates of Victoria Barracks, she joined a line of soldiers waiting to report, fingering Martin's papers and mouthing his serial number again, his regiment, the detachment he was supposed to join. There was a hush over the city. All she heard was the soft rhythm of men reciting their names and numbers, the occasional cry of a bird. As she moved on up in the line her legs grew weak and for the first time she worried about what would happen if she were caught out.

Fortunately, she didn't need to undergo a medical examination because Martin had already passed one the year before when he'd enlisted and signed up for the entertainment unit.

She was growing impatient with the slow progress of the line, half expecting to see her parents running toward her in their dressing gowns and slippers, or a police paddy wagon pulling up.

When she felt a clap on her back her heart nearly leaped out of her chest.

"Willis!" somebody cried.

She swung around, expecting to see some burly colonel who had come to have her arrested. Instead, she found a slight, slim soldier with a dimpled chin and slanted blue eyes.

"I saw your name on the roster. God, I thought I'd never see *you* again."

Pearl stared at him blankly. She knew she should say something, but was afraid her voice might not come out right.

"You don't recognise me, do you?"

She put down her backpack, confused.

"I lived up the road from you when we were kids. Charles. Charlie Styles."

As soon as he said his name she recognised the little blond boy who'd played the cornet.

"Charlie!" she cried, then, remembering she was supposed to be a man, slapped him on the back. "That's right," she said as they shook hands. "You moved to the mountains and we never saw you again."

"I'm in the band, too," he said, taking the saxophone case from her. "Come on, you don't have to register here."

Pearl shouldered the backpack again and followed Charlie across a car park. She couldn't believe her good luck in running into an old friend—and one who she and Martin hadn't seen in over ten years.

He led her down past a group of soldiers loading crates onto a truck and over to a group of a dozen or so men who were sitting around on drum cases or on their backpacks, smoking. They were all in uniform, but she noticed they were not as groomed as the soldiers she'd seen in line. One had his hat on backward; another had no laces in his boots; a few had their sleeves rolled up.

"It's about time, Willis," declared a red-faced fiftyish man with curly hair the colour of snow.

Pearl handed him her movement papers, and he glanced over them quickly.

"First time on overseas duty?"

She nodded.

"Well, this isn't going to be like the little picnic you had last year touring Australia with Merv Sent and his bloody Senders."

All the men chuckled, but she could hear the underlying tension in their laughter.

"By this time next month you'll be jumping off the stage, dodging exploding shells, living in foxholes and sleeping in your own shit—or somebody else's."

There was more laughter. Pearl shifted the pack on her back from one shoulder to the other. She wondered when she was supposed to salute.

"And I'll be right there," he added, "making sure none of you blokes plays one bum note or drops a single beat."

For the next half hour they helped load supplies onto a truck, then the band clambered onto the back of it with their instruments. They were driven from the barracks through the empty city streets until they pulled up on a wharf at Woolloomooloo Bay.

Predawn light filtered across the harbour. A huge grey ship was anchored in the bay, engines purring, with a single tendril of smoke curling from one funnel. At the other end of the wharf men carried crates of supplies up a wide gangplank.

Pearl decided to stick close to Charlie, who obviously knew his way around. She mimicked his every movement, from the way he shouldered his backpack to the brisk steps he took as he fell in line with the others. She followed his swagger across the dock and onto the gangplank that rose sharply into the air at a forty-five-degree angle. Struggling against the weight of her pack, which was on the verge of tipping her backward, she held the saxophone case tightly and with her free hand gripped the railing, scared that she'd topple into the harbour and her great escape would be abruptly halted before it had even begun.

At last she staggered onto the deck, relieved to be on a level plane. Every inch of the ship seemed to be painted the same dull, monochromatic grey. As she stood catching her breath, she was astonished to find herself up so high, as if she'd just scaled some enormous building. From where she stood she could see the sun rising behind Shark Island, the outline of the north shore, even the cluster of buildings at the top of William Street.

"Come on, Willis. We're not on holidays!" The white-haired CO jostled her forward, and she found herself standing in yet another line. After a few moments a supplies clerk issued her a yellow life jacket. Farther along the line, another handed her a cartridge belt with a water canteen attached. And then, farther along again, she was shocked to find a jowly soldier handing her a large rifle.

"I won't need one of those," she said, holding up the saxophone. "I'm a musician."

"Fartin' into that horn ain't goin' to protect you from Tojo, sonny." The soldier thrust the gun into her free hand and ordered her to join her unit.

She struggled along the deck, trying to manage the life jacket, the cartridge belt and canteen, the saxophone, and the gun that, dangling from the crook of her arm by its canvas strap, seemed more like some huge, odd, unwieldy handbag than a deadly weapon. She joined the rest of the musos, who were now lounging against the railing at the stern of the ship, smoking and trading jokes. Now that she'd safely crossed the first difficult threshold undetected she was suddenly overcome with nerves. All her moves thus far had been enacted under the veil of dawn, when it was hard to make out more than the outline of another's face or the height of the man standing next to you. But would her disguise hold up in the full light of day?

A group of teary women stood on the wharf, waving handkerchiefs and underwear, throwing streamers, blowing kisses, and for a few minutes she longed to be one of those girls wearing woollen coats and earrings, girls who'd remain in Sydney, cutting coupons, cooking cakes without butter, working in a factory every day. She suddenly felt stifled by her brother's military uniform, weighed down by the gun in her hand, and longed for curlers in her hair, rouge on her cheeks, stays against her thighs. She wanted what Martin would now have for the duration of the war: a warm bed, a doting friend, and few responsibilities.

The ship pulled away from the dock in the early rays of the spring morning. The coloured streamers stretched and snapped, drifting onto the surface of the bay like thousands of discarded ribbons. Seagulls arced and wheeled above the deck, squawking hungrily. Pearl gripped the railing and watched sunlight glancing off the water, the first ferries chugging across the harbour, the city growing smaller. As they sailed past Garden Island, she caught a glimpse of her own house at the end of the street. The blackout shades had been removed from the windows, and she could see a figure in the front yard, leaning against the fence, though she couldn't make out if it was a man or woman. She felt a rush in her head and was scared she'd start crying, right there, in front of all those soldiers. Instead, to calm herself, she made herself repeat Martin's serial number, then raised her hand and gave a little wave to whomever it was standing in her garden.

"Hey, Willis?" She turned to see Charlie Styles, standing with a thin private who looked as if he were in his midtwenties. He had wiry red hair and buck teeth, and at once reminded Pearl of a starving rabbit. "This is my mate, Blue. Second trombone."

She was about to nod and say, "Pleased to meet you," when Blue's hand shot out. She grabbed it and shook it firmly. "Martin," she declared. "Tenor sax."

"I know." Blue scratched his head, pulled out a strand of hair, examined it briefly before dropping it. "I used to listen to you at the Troc. When you soloed on 'Tuxedo Junction' my mother used to cry."

"That bad was I?"

"No, you were that bloody good."

The praise had the opposite effect of its intention, causing her to worry about the fact that she hadn't played in public for over a year.

"Us three are sharing a cabin!" said Charlie brightly, waving a piece of paper. "The boss skipper likes to keep the brass section together."

"You mean the poof section together," snarled a voice. Pearl glanced over her shoulder to see a private smirking at them. He had a thin mouth and his dark eyes were set wide apart in his head, which made him look like some kind of lizard. "So you can blow each others' horns," he added, and walked away.

Charlie, ignoring the man, cocked his head and pointed with his chin to the upper deck. "C'mon."

Pearl, surprised by the man's hostility, shouldered her backpack and picked up her equipment. She followed them through the crowd of soldiers. "Who was that?" she asked.

Charlie snorted. "Nigel Moss. First alto sax. Got a transfer from an artillery unit into our concert party—his father's a captain."

As she climbed the stairs to the second deck Pearl made a mental note to steer clear of Nigel Moss.

Now that they were up even higher, she could see that they were being joined by a convoy of three other ships and were sailing between the heads of the harbour into the infinite expanse of the Pacific. From this distance the other ships looked like toy boats in a bathtub.

"She used to be a luxury ocean liner," announced Charlie as he opened the door to their cabin. "Poor old love. Now she's just a warship."

As they squeezed into the cabin Pearl noticed that every former fitting and feature had been stripped to make room for the three tiers of canvas hammocks that took up almost all the available space. The porthole had been painted over in compliance with blackout regulations; the only other things in the berth were a cupboard and the mahogany panelling, vestiges of the ship's former life. There was an en suite bathroom with cracked floral tiles and tarnished brass taps out of which flowed streams of rusty water.

They flipped a sixpence to see who'd get the bottom hammock.

Blue won the toss. Charlie got the middle bunk, and Pearl the top. As she and Charlie stowed their gear into a corner of the cabin to make more room, Blue stepped into the bathroom and stood in front of the mirror. At first Pearl assumed that he was overly conscious of his appearance, but then she noticed he had a bald patch about the size of a penny on the crown of his head and that he was meticulously plucking his hair out one strand at a time.

She glanced at Charlie, one eyebrow raised. He shook his head briefly in a kind of I'll-explain-later gesture and pulled a pouch of tobacco from a pocket in his pack.

"We're just going out for a smoke, Blue," he called.

The convoy of ships was now surrounded entirely by the ocean, and if it were not for Charlie and his endless chatter Pearl would have been terrified. As she strolled with him around the upper deck, Charlie told her about Blue. They'd been in the same detachment in New Guinea for most of the year before, performing for troops along the Kokoda Track. Just before the Aussies took Ioribaiwa, Blue collapsed into a foxhole, and it was later discovered he'd contracted both dysentery and malaria. He'd spent the last six months in the Blue Mountains, recuperating at the Hydro Majestic Hotel, which had been converted into a military sanatorium. "That's where he started pulling his hair out," said Charlie. "I used to visit him whenever I got leave." Today was Blue's first day back on duty.

Charlie, on the other hand, seemed unfazed by the cramped conditions of the ship, by what lay ahead of them when they reached their destination. He didn't walk, but rather bounced like a pogo stick, and always seemed to be bubbling over with enthusiasm.

"I came to the Troc once, just to listen to you," he said, the wind pasting his flaxen hair against his head. "But you'd already left on your tour of duty." They were sitting on crates to the side of a volleyball court, though the net had long since been removed and the poles that had held it there were now used as mounts for artillery guns. The deck was packed with both Australian and American soldiers, some black, but mostly white. There was barely enough room to raise a rifle and many sat huddled in groups, playing cards or two-up.

"I've lost my lip a bit," said Pearl in a low voice, preparing Charlie for the inevitable moment when he realised she couldn't play very well at all. "I haven't really played or practised for ages. It's amazing how quickly it goes."

"Modest, too!" declared Charlie. "A man after my own heart. Do you dance?"

Pearl stared back at him. Was he thinking that she could perform a dance routine during the concert? "No," she replied. "My mother's the dancer." She went to cross her legs but stopped herself, remembering that it would seem too girlish. Instead, she raised her leg and rested an ankle on her knee.

At midday they joined a queue that snaked out of a wide doorway. The line moved forward, and she and Charlie edged into the mess hall for lunch. The room was long and wide, with panels of etched glass and mirrors between the windows. A stage, framed with deep red velvet curtains, stood at the other end, but instead of a ten-piece orchestra playing light dance music, a team of men on mess duty doled out food onto a parade of upturned tin plates. A five-tiered chandelier gleamed above what had once obviously been a polished dance floor; now, long trestle tables and foldout chairs stood against it and the wood was covered with dust.

It was when Pearl passed one of the panels of etched glass that she felt a quiver of recognition. She paused and glanced back. The glass was tinted pale pink and the figure etched into it was a woman in robes with a garland of flowers for a crown. Pearl picked up a tin plate and followed Charlie up the set of wooden stairs to the stage. From there the former ballroom looked both sad and elegant, like a palace whose king had suddenly gone bankrupt. The glass panels and mirrors glistened in the noonday light, radiant with refracted light from the chan-

delier, and she felt another flicker of recognition. She couldn't
be certain, but she had the distinct feeling she'd been on the
ship before, when she and her mother had returned from their
season at the Panorama Hotel in Ceylon. Pearl even remembered some of the repertoire: "Shuffle Off to Buffalo," "Sweet
Georgia Brown," "42nd Street." She and Clara had worn
matching gold outfits and identical red wigs.

Blue, she could see, was standing at the end of the queue; his
head was bowed and he was twisting a button on his jacket. Pearl
held out her plate and three ladles of brown sludge were dropped
upon it. She followed Charlie down the stairs at the other side of
the stage, and they sat together at one of the trestle tables on the
dance floor. The food was terrible—a fatty, half-warm stew—
but Pearl ate it all because none of the men she knew cared what
they ate and they all consumed twice as much as she did. While
she chewed she gazed at the etching of the woman in the robes
and had a distant recollection, more like a dream than a memory.
She had been pressed against a similar panel and kissed by a man
three times her age. While her mother had dozed in the library
after the last of the singing guests had woven out of the room
and down the red carpet to the whisky bottles in their berths, an
Indian steward had put his lips on Pearl's and moved his tongue
around in her mouth until she thought she would suffocate. Afterward, she had fled, never telling a soul about it.

During the afternoon, she and Charlie walked circuits around
the ship, while others cleaned and polished rifles, arm wrestled, or did push-ups. The ship was so crowded there was not

enough room to perform military drills. Pearl considered this a blessing, as she wasn't confident about performing drill. She simply hoped that, when the time came, she could fake it by mimicking the others.

Everywhere was the smell of the sea and the stench of vomit, as one soldier after another bowed over the railing and puked into the Pacific. It was the only thing that was allowed into the water, as any discarded garbage might form a trail the enemy could follow. Some men speculated on the probability of being sunk by a Jap torpedo or bomb. They were mostly short odds.

When twilight edged into the horizon, an announcement made over the loudspeakers ordered all on deck to extinguish every light, match, and cigarette until further notice the following morning. There was so little room onboard that many soldiers had to sleep on the deck itself, or on the dance floor of the ballroom. One unit bedded down on the tiled bottom of the drained pool.

After dinner, Charlie and Pearl joined Blue in the tiny cabin. They found him in his underwear, already asleep in the bottom hammock. Charlie yawned, stripped down to his underpants and singlet, and crawled into the middle one. Pearl locked herself in the bathroom. The sight of her clipped hair in the mirror was still a shock—she did almost look identical to her brother. She cleaned her teeth, removed her boots and gaiters, and then—what the hell, she thought—unbuckled the belt and lowered her trousers. Fortunately, the tails of Martin's shirt covered her crotch and would make it difficult to detect what she lacked down there.

She returned to the cabin and flipped off the light. She'd

made it through the first day undetected, but she knew whatever lay ahead would be much more challenging and hazardous. She tried to comfort herself by thinking that she was only a little behind James in their separate journeys to New Guinea.

"Night," she said gruffly to Charlie, as she climbed into her swaying hammock.

On the second day, the concert party CO, Art Rudolph, marched the unit of musicians onto the deck for an abandon ship drill, while the crew lowered grey lifeboats. They were told that under no conditions should any man jump directly into the water. In case of an emergency, they were to abandon the ship by way of knotted ropes that were tied between the upper and lower decks. The first time she tried it, Pearl lost her grip, and found herself dropping onto the broad shoulders of the band's drummer, which sent them both tumbling onto the deck below.

In her spare time she walked around the crowded deck with Charlie and Blue, trading jokes and looking for enemy submarines. One afternoon, they saw a big black shape rising out of a swell about two hundred yards away. The alarm was raised, torpedoes were aimed, antiaircraft artillery was held in position. After a few minutes, however, the big black shape emerged on a wave and the tail of a whale forked up and flipped in the air before sinking back into the ocean's depths.

Art Rudolph scheduled the first concert for the afternoon of the third day at sea. There was a hasty rehearsal in the dining room, during which he mostly talked them through the ar-

rangements. The musicians filed out onto the lower deck and
set up in the shade of one of the ship's huge chimneys. Pearl
pegged the music to her stand so it wouldn't blow away. So far,
she'd managed to look, talk, and behave like her brother: Earlier that morning, she'd slipped the blade from Martin's razor,
soaped up her face and, with the cabin's bathroom door ajar,
pretended to shave herself; when she rolled a smoke she let the
cigarette paper dangle from her bottom lip, pasted by a slick
of saliva as she kneaded the tobacco between her fingers; she
often sat with her elbows resting upon her widespread knees
as she played two-up with antiaircraft gunners; and, of course,
she swore as loudly and broadly as the best of them. But she
hadn't played jazz in any serious way for almost a year now.
Compared to the lightness of her old alto, Martin's tenor saxophone was heavy in her hands, with wider spaces between the
keys, a slightly bigger mouthpiece. And she'd never grown used
to playing outside, preferring instead the perfect acoustics of
the Trocadero or the dining rooms of posh hotels. Still, it was
a relief to be part of a band again, and, as the musos tuned up
and quietly ran through bits of music to themselves, a quiet
thrill rippled through her.

Some players sat on ammo crates, but most reclined on
faded deck chairs left over from when the ship had been a luxury liner. Rudolph whacked the air with his baton and counted
them in on Benny Goodman's "Stealin' Apples," which wasn't
too difficult, as it was a piano-led introduction and the brass
section just had to play harmony. But the second verse contained some fast, synchronised sax riffs, and she found herself
struggling with the fingering. She faked it, and merely pressed

the keys, but didn't blow into the mouthpiece, allowing the alto and baritone to carry her through. Fortunately, Rudolph didn't seem to notice. A few soldiers were already throwing off their hats and jitterbugging together, while others leaped into the empty pool and glided across the cracked white tiles, turning it into an impromptu dance hall.

Everyone was in full military uniform, though it was so hot that most of the musicians had unbuttoned their shirts and rolled up their sleeves and trouser legs. Pearl felt exceedingly self-conscious, not only because she was having trouble keeping up with the music; she was also the only one who remained fully clothed, with sweat patches spreading across her uniform. She feared she must seem ridiculously modest or fastidious—or just plain stupid.

The drummer was keeping the beat on the ride cymbal, but Pearl couldn't hear it properly because the wind kept carrying it away. When she had to stand up and take a solo on "Two O'Clock Jump"—a song she'd played countless times at the Troc—she sensed the tempo escaping her, as if riding away with the sea breeze. She was running out of breath and the tenor was too big and heavy in her hands and the sun was in her eyes and she was perspiring so much her uniform was wet and pasted against her skin.

"I've heard better solos from old coots in the Salvation Army, Willis," the CO said after the concert had ended and he'd summoned her to his cabin. "I bet you didn't play that drivel at the Trocadero."

Her face flushed and she could sense tears coming on. The snorts and stares from the other band members had been humiliating enough, and she'd barely made it through the final tune. The alto player, Moss, had remarked, "The great Trocadero tenor. Couldn't even fart in tune!"

Only Charlie had been sympathetic, slapping her on the shoulder afterward and reminding her it happened occasionally to every muso in a new band.

Rudolph rested his hands on his hips and demanded to know if she'd been drinking.

She bowed her head and shook it.

The CO began pacing his tiny cabin, bumping into his own hammock each time he turned.

"Well, you might think my band is some two-bit outfit touring the arsehole of the earth. But let me tell you something. . . ." His index finger jabbed the air. "Soon we'll be playing for soldiers who've been taking Jap bullets for years, sleeping in mud and living on biscuits. And let me tell you, fuckwit, if you can't deliver the performance of your life every time we do a concert, I'll have you transferred into some service unit faster than you can say 'Sayonara,' and you'll be stranded on some remote island cleaning shit from latrines for the rest of the war."

Instead of wasting time playing two-up or circling the deck, Pearl spent the next few days locked inside a linen press, practising scales and runs, rehearsing the band's repertoire, trying to get her lip back. She struggled with the additional weight of the tenor saxophone—quite a bit heavier than the alto she'd always played. It felt like an anchor hanging from her neck. She also had to adjust herself to the tenor sax's lower pitch.

The press reminded her of the time she and James had made love standing up in the linen closet of the Booker T. Club, at the beginning of their affair, when she'd been shaken by the sensations that had shimmered through her body. Inside the tiny room she annoyed no one with her noise. And besides, it was a relief to be away from the scrutiny of her fellow soldiers. Blowing into the mouthpiece for hours each day, she coaxed back her embouchure, strengthening and tightening the muscles around her mouth and lips. She repeated the breathing techniques James had taught her, and began practising slowly again, as he had advised, repeating each tune she knew in every major and minor key. At night, lying in her hammock, her jaw throbbed and her mind was riddled with jazz phrases that kept repeating themselves. And on top of that were her obsessive thoughts about James: about where he was now, what he might be doing, and how he'd react when she finally tracked him down.

Charlie thought she was nuts, rehearsing inside a closet in order to sound good for a bunch of men in the jungle, but the truth was that the effort afforded her a deep, visceral pleasure that was almost erotic in the way it exhausted her each day.

On the fifth afternoon of their journey, she was sitting next to Charlie in the ballroom, eating the usual slop they dished up. The inside of her lip was cut from a splintering reed, and she could taste her own blood mixed with the fatty mutton. Gazing up at one of the etched glass murals, she again experienced that quiver of recognition, the memory of being pressed against it with the steward's tongue in her mouth. She could no longer contain her curiosity; she had to know if this was the same ship she'd travelled on with her mother. So after they'd scraped their plates, Pearl suggested to Charlie they go exploring down into the bowels of the ex-ocean liner. He smiled, and his eyebrows arched with excitement.

She led the way out the door, along the hall, following the numbers on the doors of the berths until she found a staircase that took them down into a grinding underworld of engines, steam, and machinery. It smelled of diesel oil and sometimes the tart, chemical odour of bleach. They walked along galleries, down metal staircases, the temperature rising the farther they descended, as if they were inching their way into hell. On the sixth level belowdecks, the engines groaned like dying animals. The navy hadn't bothered applying the same monotonous grey paint to everything down there, and dry green flakes peeled off the walls and stuck to the soles of their boots. She reached a waist-high metal gate that looked familiar, and vaguely remembered a sign that had once hung from it: PASSENGERS STRICTLY FORBIDDEN BEYOND THIS POINT. She pushed the gate open and counted the doors on her left until she reached the fifth one. She opened it and entered a tiny cabin with a narrow single bed and a sink. Yellowing newspapers and magazines from 1939 were strewn across the carpet. The upper corners of the cabin were netted with sagging cobwebs. When she walked into the cabin, she was surprised to turn around and see the outline of her boots imprinted in the dust on the floor.

She rushed to the bed, and pulled back the mattress: there, carved into the wall, were the initials PW and a crooked semiquaver. Eight years before, the unused berth had been her secret hideout. While Clara had caroused with wealthy patrons on the ship, she'd slipped down here to play on her own, listening to every creak and rumble of the liner, pretending she was a stowaway.

She pushed the mattress forward again and was straightening up when she felt a pair of arms engulf her from behind and push her face-first onto the bed. She struggled, cried out, turned onto her side. Charlie was suddenly all over her, kissing her neck, kneading her arse, trying to stick his tongue into her mouth. He was breathing heavily, the bulge in his pants pressing against her. She shoved him away, but he seemed to take it as encouragement and lunged forward again, his full weight against her, biting her earlobe and neck.

She cried out in pain, and when he jolted his head back she raised her fist and punched him hard in the face. Without a sound, he rolled over and hit the floor. They both lay still for a moment, Pearl shocked by what had happened.

"But I thought this was what you wanted," said Charlie, rubbing his eye.

Pearl was breathing heavily. She didn't know what to say. "I'm—I'm not like that."

"It's always the blokes who are secretly scared of being queer that hate queers the most."

"I don't hate queers. I don't hate you."

"Well, then . . . " Charlie got to his feet. His eye was already beginning to swell. "You led me down here. You led me on." Then, to Pearl's great surprise, he undid his trousers and let them drop to his ankles, revealing a hard pink penis about the length of her hand.

"That's how much I want you," he said in a quiet voice.

Pearl flushed with embarrassment and was overcome with pity for him: for all his furtive desires, for the lies he must have had to tell for years, and for the ones he would have to keep on telling throughout his life. He wasn't so different from herself, or even James—an outsider pretending to be an insider. She scooted forward and stood up. His erect member was nodding at her impatiently. Mimicking Charlie, she undid the buttons of her shirt to reveal her bandaged chest, then she unbuckled her belt and let her trousers and underwear drop to the floor.

"You still want to do it?" she asked.

Charlie stared at the blond triangle of hair between her legs. His face paled and he stopped breathing. His eyebrows fluttered then his cock sank into a limp, tiny finger, pointing at the ground.

13

After eight days at sea, the troop ship anchored in Port Moresby just before daylight. All the soldiers fell in and formed lines across the deck. Sequins of moonlight shimmered across the harbour, the only illumination against the blacked-out town. The air was heavy with humidity and already mosquitoes were nipping at the hands and necks of the troops as they crawled into the rocking barges. Pearl sat clutching her rifle as they were ferried away from the troop ship, both terrified and exhilarated. The breeze smelled of rotting fish. The stars above her were so bright and iridescent they looked like a mosaic of diamonds—so much sharper than in the sky over Sydney.

It was a relief to have finally told someone about her real identity. Back in the tiny cabin, when she'd explained why she was dressed as her brother, why she'd taken such a risk, Charlie shook his head and murmured, "You haven't changed a bit." He squeezed her arm and assured her that he'd keep her secret and guide her through the rigours of army life. He explained that queers, too, were banned from the military, but he and his friend Blue had been getting it off for two years, since their first tour of New Guinea.

"Sometimes you get so scared," he said, "the only thing you can do is fuck."

The relationship, however, had been severely tested since Blue had been sent back to Australia and hospitalised. Charlie added that now, when they made love, Blue would sometimes begin to weep. He could offer no explanation for his tears, and it made Charlie feel powerless to help him, as if Blue were a man teetering on the ledge of a building, just out of reach.

At the wharf, the musicians assembled under the command of Rudolph. They picked up their gear and were marched to waiting trucks. As dawn began to press over the hilltops, faint images of the township began to emerge: the rubble of destroyed buildings, shopfronts pockmarked with bullet holes, shattered windowpanes, awnings lying on a narrow footpath. Three coconut trees had fallen against a house, demolishing part of the roof. An awful fear itched across Pearl's skin. Already, a few locals were moving about the streets, the men slim and bearded, the women wearing loose, tentlike frocks; she glimpsed a group of four or five walking languidly, with bundles of what looked like fruits and vegetables balanced perfectly on their heads. Naked youngsters wove between them, chasing a long-necked feathered creature about the size of a small kangaroo.

They were driven past rows of army huts, thatched with palm fronds, some with little rock gardens out the front with vines of bougainvillea and the odd ficus tree. Some units were already performing morning drill, their abrupt, puppetlike movements silhouetted against a blushing sky. Pearl glimpsed a group of black men marching around a long hut without walls and her heart leaped. She half expected to see the face of James amid the passing parade of men, but the truck abruptly turned a corner.

They pulled up beside an old, double-storey wooden hotel by the water with two wilting palm trees out the front. The reception area had its front wall missing and there was a giant crater in what once must have been the floor of the adjoining foyer. The CO announced that the U.S. military had occupied the hotel since early '42, that they were being billeted here because the nearby Murray Barracks was overcrowded. In spite of her apprehension, Pearl was glad to be staying at a hotel full of American GIs; perhaps James was there, or somebody in the building would know where to find him.

Charlie, Blue, and Pearl were assigned to share a single room again, along with the alto player, Moss. On the way over on the ship he'd been assigned latrine duty every day for giving the CO lip, and he was still in a filthy mood.

Blue walked into the room first and immediately went to stand in front of the bamboo-framed mirror on the wall, examining the widening bald patch on his head.

"Oh, great," announced Moss as he claimed the cot by the window. "I got stuck with all the loonies."

A humid, musty pall hung over the town. As Pearl combed the streets with Charlie, the heat felt close and suffocating. Their sweat-stained shirts stuck to their skin, and mosquitoes swarmed around them incessantly. The roads were slippery from the early morning rainfall, and trucks ground tyre marks into the red mud as they transported men between camps. A few army nurses in khaki trousers and slouch hats walked arm in arm with soldiers who limped or hobbled with walking sticks. At each intersection of the city, American MPs directed steady streams of traffic: army jeeps, trucks, donkeys, bicycles, ambulances, even the odd horse and cart. Pearl looked for James in the face of every black GI she saw, but found only strangers, who glanced away as if she were invisible.

They walked up the hill toward the Murray Barracks. It had been Charlie's idea to look for him there, where most of the GIs were stationed. They found a thatched hut with a sign out front that said OFFICE painted in white, and walked along a path of wooden planks that led to the open door. Inside, an electric fan whirred on a desk at which a bespectacled private was hitting the keys of a typewriter. A red and green parrot, gnawing on a piece of chalk, sat on the radio transmitter that was set up behind him.

"Can I help you?" he said, not looking up from the form he was filling out. His voice had a slow, midwestern twang.

Pearl approached the desk. "I'm looking for someone."

"Name?"

"Washington."

"Division?"

"Uh, I'm not sure."

The private pursed his lips as he hit the return lever and continued to type. "What regiment?"

Pearl threw a helpless look at Charlie, who shrugged.

"He's a mechanic," said Pearl.

The private stopped typing and finally looked up. "You mean you're looking for a Negro?"

Pearl explained that he'd been stationed in Australia for a year and would have only arrived in New Guinea a day or two before.

The private, who had a wide nose and a long, lantern jaw, regarded her through narrowed eyes then turned to the parrot, which was still scratching at the piece of chalk. "You reckon we can find him, Petey?"

The parrot looked up and squawked.

"What's that, Petey? Is that a yes or a no?"

The bird squawked again once, then twice, lifting its wings and flapping nervously along the transmitter.

"Gee, fellas, I'm sorry," said the private, smirking. "I guess that's a no."

Pearl sighed and asked him how she should go about finding her friend.

The private shrugged. "Petey and me ain't got the time to track down some raggedy-assed coloured boy for some raggedy-assed Aussies who don't even know his goddamn regiment."

"We know his name. What he does."

"I've got rosters to type. Supplies to order. So get the fuck out of my office before I kick your ass."

The parrot let out a piercing screech and cried, "Ass! Ass! Ass!"

They wandered, dejected, through the city streets. The temperature was rising and the air smelled of putrid, oil-slicked mud. Men squatted in front of bombed-out buildings, passing between them huge cigarettes that smelled like burning rope, rolled from pieces of newspaper.

The sheer weight of what she had recently undertaken pressed down on Pearl in the heat, and it only occurred to her now that all the risks she had taken, the people she had hurt would probably be for nought. She'd managed to keep her disguise a secret from everyone but Charlie and now Blue, but how long could she maintain the ruse before someone else found her out? She glimpsed a dark-skinned girl with a white sheet wrapped around her, swaying in front of a fruit stall. Today, she realised, should have been her wedding day. She thought of Hector and how she had probably ruined his life.

When they arrived back at the hotel, dehydrated and disappointed, they found Blue lying naked on his cot, plucking out the fine hair that grew around his navel. Moss, fortunately, was out, and after they drank some water and pulled off their heavy boots, Charlie began to show Pearl how her .303 worked, how to load and aim. She'd missed out on the six weeks' basic training that the other musicians had been given, and needed to catch up. The weapon felt heavy and important in her hands. She raised the barrel to the open window and aimed it at a palm tree out the front, murmuring, *"Bang! Bang! Bang!"*

After lunch, she disappeared into the back garden of the hotel, rifle in one hand and tenor saxophone in the other, in the hope of finding some privacy. She'd been quietly crushed by the fact that it was going to be nigh on impossible to track down James. Pearl swallowed the anger rising in her throat, trying to control her sense of futility.

She wondered what kind of craziness had caused her to do

this; she certainly didn't feel like the same person who'd talked her brother into switching identities only a week before. The sheer danger and stupidity of it all threatened to overwhelm her. She sat in the dappled sunlight in a kind of dumb, bewildered silence. Sweat rolled down her temples, over her cheeks, and dripped from her chin. A kingfisher cried from the branch of a sago palm. She wasn't sure how long she sat there, overcome, but when a huge yellow butterfly fringed with black fluttered down from the branches of a crocus tree and landed briefly on her hand, it was so beautiful and unexpected that she convinced herself that something good was about to happen. She wiped the sweat from her brow, drew in a deep breath, picked up her brother's tenor saxophone, and began to practise her scales in the dying light.

Rudolph ordered drill the next morning, between the wilting palm trees in front of the hotel. Pearl stood at attention next to Charlie, and when Rudolph barked his orders she saluted, turned, wielded the rifle—dropping it only once, when they were marching around the building. Fortunately, most of the other musicians were not much better at it than she was, and Rudolph didn't seem to notice or care about her few mistakes.

After breakfast they collected their instruments and filed onto a bus that rumbled through the muddy streets of Port Moresby, passing wooden buildings and squat huts splintered by bullet holes and shells. The concert party's first performance was to be in a small hospital camp about twenty miles up into the Owen Stanleys. She'd practised for hours each day since her embarrassing performance on the troop ship, and she was finding it easier to get her hands around the larger instrument, but it had been so long since she'd performed professionally in public that she was still anxious.

The road out of town rose gently into green fields, carved up into several runways, and every now and then an Allied plane flew so close that everyone cringed at the noise. Sometimes the bus had to detour around bomb craters, or churn through the overflow of flooded ravines. As they ascended farther into the mountains it began to rain and one windshield wiper fell off, slowing their progress further.

Toward lunchtime, they pulled into a clearing dotted with canvas tents and a few dwellings built native-style, their roofs thatched with palm leaves. There was one large shelter that had been built without walls. The dirt floor was lined with logs, and already a dozen or so men—some with bandaged heads and limbs—were sitting on them, smoking and waiting for the show to begin. Others were making their way across the clearing on crutches. When she looked closer, she could see that some of the crutches were fashioned from the boughs of trees.

As the party clambered off the bus, Pearl saw a tall black man standing on a platform, on guard duty, rifle poised, his uniform caked with mud. She broke away from the group and ran toward him.

When she reached the platform the man turned and gazed down at her, and up close she could see his face was too long, his chin too prominent, his eyes too wide.

"Can I help you?" His voice had none of James's Southern lilt.

She hung her head, feeling foolish. "I thought you were someone else."

"Oh yeah?" he said. "And who's that? Ain't too many Aussies runnin' round lookin' for the likes of coloured folks like me."

Pearl explained that she didn't know his division or his regiment. All she did know for sure was his name: James Washington.

The guard frowned. "Don't know him. Why you lookin' for him, anyway?"

"My twin sister used to date him back in Sydney. Still sweet on him, I guess."

The guard lowered his rifle and leaned on the railing around his post. "Best bet is the airfields," he offered.

She edged closer to him, waiting for him to elaborate.

"Talk to the pilots. They flyin' all over the place every day. They know what's happenin'." He shrugged. "Long shot, of course. Be mighty hard to track him down."

Pearl nodded briefly, thanked the guard, and returned to the large hut without walls to begin warming up with a few quick runs on the saxophone. When she paused, she realised she was shaking—from fear or anticipation, she couldn't tell which. Charlie must have noticed it, too, for he called, "Hey, Willis," and led her out of the hut and into the dense green foliage beyond the clearing. When he was sure no one could see him, he pulled out his water canteen, flipped the top and took a sip, then passed the canteen to her. She was confused at first, until she caught a whiff of the rough grain alcohol. She took several gulps before Charlie snatched it back.

More and more soldiers gathered before the band. Local

men carried some in on stretchers; Pearl was shocked to see a couple of them had no legs. Others arrived in rusting wheelchairs pushed by medics and nurses. Before her was a sea of gauze and bandages, makeshift slings and crutches. Everything seemed bruised and broken and sore—except their eyes, she noticed, all of which were fixed on the band, bright with anticipation, and she found herself curiously moved by their expressions, all somehow childlike, despite their suffering.

As she stared at these men, her own problems receded, became remote and insignificant. She had her health; all her limbs were intact; she'd never had to face, repeatedly, the threat of her imminent death. It occurred to her that these men needed music as much as they needed morphine or antibiotics, and, as she began to play, as she followed the circumlocutions of each chart, as she saw the glowing faces of the wounded men, a strange kind of urgency welled up through her until nothing else mattered but trying to ease their pain.

14

After a week or so in Moresby, as the band was eating dinner in the gutted dining room of the hotel, the CO stood up, cleared his throat, and informed them that the famous American comedian Bob Hope was due to arrive the next day. He'd be performing in a warehouse on the other side of town, along with the great Australian soprano Gladys Moncrieff. A huge stage was already being erected inside the warehouse, and the entertainment unit had been scheduled to accompany the stars.

Later, Pearl lay on her canvas cot, trying to prepare herself mentally for the upcoming concert. She was terrified of being exposed as an impostor, yet excited to be performing with such big names. That week, they'd already performed a concert in the market garden of a village, another beneath a leafy cathedral of palms in a forward camp in the Owen Stanleys, yet another amid the debris of a bombed community hall. The acoustics were appalling at all these venues, the heat stultifying, and Pearl's fingers were so sweaty they occasionally slipped from the brass keys. On top of that, she was still struggling with the nuances of the tenor sax, though each time the band struck up she found it a little easier to adjust her lips and coax a deep, fluid tone from the S-shaped bell. Now that she knew the company's entire repertoire by heart she could concentrate on her breath, her tone, and improvising on her solos. And she could focus on finding James.

During their one free morning that week, she and Charlie had taken the black American guard's advice and headed out to one of the nearby airfields. They chatted with ground staff, shared cigarettes with pilots, and ingratiated themselves with a unit of black Americans who loaded planes with supplies. None of them had heard of a Washington who used to play the tenor sax back in the States and who now worked as a mechanic—until Pearl and Charlie were introduced to a copilot named Sol Leiderman, a jazz buff from New York City who said he'd actually once heard James Washington play in a Harlem club before the war. His wife even owned one of the records he'd made with Count Basie in 1939. It was a long shot, but just in case Leiderman did happen to come across him in his travels, Pearl wrote down Martin's regiment number so that he'd be able to track her down.

As she lay perspiring in her cot, the constant buzz of mosquitoes and the sound of Moss's snoring made her head throb. And the more she tried to fall asleep, the more anxious she became, worrying about the big concert the following day. Her throat was parched and there was another pain, lower down, in her belly. For a moment she feared it was the onset of one of the local diseases: dysentery, perhaps, or even malaria. But then she felt wetness between her legs and stifled a groan; her period had arrived.

Wads of army-issue toilet paper were stuffed inside her underpants, chafing against her skin, as she performed drill the next morning. She was scared she'd bleed through her khaki trousers. She had an extra toilet roll stuffed in her pack for the long day ahead.

Three U.S. jeeps collected the band members and Rudolph late in the morning, and they were driven around the curve of the harbour, through hot, humid air and the ubiquitous smell of rotting seaweed.

The warehouse was as big as six tennis courts. Inside, men were still nailing together the floor for the stage and erecting a curtain sewn from parachute silk. The smells of sawdust and the petrol that had once been stored there were pervasive. The American band they were to join was gathered down the back, tuning their instruments and warming up. Rudolph led Pearl and the others across the concrete floor toward them, and as they drew closer she saw a black GI play a run on an alto saxophone that sounded so familiar a shiver ran through her body. Up close, however, he looked nothing like James: His skin was darker and his cheeks were marked with acne scars.

The CO of the American band, Captain Simon Rowe, was to lead the united outfit. Gladys Moncrieff had already forwarded her charts, and Rowe passed them around to the twenty-five musicians.

"Okay, fellas," said Rowe, "there's no time to run through all these but they're pretty straightforward. Any questions?"

Pearl and the others thumbed through the charts. Rowe was right: There was nothing tricky or demanding. She'd been playing stuff like this since she was eleven years old: "A-Tisket, A-Taskit," "I Can't Give You Anything But Love, Baby." Rowe then passed around an additional set of jazz charts for the opening set of the show, to be played before Gladys and Bob came on. These were much more complicated, with additional codas and extra instructions written in pencil on top of the bar lines. There were only about ten foldout seats set out along the side wall, reserved for the Australian and American top brass. The band hurried to help the service personnel set up the music stands and seats on the stage, for the show was due to start in less than half an hour. Soldiers were already filing into the warehouse, bringing with them boxes, empty ammo crates, and anything else they could find to sit on.

A flurry of panic erupted onstage, behind the drawn curtain. "Miss Moncrieff's arrived!" "Glad's here!" "Our Glad just pulled up." Rudolph, who was helping to erect the microphone into which she would sing, tripped on the cord and knocked over the baritone sax. Rowe was pacing the boards, giving orders. Most of the musicians were still warming up or rearranging the sheets on their stands.

Pearl was sitting in her assigned chair, holding the tenor and trying to remain calm, when she felt a warm gush between her legs. Leaving the sax on her seat, she dashed toward the back of the stage and leaped off it. She rushed through an open door and almost bumped into a woman who was standing in the shade of the warehouse, her hair lacquered up into a towering bun, sweating through an apricot satin dress and fanning herself with a magazine. Gladys Moncrieff. There was a sudden roar of engines overhead, and when Pearl looked up she saw a small aeroplane soaring through the clouds.

There were two latrines set up roughly thirty yards away, each with a line of about ten or twelve men. She squinted and could see Moss and the drummer joining one of the queues. She knew there was no way she could wait that long, and anyway she was unable to piss standing up, always having to find some secret place behind a building or in the long grass of the jungle. Beyond the clearing, the land sloped up gently into a rainforest thick with tall trees and vines; a stream ran down between banks of high grass. She followed it up into the tangle of vegetation, into a chorus of insects and twittering birds. Another plane roared overhead.

She had just squatted beside a smooth rock and lowered her trousers when an air-raid siren sounded. Her hands were wet with blood as she tossed the soiled paper into a bush. She fumbled in her pocket and pulled out a long, fresh piece, then folded it over and over to make a new napkin, noticing to her dismay that her trousers were now splattered with blood. The siren was so loud it made her ears hurt. When she glanced down the hill she saw men running out of the warehouse, diving for split trenches near the latrine. There was a distant stutter of gunfire. She was just about to shove the paper into her crotch and pull up her underpants when she caught sight of a man standing on the other side of the stream, pissing. She couldn't be sure but she thought it was Moss.

Gunfire hammered around her and she threw herself to the ground. A smaller plane streaked across the sky and another shell dropped, closer this time, and she was splattered with dirt and rocks. She crawled along the ground on her elbows and knees. She could see the man who'd been pissing was now running down the hill, on his way back to the warehouse. She wished she could follow him, but was too terrified to move. Between the wails of the siren she could hear someone shouting orders and the stutter of ack-ack guns. A plane flew so close she could feel the wind from its propellers. She flattened herself against the ground and rolled into a hole, pressing her face into the mud. The earth shuddered as a third shell exploded farther down, near the warehouse. She could hear people wailing and yelling, and the air was thick with the stench of gunpowder.

After five or so minutes, silence settled over the valley. She raised her head warily and glanced down the hill. Between the trunks of palms she could see that one corner of the warehouse was on fire and soldiers were already ferrying buckets of water from the beach, trying to put it out. Smoke rose from a crater in the ground. She crawled out of the hole and hurried down the slope. Someone was barking orders, and there was the rumble of ambulances and trucks speeding toward the site. Two Americans were already lifting the limp body of a fellow soldier into the back of a jeep. She was striding past a drain at the back of the warehouse when she noticed a pair of boots, upside down, sticking out of it. There seemed to be a soldier wedged head first inside it, though he wasn't calling for help or making any noise at all. Pearl called to Farthing, the organist, who was collecting some musical arrangements that were scattered all over the ground. Farthing grabbed one ankle and Pearl took the other, and, after counting to three, they bent their knees and pulled, clutching various parts of the man's uniform—his trouser legs, his belt—for a better grip. As he rose from the hole, she could feel that his body was as limp as a puppet. They

laid him on his back on the ground. He was covered in a con-
fetti of blood and dirt, but Pearl recognised him immediately.
It was Moss, and his eyes were open, looking directly up at her.

The front wall of the warehouse had been burned down, smoke
rose from the roof, and several rows of chairs had been reduced
to clumps of ash, but once the wet, charred mess had been
cleared, the soldiers filed back inside. Some sat quietly on the
ground, heads bowed, waiting for further orders. Fortunately,
the stage had been spared and none of the instruments had been
damaged. Moss had been taken away in an ambulance, along
with an American trombone player who'd also been killed. The
Australian musicians stood around anxiously, smoking cigarettes, not saying much about the air raid, about losing one of
their own.

"Okay, fellas," announced Rudolph, "the show's going on.
Let's blow the roof off this joint."

"Shouldn't be too hard—it's already half gone," joked
Charlie.

As the curtain finally rose to the sound of "One O'Clock
Jump," cheers mushroomed out of the soot and rubble. Above
the music, ambulance sirens could still be heard wailing across
the bay. Men in the audience began slapping their knees and
clicking their fingers in time with the beat. Pearl was still in
a kind of daze after the shock of the falling shells and finding Moss's corpse wedged into the drain. She'd never seen a
dead body before, and had been surprised by how heavy it was.
And as she was thinking about this, she suddenly realised that

Rudolph was pointing his baton at her, drawing tiny circles in the air, and she remembered her first solo was due to begin. She glimpsed Moss's alto on its stand. Before she had time to stop herself she was unclipping Martin's tenor from the noose around her neck. She reached forward and snatched up Moss's sax and raised it to her lips.

For the first time in nearly a year, she was holding an alto in her hands, in her mouth, and it felt as if she were embracing an old lover from whom she'd been separated for years. After practising and performing on the much larger tenor, playing Moss's sax was a comparative breeze. As she stood in the spotlight, the air sang in her lungs and her fingers moved effortlessly against the keys. Her stomach was giddy with adrenaline, there was a gorgeous tingling between her legs that was almost sexual, and these sensations soared out of the bell of the sax in a fast, excited rush. She glanced to her right and was astonished to see Bob Hope and Gladys Moncrieff in the wings, dancing together. To her left, in the audience, was the line of top brass: the captain of the Pacific Entertainment Unit, Jim Davidson, Australian and American officers. When she completed the solo with a descending riff that James had taught her, the men jumped to their feet and applauded loudly and the locals in the audience tossed flowers at her feet.

Afterward, the top brass came backstage to greet the band and to have their photos taken with the visiting celebrities. Pearl cleaned Moss's sax before packing it back into its case.

"That was fantastic, Willis!" boomed Rudolph. He clapped her on the back. "You play a wicked alto. Why didn't you tell me?"

She shrugged, lost for words.

"That thing you were doing at the end of 'Cherokee,' that was a knockout. And your *tone*. Like honey. Bit of the old Lester Young there."

"Thanks, sir."

"Shame about old Moss. But you know the old saying . . . "

Pearl nodded. "Only the good die young."

"No—the show must go on. I don't want any arguments about this, Willis: you're playing alto from now on, *and that's an order*." And with that he made a beeline toward Bob Hope, who was standing by the door chatting with the musicians and signing autographs.

15

Through the windows of the plane, the sea looked as smooth as a pane of glass. It was the first time Pearl had been on an aircraft and she was absolutely terrified. Charlie sat beside her with his arms crossed over his chest, hands clamped under his armpits to keep them warm. Blue was so tense about flying his eyes were shut, hands clenched together on his lap. Pearl could see a patchwork of ploughed fields pockmarked with bomb craters and trenches. Suddenly the plane banked on a forty-five-degree angle, and she found herself looking down on a series of uneven peaks that resembled a line of knuckles. Inside the cabin it was so cold her breath fogged the air and her ears began squealing due to the lack of air pressure.

The unit had received orders from Sydney only the day before to move on to the Huon Peninsula, due north of Port Moresby. The region on the map the CO had shown them was a peninsula of land framed on three sides by the Solomon Sea. The Allies had taken the peninsula only a few weeks before; there'd been many casualties, and some of the men isolated on island posts hadn't heard music or even seen a newspaper in over eighteen months.

The old bomber coughed and spluttered. Occasionally, it lost altitude for a moment and began to rattle. From the air, Pearl could see the area around the gulf had been heavily bombed. Big black bald patches mottled the rainforest. The wings of crashed planes forked up between palm trees. As they began descending she could see overturned jeeps lying in the tall kunai grass. The plane circled an airstrip and landed with such an impact that some of the instrument cases were flung around the cabin.

The musicians leaped out of the hold and into a hot wind that smelled like putrid meat. A group of American soldiers began unloading the plane.

"What's that stink?" Pearl asked one of them.

The man nodded at the ranges to the north of the airfield. "Corpses up in the mountains. Too many to bury."

"Allies or Japanese?" asked Charlie.

"Both."

They were driven to a small barracks close to the airstrip. After stashing their gear beneath canvas cots in a dormitory, they followed Rudolph's orders and marched into the mess tent. Soon, a clerk lugged in a bulging canvas bag, and everyone lined up to receive mail. Pearl was surprised when a clerk handed her a package addressed to Martin Willis. She cut the string, ripped off the paper, and found a square tin she recognised from the kitchen cabinet at home, with a faded picture on the lid of a pretty girl sitting on a swing and eating a green apple. Inside were twenty-four of her mother's cinnamon biscuits and a long letter which was full of bad news, all related with blue ink in her mother's spidery longhand. Clara wrote that Pearl had *really gone off the deep end* and had *vanished into thin air*. The police could *find no trace of her*. The wedding had had to be called off. Pearl ate five biscuits in quick succession as she reread the letter. Hector was *beside himself*. And one day Pearl would *get what was coming to her*. There were also items of domestic trivia—Mr. Bones had moved to a local nursing home; Lulu's false teeth had been misplaced; Clara had hosted a tea party for the local chapter of the civilian army. She closed by begging Martin to look after himself.

More than anything, Pearl had hoped to receive a letter from Martin, to be reassured that he was safely hidden on Nora and Pookie's farm. That afternoon she sat down and wrote him a short letter, telling him she was safe and well, and that she'd met and performed for Bob Hope, who'd autographed one of her musical arrangements. She asked him to reply as soon as possible and signed off with *Your brother, M.*

Over the next few weeks, Pearl almost began to enjoy herself. No one questioned her identity or her position in the band, and she was allowed to play the alto saxophone.

From Finschhafen the musicians travelled by barge down the coast toward Lae, leapfrogging from island to island, camp to camp. Their instruments were packed inside an army truck, and each day, after the barge had ploughed through the chartreuse-coloured water to another island, the truck was driven off onto the sand, where native children would dance and cavort alongside it like a flock of excited birds, walking on their hands and throwing fruits and flowers.

The troops would help clear the jungle scrub for the portable stage, which folded out from the back of the truck. The band members would wash and refresh themselves and then the ninety-minute performance would begin.

The soldiers sat on boxes, jerry cans, and biscuit tins—anything they could find to keep their backsides out of the mud—clapping in time and shouting requests. At night, the band used the taillights of the truck to illuminate the stage. Some island-bound troops hadn't had leave in two years, and when the concert was over, the musicians were often asked to do the entire show all over again. When they did, Rudolph would throw in extra material that Pearl had arranged in her free time, to see how it sounded and to provide some variety. Rudolph would tell a few jokes and Charlie Styles would do his impression of the bombs over Darwin that had happened two years before. Once, while he was performing it, a real shell was dropped, and everyone grabbed their instruments and dived into the trenches.

"Special effects are good!" cried a guard as he gunned at the sky, laughing.

Afterward, the troops were usually so grateful that they gave Pearl and the other musicians gifts—small boxes and masks carved from tree trunks, shells filed into talismans, palm leaves woven into mats.

When they weren't performing, Pearl, Charlie, and Blue avoided the rest of the band. Blue was fastidious about hygiene, and when he wasn't pulling out his hair he was polishing and oiling his treasured trombone. He always nagged Pearl if she didn't wipe out her sax after a show. When her last reed split he showed her how to file down a piece of bamboo and insert it into the mouthpiece instead.

Sometimes they went fishing, and if they caught anything they'd build a fire, roast the catch, and eat it with warm coconut milk. Other times they'd slip off with the locals and look for turtle eggs to eat; they were round and dimpled, like golf balls. Occasionally they'd find an isolated beach, and when Pearl was sure no one was near she'd strip off her clothes and swim in the turquoise sea with Charlie and Blue, ducking and bobbing between tropical fish. In spite of the occasional air raid, those weeks felt like an endless holiday—she was free to experiment with different musical ideas, and there was no Clara or Hector to tell her what to do.

Their barge chugged through the low tide of the Huon Peninsula in late January 1944. As it edged its way toward the harbour, the bow of a sunken ship could be seen rising above the surface of the sea. Lae had been taken by the Allies only a few months before and everyone knew there were still units of Japanese hiding out in the ranges. The outline of the township grew more distinct as they approached, jagged silhouettes of bombed buildings and flattened houses, felled trees and overturned jeeps. The bay reeked of shit and rotting vegetables. Mangy dogs roamed the wharves, nosing through garbage and barking at the moon.

The musicians camped at a barracks on a ridge above the bay, sleeping in double bunks with wooden frames; the legs stood in kerosene tins full of water to keep the ants away. Every now and then gunfire hammered in the mountains. During the second night, an air-raid siren sounded and everyone stumbled out of bed and into a foxhole and had to doze against one another until dawn.

On the third day of their stay in Lae, Rudolph received movement orders from Sydney, delivered by a skinny, big-eared clerk.

Rudolph's eleven-man unit was to be divided temporarily into two groups. One would stay in Lae, unloading supplies from Australian ships and helping the Allies repair the damage to buildings in the area; the other would travel independently into the more remote areas of the country, to camps close to the combat zones, where soldiers had been isolated for months without adequate supplies, let alone entertainment. It would be tough, exhausting, and extremely dangerous. The orders stated that no more than five men should form the troubadour detachment, for reasons of mobility as well as security.

"These soldiers," said Rudolph, "haven't had a proper hot meal or seen a movie in ages. So they need more than a tune or two. They need song-and-dance routines. Comedy. Maybe even a magic act."

The party was standing at attention between the company clerk's office and the mess tent. It was already hot and flies buzzed in circles around their heads.

"Now I'm asking for volunteers," continued Rudolph. "You're all welcome to try out. There's no extra pay, of course, but think of what you'll be doing for your comrades."

Everyone looked at the ground, nodding briefly, swatting at flies and mosquitoes.

Charlie asked what they would use for props and costumes.

"We can probably borrow some from the Yanks. There's a supply hut near the latrines." Rudolph nodded to a small square building on the other side of a creek, made from logs and corrugated iron.

Blue then asked, in a trembling voice, for the exact location of the combat zone.

Rudolph glanced at the orders he was holding. "The troubadours will play three isolated camps through the Markham Valley between here and Nadzab. At Nadzab they'll receive orders either to return here or to continue farther toward the front. Any questions?"

Pearl asked if the troubadours would be performing in American camps.

"Of course," said Rudolph, who was growing testy in the heat. "Now there's not much time. This new outfit'll have to be rehearsed and polished by the end of the week. So who's going to try out?"

In the mess tent later that day, Charlie stood in a pair of baggy trousers held up by braces and performed a set of impersonations of various famous people, from James Cagney to Hitler to Oliver Hardy. He then did a comedy routine with a hand puppet he'd made from an army sock. Blue, while terrified at the prospect of such a dangerous mission, was even more frightened of being separated from Charlie. He surprised everyone by sitting on a foldout chair and playing the trombone with his feet, something he used to do as a child back in Orange. The drummer, Marks, painted his face white, dressed up in a clown costume, and did a softshoe on top of an oil barrel, using his bayonet as a cane. Marks was also able to walk on his hands. The organist, Farthing, a hefty, muscular man with legs like tree trunks, donned a blond wig from the supplies hut, painted on red lipstick, and squeezed into a spangled pink dress. He balanced a broomstick on his nose, then a rifle on his head. After that, he stuck two pineapples down the front of the dress and imitated Mae West.

Pearl was keen to tour the American army camps, even if it meant performing close to the front, and she wanted to stick with Charlie and Blue, who were the only ones who knew her secret. When her turn came, she stood in front of Rudolph and began to play "In a Persian Market" on her alto.

Rudolph waved at her to stop. "We all know you can play the saxophone, Willis," he barked. "But this detachment needs *variety*."

Pearl told an old joke of her father's about a priest with constipation, but when she delivered the punch line Rudolph just coughed.

"Can you do any routines?" he asked. "A bit of dressing up?"

She glanced at the other band members, standing there with their sock puppets and broomsticks and funny hats. "As what?"

"Well, like what Farthing here just did—as a sheila."

Pearl swallowed. Her face began to colour. The organist pursed his lips and blew her a kiss.

"I'm sure you could get away with it, Willis. You're a lot prettier than Farthing."

A wave of panic moved through her. "No I'm not, sir."

"You can't just play the saxophone!" bellowed Rudolph, exasperated. "The men in these camps haven't seen the likes of a woman for years! Haven't had mail or tasted a steak in months."

"I wouldn't know what to do," she protested.

"Just do what Farthing did! Get your arse over to supplies and pick out a nice frock."

She opened her mouth to object, but Rudolph interrupted. "Do it, Private. Or you can forget the whole thing."

Pearl stormed out of the mess tent. She couldn't believe her bad luck, after having come so far, after having fooled so many people. If she impersonated a woman, she suspected, she'd be far too convincing.

She was sitting in the shade of a bombed requisition hut, trying to hold back her tears, when the skinny, big-eared clerk appeared before her, squinting in the sunlight.

"You Willis?" he said. He shooed away a fly with the piece of paper in his hand.

Pearl took off her hat and nodded.

"This just came through from Moresby." It was a cable from Sol Leiderman addressed to Martin: PRIVATE WASHINGTON BASED IN NADZAB.

Her heart did a little dance in her chest as she read the words over and over, hardly believing the message in her hands. On the other side of the creek, heat waves rose from the iron roof of the supplies hut. She looked up to see Charlie standing over her, hands on hips. "He's in Nadzab," she breathed. "Only thirty miles away."

*   *   *

Hoots and wolf whistles ricocheted through the mess hall as she marched toward Rudolph, who was still in his seat, scribbling on a clipboard. A few men clapped, and a cook rushed up and asked her for a root. On her head was a long, blond wig. Charlie had painted her face with garish makeup—scarlet lipstick that exceeded the perimeters of her lips, eyeliner, a smudge of rouge on each cheek. She wore a full-length dress made of a filmy red imitation silk that swayed and caught the outline of her body as she moved; beneath it was a 40D brassiere stuffed with surgical hemp, creating a pair of enormous breasts that stood out in front of her like two cannonballs. On her hands were long black gloves that stretched up over her elbows. She still wore her army boots, and in them she walked heavily, swinging her arms from side to side, grimacing at the cat calls. She affected a humiliated pout—nostrils flaring, downcast eyes—that sent the rest of the party into paroxysms of laughter. She came to a stop before Rudolph, raised one gloved hand, and saluted. She noticed her breasts were crooked and rearranged them.

"That's more like it, Private," said Rudolph. "Now give us a tune."

She hadn't planned the ruse this far, and hesitated. If the song were too romantic, she'd risk sounding like a girl. But if she didn't sound a little feminine, she wouldn't get the gig, and then she'd be left behind on the wharves of Lae. The trick was to sound like a man trying to sound like a girl, which wasn't the same as a girl trying to sound like a man.

"Come on, Willis," prompted Rudolph. "Give us a fucking song."

She cleared her throat and took a deep breath. Suddenly, she heard her father singing one of his old vaudeville tunes, his high, soprano voice as he played the ukulele, pulling faces at the crowd and wagging his bum from side to side. And when she opened her mouth, out came Aub's warbling, comic vibrato, crooning "Fan Dance Fanny, the Frowsy Nightclub Queen." One by one, soldiers appeared at the flap of the tent and came in to get a better look. When she hit the last high note, she parted her legs, raised her arms, and held it as if it would never end, and when it did, the crowd that had gathered clapped and whistled, throwing betel nuts at her feet.

16

There were now costumes to be made, songs to rehearse, comedy routines to sharpen, arrangements to be written. Pearl didn't mind all the extra work, however, because she knew she was only two or three days away from finding James. They made dresses out of parachute silk, wigs from surgical hemp, and dyed them different colours with Condy's crystals, iodine, and chemicals from the barracks hospital. She also begged a roll of canvas from the ordnance store and painted on it the Sydney Harbour Bridge and a cove of water; she then attached two wooden stakes to each side so that they could be driven into the ground to hold up the scenery. Farthing already had a portable organ; Marks cut his kit down to one drum, a cymbal, a cowbell, and a woodblock. Rudolph appointed Pearl the musical director, and she began to write arrangements for the five-piece band. Charlie complained that there were no slow tunes in the repertoire and Pearl retorted that they would bore the soldiers.

"There's only one thing worse than a ballad," she said. "And that's a ballad medley."

*   *   *

The troubadours set out early on a Sunday morning.

Wanipe and Dogare, the two black trackers, carried the heavier instruments and props: the portable organ, the scenery, and the small kit of drums. The rest of the band carried costumes, wind instruments, a ground sheet and blanket, mosquito nets, antimalaria tablets, and food rations. They each had a water canteen attached to their belt and carried a rifle in one hand.

They walked toward the foothills that ringed the township of Lae, avoiding the direct road to Nadzab, where they could be easily ambushed. Pearl had had her hair cut the day before by a company barber and he'd shaved it so close that she was now almost bald. It pleased her to look even more like a man, but she had to keep her hat pulled tight over her ears to prevent her scalp from getting sunburnt.

The river they followed was a deep turquoise with islands of red silt and white sand marbling into swirls. As the day passed, the trees loomed taller, the jungle thickened into curtains of vines and leaves. Sometimes the river curved into itself and they had to cross it, holding their instruments and rifles high above their heads.

Late afternoon, the convoy approached a small base camp consisting of half a dozen sagging tents alongside the river. Dotted throughout the clearing were scrawny, bare-chested men sitting on jerry cans and bits of wood. Some cleaned their rifles, others smoked, two soldiers were stacking logs by a tent. The nearby trees were festooned with drying shirts, and rudimentary hammocks were strung between the boughs. Green lichen carpeted most of the ground and everything smelled of mildew. There was a washstand built into the trunk of a sago palm with a plate of reflective steel nailed above it.

The troubadours' first concert was a total disaster. The portable scenery sagged into the ground, the costume changes were too slow, and the men in the camp knew the punch lines to most of the gags and yelled them out prematurely. The wind blew the sheet music away and the pages glanced across the surface of the river and were swept downstream. Farthing lost his way without the charts, and the music lurched on in a retarded grind of dropped codas, missing notes, and dissonant harmonies. When Marks attempted to walk on his hands he slipped in the mud. Behind some bushes, Pearl donned her wig and then the red dress, pulling it over the top of her still-wet trousers so she wouldn't look too feminine, and applied a thick coat of makeup. In her attempt to sound manly, she accidentally started off in the wrong key and had to begin again. She sang in her father's voice but the long hike and the many mishaps had unnerved her. And by this time the men were growing restless with all the mistakes and were wandering off toward the mess hut. But one of the carriers, Wanipe, stood by shyly. He wore only a burlap sheath, and a dog's tooth hung on a piece of string around his neck. In his hands he held three kauri shells. It was hard for Pearl to tell how old he was—maybe forty or even older.

After she finished her number, she saw that he was holding the shells out to her. She took them, nodding. No sooner had she murmured her thanks than he swooped down upon her and began kissing her face, her neck, her shoulders, pressing himself onto her, until they both slipped over in the mud. All the musicians burst into laughter and Farthing pulled Wanipe to his feet, explaining in rudimentary pidgin and accompanying hand gestures that the object of his desire was really a man. Wanipe frowned and shook his head; Pearl couldn't tell whether it was in astonishment or disbelief.

The tracks through the rainforest were slippery with mud; the air buzzed with mosquitoes and flies; everyone grew weary with the heat and the constant dehydration, but they wouldn't allow themselves to complain, let alone turn back. Coconut trees stretched into the sky, along with sago palms, breadfruit trees, bamboo, and wild sugarcane. When they were sure they were in a safe area, they rehearsed the show again, tightening up the costume changes and changing the jokes and routines. The scenery that Pearl had so carefully painted was too heavy to carry and was soon abandoned by the river.

The carrier who'd offered Pearl the kauri shells, Wanipe, always led the way. He was not only familiar with the local territory, he was one of the few coastal people who'd traversed the hundreds of miles of the western highlands, walking up mountains as high as fourteen thousand feet above sea level to trade shells for gold and pigs. His skin was a deep ochre in the sunlight. The whites of his eyes were always a little red, as if he were suffering from a permanent hangover. His cheeks creased into gentle corrugations when he smiled. Sometimes Pearl caught him gazing at her with a knowing look, as if he could see through her clothes and detect the slight curve of her breasts and the triangle of downy blond hair between her legs. Farthing and Marks had done their best to convince him that she was a man, but she often felt he knew the truth and that this knowledge was a source of amusement to him. The other carrier, Dogare, didn't give her a second glance. He was younger than Wanipe, and lighter skinned, with a thin, wiry body that always held the scent of sweat and coconut oil. In a certain light, he looked like James, though his expression was more surly and unsure.

They didn't walk a direct route toward Nadzab but zig-zagged back and forth through the jungle, from one post to an-other. The tracks they walked wound like long brown serpents through stands of sago palms and clusters of cane, the stalks of which stood twice the size of a man. Sometimes the river flooded and the party would be thigh-deep in mud and sour water, struggling past water lilies and ferns. Sometimes they'd spot snakes undulating in the water. Blue, in particular, was terrified of them, and whenever he spotted one he would splash toward Wanipe and Dogare for protection. But the greatest fear of all was the one generated by the presence of the Japanese, who were hiding in the area through which they now moved. Several times a day they heard the whistle of a falling shell or the heavy stutter of gunfire, and they'd dive into the mud or a shallow ravine. Now that they were closer to the fighting, they were under orders to always end their shows before dusk, as any artificial lighting would be a beacon to the enemy.

Apart from the carriers, the only other people who didn't know Pearl was a girl were Farthing and Marks, and she was always on her guard. She never went swimming with them; instead, she briskly bathed on her own in the dead of night. In her pack she carried her brother's razor, without the blade, and each morning she lathered her face and drew it across her cheeks and chin until the soap had been scraped away.

When they all lounged around a fire at night, Farthing and Marks often bantered about ex-wives, old girlfriends, and bad cooking. Pearl was startled by their talk—she'd never heard men speak so directly, so candidly about themselves.

"That's the trouble between men and women," remarked Farthing one night. "For a man, the first fuck with a girl is always the best one, but over time it just goes downhill." He shook his head. "But for a girl, the first fuck with a bloke is always the worst one, but over time it gets better and better."

Marks roared with laughter and Pearl, a little shocked, quickly joined in. Blue and Charlie were already in their tent, asleep.

"Whaddya reckon, Willis?" Farthing prompted.

Pearl nodded. "Mate," she said, flicking the butt of her cigarette into the fire, "don't talk to me about first roots. I used to go out with this one girl—you know, the first time we did it was in Luna Park."

"Bullshit," said Farthing.

"True."

"On the Big Dipper?"

"Did ya sell tickets?" added Marks.

"It was the night the Japs invaded Sydney. In a carriage of the Tumblebug."

"Like doing it outside, eh?" asked Farthing.

"I tried that once," said Marks, "but it was too fucking cold and my John Thomas shrivelled up."

"I didn't want to at first," said Pearl, trying to be just as brazen, "but she begged me. And right after we're done—I've hardly had time to pull out of her—and what does she do but turn around and beg me for a favour."

"There's always a catch," mused Marks.

"She want money?" asked Farthing.

"Let me guess," said Marks. "Probably wanted to move straight into your place and start rearranging your whole life. That's what my first girlfriend did. After six months I got pissed off and left her there with all my gear. She got the lot."

"Better off tugging," said Farthing.

"This girl wanted me to teach her how to play the saxophone." Pearl rubbed her hands together over the fire. "One root," she sighed, "and they reckon they own you."

"Just for spreading their legs . . . "

"And lying on their backs for five minutes."

"Three minutes if it's you," joked Farthing.

"You'd only take sixty seconds!" Pearl laughed, relieved to be accepted as one of them.

They'd been on the trek several days when Farthing and Marks guessed that Charlie and Blue were, as they joked, "playing bottoms with one another." There were several telltale signs: a hand on a shoulder, one straightening the other's hat, the traded glances. Any doubts Farthing had had about the intimacy between the couple were put to rest when he stumbled into the wrong tent one night and saw, in the dim moonlight, the outline of Charlie's head bobbing against Blue's groin.

As the caravan pressed north, the affair between Charlie and Blue became the source of good-natured ribbing. Charlie would ask something like "What'll we have for lunch?" And Marks would retort, "Why don't you ask your missus?" When Blue would clean and polish his trombone every night they'd tease him about doing his housework. The ease with which Farthing and Marks accepted the couple allowed Pearl to relax a little, but she was always wary of being caught out, especially when she had to dress up as a woman and sing love songs to lonely soldiers.

They were only a few hours outside of Nadzab when the unit reached a company of Americans that had, only the day before, taken a nearby airstrip. The Japanese had been driven back into the hills. But twice while the band changed into their costumes and applied their makeup they could hear exchanges of rifle fire and bullets ricocheting off trees and rocks. Blue grew pale at the sound and began to tremble, and Charlie had to straighten him up with a bottle of brandy he'd cajoled from an American gunner.

It was about an hour before dusk. They set up their instruments and props between two L-shaped split trenches. A group of about forty soldiers sat before them, some bandaged. Three men lay on stretchers, heads supported by sandbags. Guards patrolled the grassy clearing that served as an airstrip, the piece of land everyone had been fighting over the day before.

The band struck up the overture, a fast rendition of "In the Mood." They were into the third chorus when Pearl saw two men carry a body out of a thicket of trees at the edge of the clearing. As he was ferried past the band and into a tent she noticed his shirt and trousers were caked with dried blood; his head, arms, and legs flopped limply.

As the show progressed, the soldiers clapped and laughed. Charlie dressed up in a frock sewn from surgical gauze and sang "Chattanooga Choo Choo." All the men joined in, crooning the words and swaying from side to side, while intermittent rifle shots from the surrounding hills provided an unsteady counterpoint. Marks balanced a rifle on his head, next a bayonet, next a bamboo canvas stretcher. He then turned over a huge wire reel and did a tap dance on what was now a round wooden platform. Blue played the trombone with his feet but the occasional gunfire made him so nervous the slide kept slipping out of his toes and the tune was cut short after only one chorus. After that, he rested his trombone on his case and walked away from the band, around the split trenches and into the bush, because there weren't any latrines in the temporary post. While Blue was relieving himself, Pearl emerged from the costume-change tent in her red dress, long gloves and blond wig, carried by Wanipe and Dogare. She lay stretched out on her side, elbow cocked and head resting in one hand, singing "We'll Meet Again" while the soldiers cheered and shouted, "My place or yours?"

Wanipe and Dogare were clearly enjoying themselves. It was the first time they'd been included in the show, and they'd painted ceremonial stripes on their faces and necks with Pearl's red lipstick; their fuzzy hair was speared with cassowary plumes and the iridescent feathers plucked from birds of paradise. They deposited Pearl on the wooden reel, placing her upright on her feet, where she continued to sing while the soldiers blew kisses. Hoots and wolf whistles rose like sirens up into the trees.

Then the real sirens sounded, a high, ominous howl echoing through the valley. The band stopped playing. The soldiers jumped to their feet and began to run. Suddenly, the whine of a Japanese Zero could be heard in the distance. Charlie dashed toward the trench at the edge of the clearing with his cornet still in his hand, followed by Marks and Farthing, who carried the portable organ. Pearl jumped off the wooden reel but found it difficult to run in her tight dress and she stumbled over in the mud. The roar of approaching aircraft made her ears throb. She was struggling to her feet when Wanipe swept her into his arms. Looking up, she could see the scarlet balls of the fuselage of a plane and the silver underside of its wings, and then the first bomb was released, whistling loudly as it fell. Wanipe dropped her into a trench and dived in after her. The bomb hit the top of the airstrip, just missing an Allied Boston Havoc, and the valley shuddered, showering the clearing with dirt and rocks. Inching her head above the lip of the trench, Pearl glimpsed two gunners leaping onto antiaircraft mounts.

And then another Zero appeared in the sky, casting a shadow across the hills. The plane roared closer and the ack-ack men began firing at the sky. Pearl could hear the short, sharp barks of the guns, and then the plane, which was about half a mile away, exploded into a fireball.

It was only then that Blue came running out of the bush,

pulling up his zipper. He was making a beeline toward the trench when he glanced over and saw his trombone lying on its case, where he'd left it, about fifty yards away. He changed direction and bolted toward it, his shirttail fluttering behind him like a waving hand. The burning plane was losing altitude as it dropped toward the camp.

"Blue!" cried Pearl. "Come back!" Charlie shouted at him to leave the damn trombone, but Blue either didn't hear them or didn't care.

The plane was almost overhead now, falling faster. From the ground it looked like a huge, flaming comet. Just as the gunners abandoned their mounts and ran for the trenches, Blue grabbed his trombone. And then the inferno of burning metal and oil ignited the sky, leaving a thick black trail of smoke as it hurtled toward the camp.

17

The plane burned and smouldered throughout the night. The stench of smoke, charred rubber, and wood filled Pearl's mouth. For a long time she merely sat in the trench, huddled against Charlie, trying to comfort him. Farthing, the organist, had gone berserk after the crash and had begun screaming at the American gunners who'd shot the plane down, threatening to shoot every one of them. The drummer, Marks, had had to wrestle the rifle away from him, and then a fuming sergeant handcuffed Farthing's wrists and marched him away.

Through it all, Pearl was vaguely aware of the rest of the soldiers carrying buckets of water from the river and pouring it onto and around the crash site to contain the fire. Not only did it threaten to burn down what was left of the camp, the flames provided a target for the enemy. Later, Pearl kissed Charlie on the forehead, picked herself up, and joined the men ferrying water. Hour after hour, she performed the backbreaking routine in a shocked kind of sleepwalk, hardly believing what she'd just witnessed, the ease with which Blue had lost his life.

The fire burned itself out by sunrise and left in its wake a wide hearth of grey ash and blackened metal. The plane had crashed onto the very spot where the band had been performing. Amid the rubble Marks found the distorted metal rings that had once been the shells of his drums. The wire reel on which Pearl had sung had been reduced to a charred stump. Beneath a cylinder of the fuselage Pearl found two mangled bayonets and a trombone mute.

It wasn't until she and Marks pulled back the remains of a wing that they discovered what was left of Blue: two black clumps that were once his army boots, dog tags dull and tarnished in the early light. The rest of him was unrecognisable, so ravaged and burnt there was only the uneven shape of what had once been his body, covered in a caul of blood, ash, and bits of melted brass, relics of the trombone for which he'd risked—and lost—his life. Charlie, devastated, fell to his knees and just stared for a long time. Then he took the mound of charred flesh that had probably once been Blue's hand and held it.

For hours, he sat by what was left of the corpse, touching it occasionally. Every now and then Pearl or Marks would approach Charlie with a cigarette or a flask of whisky, which he accepted wordlessly, as if his vigil could, like a movie running in reverse, raise the plane back into the sky and resurrect his lover. Whenever anyone approached him with a stretcher or a body bag he spat at them to go away and threw handfuls of dirt.

The band was supposed to be in Nadzab by midmorning to perform another concert, but since Blue's death had been reported back to Rudolph in Lae, along with the news of Farthing's attack on the Americans and his subsequent detainment, Rudolph postponed the Nadzab concert until the following afternoon.

Around midday, Charlie finally allowed Wanipe and Pearl to lay the remains inside a body bag. They also inserted Blue's tortoiseshell comb and what was left of his trombone. Late that afternoon, Farthing was released from custody, and the band surrounded the bag and held a ceremony for their fallen mate. Charlie performed a wavering solo of "We'll Meet Again." Farthing told a story about the first time he'd met Blue, at a gig at the Albert Palais. Blue had come careening into the ballroom—dressed in a tuxedo, carrying his trombone—on a pair of roller skates. He'd skated the four miles from his home in Chinatown because it was cheaper and faster than taking the bus. Marks told a tale about Blue once turning up to a show at Roosevelt's impeccably dressed and groomed, but wearing only one shoe. When the bandleader confronted him about it, Blue explained that on his way to the gig he'd sat in the back of the tram playing two-up with a handicapped man. "So?" said the bandleader. "That's no excuse!" "The guy only had one foot," explained Blue. "And I lost."

At dusk the bag was carried to the airstrip and loaded onto a plane with six other body bags to be flown back to Finschhafen and then on to Sydney, where Blue would receive a proper Catholic funeral and be buried in Rookwood, only a mile from where his mother now lived. The band watched the plane taxi, then put their arms around one another as it lifted above the frill of trees around the camp, the foothills, and on, until it became as small as a sparrow and vanished into the clouds.

*   *   *

The jeep rumbled along the narrow road toward Nadzab. It was a clear, warm day. The CO of the artillery unit had ordered a military escort for the band, as enemy soldiers were still scattered through the area, and the danger would increase the farther north the musicians travelled.

Gunfire continued to stutter in the hills. Charlie sat in the backseat with Pearl, his hands folded on his lap. He'd been silent all morning, automatically going through the motions of changing his clothes and packing his gear with an air of quiet resignation. At one moment, Pearl had caught him pressing Blue's spare shirt to his face, inhaling deeply the lingering odour of his lover.

After driving for ten or so minutes, they passed a body lying facedown in the mud on the side of the road. The driver hit the brakes and Pearl jumped out of the jeep. They turned the body over. The man, a Japanese, still had his eyes open, and in his hand he was holding something. Pearl peeled back his fingers: It was a photograph of a pretty Japanese woman, dressed in a skirt and long-sleeved blouse, glittering combs in her hair, sitting on a bench by a stream. She was holding a flower, perhaps a chrysanthemum, and smiled shyly at the eye of the camera. Gazing at it, Pearl was both disturbed and profoundly moved, and she found herself blinking back tears. The face of the woman he loved would have been the last thing the man saw before he died. The Japanese soldier must have loved the woman in the photo as much as Charlie loved Blue, as much as she loved James, and for a moment all that they were fighting for seemed a waste of time and life, so futile.

Pearl suggested to the driver that they load the corpse onto the jeep and transport it to the next camp, where his identity could be registered and he could receive a proper burial, but the driver grimaced and shook his head. "Leave the bastard to rot," he said. "That's what they do to us."

Not knowing what else to do, Pearl slipped the photograph back into the man's hand, folding his stiff fingers around it.

The camp finally appeared in the distance, a ramshackle collection of shelled huts and sagging tents built against the slope of a valley. Pearl could see the outlines of snipers balanced on the tops of coconut palms, rifle barrels poised. Carriers moved back and forth, ferrying supplies farther into the hills. As they drove into the camp they passed a few shirtless black Americans, covered in dust, digging split trenches near some artillery positions. Pearl tried to see if any of them were James, but most had their backs turned, and they all went by in a blur.

The troubadours pulled up in front of the head office, a squat square hut made from palms and sheet metal. Marks and Farthing were joking back and forth, trying to enliven the atmosphere, to cheer up Charlie. The CO appeared, a fat, red-faced sergeant with acne scars and bulbous blue eyes that made him look like a toad.

He glanced at their instruments in the back of the jeep. "Jesus!" he cried in a hard American accent. "We need reinforcements, not musicians!"

"The drum is mightier than the sword, sir," cracked Marks.

The CO scowled. "Name's Thomas. Sergeant Thomas." He

shot Marks a withering look. "I never saw a Jap die from a jazz riff, soldier."

"You've never heard Marks do a solo, sir," said Farthing.

"Yesterday we had another air raid," snapped the commander. "Thirteen dead. And those fucking idiots in Lae send me a bunch of Aussie jesters!"

Pearl decided this wasn't the right time to ask him about James. Instead, she leaped out of the jeep and surveyed the camp. There was a team of black men unloading supplies from a truck parked next to the post exchange. She squinted in the sunlight. He was somewhere close by, she was sure; somewhere in the camp, or in the surrounding area. Maybe he'd already noticed the band from a distance, had seen her, not knowing who she really was or what she was doing there.

The captain spat on the ground. "You guys have got it easy. Carousing around, blowing your trumpets."

"We've been fully trained in combat, sir," said Farthing.

"Great. You can stand guard duty tonight. Replace the guards I lost yesterday."

The band was directed to two tents near the post exchange, where they could clean up and prepare for the concert. While the others unpacked, Pearl slipped away and circled the camp, eyeing the face of each black man she encountered, her heart pounding. She glanced over the GIs unloading supplies, the others digging trenches. She checked the mess tent, the latrines. There was a small group bathing over near a swampy pond, filling their helmets with water and pouring it over their heads, down their backs. She hurried toward them, but his was not among the wet and glistening faces that looked up at her.

Finally, she walked into the rudimentary hut that served as the PX and ordered a Coke. There was a tiny fawn puppy asleep in one corner of the hut. Two Australian men came in and bought a can of baked beans. After they left, she sat on a stool and rolled a cigarette and offered the packet of tobacco to the attendant. The white man behind the counter had hooded eyes and a grim, downturned mouth. He shook his head.

Pearl drained her Coke and looked squarely at the man. "I'm looking for a Private James Washington," she said. "A Negro. Ever heard of him?"

The attendant looked as if he'd been startled by a sudden noise. "Who hasn't?"

"He's not dead is he?"

The man shrugged.

Pearl followed the attendant along the counter. "What's that supposed to mean?"

He popped the metal top off a bottle, and beer frothed over the rim. "Hey, Billows!" he cried. "The Aussie here wants to know what happened to the Great Black Hope!"

The man called Billows rolled his eyes. The puppy stirred and stretched. "Hell, that's one crazy motherfucker."

Farthing burst into the store, panting, "Willis! Hurry up. We're supposed to be on at one!"

Pearl grabbed the attendant by the sleeve and asked him again about Washington.

The man jerked his arm away. "What's it to you?"

"We're already late," said Farthing. "They're all waiting."

"He's a friend of mine," said Pearl.

"Willis . . . " pleaded Farthing.

The man called Billows smirked. "Are you some kinda nigger lover?"

Pearl swung around. "Yes, I'm some kind of fucking nigger lover!" She advanced upon him, fists balled. In her anger, her voice rose into its old feminine tones. "Now where the fuck is he?"

"Bit of a pansy man?" said Billows, and the attendant laughed.

Pearl lunged at him, but Farthing leaped forward and grabbed hold of her arms.

"Christ, Willis! C'mon, the captain's gonna kill us." And he wrestled her out the door.

There were probably about forty or so whites in the audience—both Australian and American—and half as many blacks. She learned later that some had walked as much as twenty miles through the hills just to hear some music from home. They sat patiently in the mud, waiting for the show to begin. She saw the grimacing CO leaning against a gun mount. The two men from the PX appeared and stood in the doorway of the hut.

Marks's drum kit had been destroyed when the plane had crashed and he had to improvise on a set of tin oil drums. They replaced Blue's novelty number with an act in which Marks inflated surgical gloves and twisted them into the shapes of various animals. Pearl wondered where Blue was now. In a morgue in Finschhafen? Packed in ice on a hospital ship? Or on a plane back to Sydney? And where was James? Was he alive or dead? Was he perhaps so close he'd soon hear her playing "Cherokee," would recognise the way she imitated his own distinctive triple-tonguing technique?

All through the overture, she scoured the faces of the audi-ence, their gestures, the way they swayed and tapped their feet, trying to reconcile them with the man that she remembered. It was like trying to recall a forgotten part of a dream, the missing fragment that would allow all the other parts to make sense. At the same time, she was aware that she had to play the best she could, for if he were out there she wanted to impress him, not only with the journey she'd taken to find him but also with the journey she'd taken with the music he'd taught her.

When the show was over, the soldiers lined up to have their helmets signed, but not one of the dozens of men who shook her hand was James. She didn't bother changing out of her red dress and blond wig before striding back to the main office. She found the sergeant with his feet resting on a box of whisky and reading a yellowing newspaper.

"That was a big goddamn distraction," he said, not looking up. "And you might as well know now, Private, you're in my territory now, so I'll be requesting you clowns return to Lae."

She tried to protest, but the sergeant cut her off, explain-ing that it was too dangerous to travel any farther, that the Japanese still had control of the hills. "What you gonna do when they catch one of you?" he sneered. "Hit him with your handbag?"

Pearl reminded him again that all the musicians had had combat training.

"I've been in the army for twenty-five years, Private, and I won't be told what to do by some runty little Aussie in a red dress and wig. Tonight you're on guard duty and then you're goin' straight back to where you come from."

Pearl knew it was pointless to argue, so instead asked him if he knew a Private James Washington.

The CO put down his paper and fixed his bug eyes upon her. "What do you want with him?"

Pearl shrugged.

"Wanna turn your concert into a little coon show, do you?"

"I heard that Washington was in the transport company in Nadzab."

"And when did you hear this, Private?"

"Six days ago."

The CO swung his feet off the box. "Well, about six days ago your dear friend *was* here under my command. In fact, if you'd arrived yesterday, when you were scheduled to, you and your buddy would've been able to sit down at the PX and have a beer together."

"Well, what's happened?" asked Pearl, exasperated. "Where is he? Is he wounded?"

The CO stood up and leaned across his desk. "Yesterday afternoon, your friend Private Washington deserted the U.S. Army. An act of treason, as far as I'm concerned. What do you think of your nigger now?"

18

The glass she drank beer from had been made from a bottle, the neck of which had been sliced off with hot wire. The rim was rough against her lips, and the beer was warm, yet she continued to drink with morose determination. She didn't care if she got stinking drunk and let her guard down, even if her disguise were discovered. She was still wearing her red dress and wig, sitting on a stool in the oppressive gloom of the PX. She sweated through her makeup and the mosquito cream mixed with rice powder ran down her face in milky rivulets. She drummed the primitive glass against the bar twice and the attendant served her another beer. The little puppy wandered into the PX and found its way to the same corner of the hut. It lay down on its belly, resting its head between its front paws, and stared at Pearl as if awaiting instructions. It was no bigger than a dinner roll, with floppy ears and light brown fur soiled with mud.

Pearl rested her chin in one hand and fixed her eyes on the bar mutilated with carved initials and names. There was no point now in going on with the band, she realised, in keeping up the pretense.

For the last couple of months, everything in her life—every choice she'd made, all the risks she'd taken, the music she'd played, each step through the swamps and rainforests—had been straining toward Nadzab, toward him. It was like running a marathon for weeks on end and finding when it was nearly over that the finish line had been erased.

The attendant's shift in the PX was over and he hung up his apron. Another man took his place, a private with blue-black skin and small, birdlike hands. He began wiping down the counter, as if he were trying to erase every chip and crack in the wood. Pearl crossed her legs glumly, not caring if she seemed too feminine, if her identity were discovered. To be found out would be a relief, a kind of gift amid all this disappointment. The more she drank, the more she considered the idea. There'd be interrogations and inquiries—maybe she'd do some time in the brig—but after all that there'd be a free trip home to Sydney, back to the comfort of her own bed. She even fancied it would be possible to get her old job at the Trocadero back. Of course, the controversy would get into the papers and cause a stir. And then there was her mother. And Hector. And they'd probably try to have her hospitalised, even committed to an institution. Though after what she'd endured recently, even the thought of a permanent bed in a psychiatric unit was appealing: free drugs, free food, a manicured garden, finger painting. No shells to dodge, no deaths to witness, no breasts to hide, no friends to grieve. Everything would be as quiet and calm as a church. It was better than ending up beneath a crashed plane, like Blue, better than pining for a man she knew she'd never find. James was right: Even in the event that she did manage to find him and they returned to Australia, they'd probably never be able to live as a couple. It'd be too hard on them both.

She rested her boots on the rungs of the stool and sighed heavily. When Charlie pulled up a stool beside her and ordered some water, she didn't even bother to acknowledge him.

"Well, where is he, then?"

Pearl shrugged.

The puppy stood up and walked across to them, sniffing at Pearl's boots. Its tail curled up at a weird angle, as if it were pointing over its head to the left side of the room. Charlie suggested that she change out of her costume before somebody twigged that she was a girl. "I'm turning myself in." Pearl drained her glass. "I'm going home."

"You can't leave now. We're a team. We need you."

She rested her forehead against her folded hands on the counter and groaned. The puppy began gnawing at her bootlaces.

"What about James?" Charlie reminded her.

"James is gone. Deserted yesterday."

She leaned down, scooped up the puppy and placed it in her lap, where it curled up under the touch of her hand. It smelled a little strange, like rotting fruit. It whimpered for a moment and nosed her stomach.

"I didn't chuck it in after Blue died," Charlie complained.

"You *can't* chuck it in," she said. "You've been drafted."

They sat in silence for a few minutes, gazing down at the puppy.

"You're just like a gutless little girl," Charlie said at last.

"I *am* a girl."

"Go on, then," he dared. "Hand yourself in. I'm really surprised though. I thought you had more balls."

Pearl drained her glass and slammed it on the bar. She was angry with herself and also with Charlie, because she half suspected he was right about how cowardly she was behaving.

He pulled an envelope from his shirt pocket. "Here," he said, throwing it down on the bar. "This came for you."

She picked it up and recognised her mother's handwriting.

"At least *your* man's alive," Charlie added.

She ripped open the envelope, and began reading her mother's letter. *My Dearest Boy* . . . The censors had blacked out some passages. She skimmed the legible parts, detailing the death of another neighbourhood boy in Crete, and the fact that Mikey Michaels's mother had moved them both in with her sister's family. There was a paragraph about Hector, who, within a period of three weeks, had met a woman ten years his senior, had proposed to and then married her. They were now honeymooning at the Windsor Hotel in Melbourne. The letter finished with a reference to her ongoing anxiety over her missing daughter. *Frankie the Butcher swore that he saw Pearl just the other day, walking down Macleay Street with a tall blond woman, but we haven't seen her since you left for Port Moresby.* The tone, as usual, was slightly hysterical, and hearing her mother's voice in her head again was unnerving, confusing her now about what she really wanted to do. At least Hector was happy, and the news of his marriage relieved a little of her guilt. But she still hadn't had word from Martin. Was he on the farm with Nora and Pookie or not? She folded the letter and pocketed it.

Charlie called to the attendant and ordered more beers.

The man nodded, pulled two bottles from a cupboard.

"Hey," said Charlie. "You know the bloke who deserted yesterday? A Negro?"

The attendant smiled. "If he'd a been here, he woulda jammed with you all today. Washer plays a mean sax."

Pearl sat up straight and looked more closely at the man. He seemed curiously familiar. "You know him?"

"Hell, man. Wash and me done many a detail together."

"Well, what happened to him?" she demanded.

The man looked surprised. "Ain't you heard?"

"All the CO said was that Washington had deserted. Didn't know where he was."

The man threw his head back and laughed. "Ol' Washer stuck a rifle up the CO's ass, I tell you." He nodded at the puppy, still nestled in Pearl's lap. "That there's his dog. Or was."

"Washington's?" said Pearl. "This was Washington's dog?"

"Loved that pooch more'n anything. Bought her off a native kid last month for a pack of cigarettes, right after she was born. Fed her canned milk through an eyedropper. Can you believe that?"

Pearl looked at the puppy in an entirely new light. She patted it gently and it whimpered again and licked her hand. This same tongue would have licked James's hand; he would have run his fingers through the same fur. She picked a burr from behind the pup's left ear.

"If he loved her that much, why didn't he take her with him?"

The man shook his head. "It's fucking dangerous out there.

Can't be marching with commandos and playing fetch at the same time."

"Marching with commandos?" asked Charlie, sliding forward on his stool. "But I thought he'd deserted."

"He deserted the U.S. Army, man. The segregated Labor Corps—not the cause."

A white GI walked into the PX and ordered a beer from the other end of the counter.

The attendant eyed him. "Tell you later," he murmured. He walked down to serve the man, leaving Pearl numb. She picked up the puppy and cuddled her, and felt a warm wet tongue against her earlobe. When the attendant turned toward her again, she suddenly recognised him.

"Your name wouldn't happen to be Tyrone, would it?"

The man looked puzzled. "How'd you guess?"

She smiled. "Do you reckon you could meet up with us later tonight, when there aren't so many people around?"

As he had threatened, Sergeant Thomas ordered Pearl and Charlie to do overnight guard duty. But instead of guarding one of the posts of the camp, they were ordered to stand duty at a single hut. Pearl thought this must be some kind of joke until a GI later explained that great quantities of canned meat, crates of beer, powdered milk, and eggs were disappearing from the hut, so much so that the camp was now running out of supplies. Snap inspections of every tent had yielded no clue as to where the goods were being stashed. White soldiers reckoned that the Negroes had stolen them and buried them in the forest for themselves. The Negroes speculated that the mess sergeants were responsible, and Sergeant Thomas was the ringleader. Morphine, anaesthetic, and antibiotics had also gone missing from the supplies hut, but no one could really account for that.

The hut they had to guard was about the size of a three-roomed cottage, thatched with palms and with a door of bound bamboo, and had been built at the edge of the camp near a mangrove forest. It stood on two-foot stilts to keep the supplies out of flash floods, with a little gallery that ran around the outside walls.

At first Pearl and Charlie stood on the gallery, almost at attention, poised for an attack. But after half an hour of hearing only hooting owls and the odd, distant snoring of sleeping soldiers, they sat and leaned their backs up against the wall. They'd only been sitting there for a few minutes when they heard a whistling sound coming through the trees. They jumped to attention and raised their rifles, aiming blindly into the darkness, until they heard a voice, much closer now, say, "Hey, boys, it's only me: Tyrone."

He joined them on the gallery, rolled a cigarette, and lit up. Between drags, in a hushed, uneasy voice, he told Pearl and Charlie everything they wanted to know.

"Our CO, Thomas, he's from Georgia. Washer, he grew up in Louisiana, so he used to dealin' with crackers like him. Anyways, Washer asked for permission to marry an Australian girl—a white girl, that is—and from then on Thomas had it in for him. He made him wash the same jeep ten times in one day. He'd deny him passes for no reason, and make him do ten-mile hikes in the mornings. When we got to Lae, Wash tried to put in for a transfer into one of the entertainment units, but Thomas wouldn't allow it to go through."

The trouble escalated, Tyrone explained, when James, angry at having his transfer denied, tried to enter the PX in Lae for a beer. A runty little private from Texarkana refused to serve him, and James, furious by now, picked up someone's beer and threw it into the private's face. A brawl broke out. Glasses were smashed, about six or seven guys jumped James, and a couple of MPs finished him off, punching, kicking, pistol-whipping his head. He spent four days in the company hospital, followed by three weeks in the brig.

Pearl was shocked. There seemed to be more fighting between the black and white Americans than between the Americans and the Japanese.

After that, Tyrone continued, James tried to stay out of trouble. He came out of the brig quieter, and he rejoined the Labor Corps, unloading ships, washing out mess tents, scrubbing floors. He bided his time and tried to keep his nose clean.

"But it was hard for Wash to stand back with a mop in his hand while we was all being shelled and strafed by the Japs, and Thomas not letting us arm ourselves."

"Not enough ammunition?" asked Charlie.

Tyrone snorted. "Whitey's already fighting a bunch of coloured folks—the Japanese. He don't want no niggers with guns. Hell, they might band together and turn. Run off with ol' Tojo."

The transport company was then transferred from Lae to Nadzab. There were many casualties at the time, and James, Tyrone, and the rest of the unit worked around the clock, digging foxholes, ferrying ammunition to observation points, carrying the dead and injured out of the jungle to the camp's makeshift hospital.

It was around this time that an Australian independent company was flown in from Moresby. Most of the soldiers were big jazz fans and they had an old gramophone. At night they'd play records they'd bought from an American. One night, they discovered James and Tyrone sitting outside their tent, listening to the music, and invited them in to join the party. They passed around their whisky. Shared some cigars. They allowed James to play any record he wished. "But things really hotted up," Tyrone recalled, "when they found out who Wash really was—the famous tenor player from the Basie band. They even had one of his records! Man, they treated him like a king." James would sit around with them at night and reminisce about his gigs in New York, when he was on the road with Jay McShann. And then one day an Aussie turned up from Wau with a soprano saxophone. "Well," said Tyrone, "Washer went to town, playin' so loud and swingin' that Thomas went nuts and threw him in the brig again for three days."

"For playing music?" asked Pearl.

"Thomas reckoned the music'd attract the Japs. And after that, things got real bad."

The tensions had peaked only two days before Pearl had arrived at the camp, when enemy planes had bombed the valley. Shells and gunfire blasted out of the mountains as the Japanese tried to regain the territory they'd recently lost and reclaim the nearby airstrip. As pockets of earth exploded around them, James and Tyrone carried out Thomas's orders, filling sandbags with dirt and hauling them off to the trenches.

The Aussies were positioned in a shallow foxhole near the river. James and Tyrone were each carrying a bag toward it when they saw bushes moving on the other side of the stream and realised that the enemy was only about forty yards away. A mortar exploded, and Tyrone dropped his bag and jumped into the hole. One of James's Australian jazz buddies stood up and fired his rifle three or four times. They heard a Jap yelp, and then suddenly the Aussie was hit, too, and as he fell backward he dropped his gun. The next thing Tyrone saw was James ditching his sandbag and snatching up the dead man's rifle. He fell to the ground behind the bag, then writhed through the mud, beyond the foxhole, pushing the sandbag ahead of him for protection. The crowns of palm trees were swaying, even though there was no wind. He slowly raised the rifle, squinted, and aimed at the crown. Tyrone glimpsed a flash of black amid the palms, and James pulled the trigger and fired. A Japanese soldier arched backward, head first, and dropped to the ground. Tyrone lurched back to see James reloading, when he glimpsed, out of the corner of his eye, the barrel of a rifle pointing from behind a tree trunk to his right. Before he had a chance to shout a warning he heard an explosion, and saw James collapse.

"And then I saw the most scary thing of all," Tyrone told them. "It wasn't a Jap firing from behind the tree to the right. It was Thomas."

Charlie snorted in disbelief.

"Listen, man, I was in the foxhole. I saw it all. Washer, he rolled into that hole with us faster than you can say Ku Klux Klan."

"Was he hurt?" Pearl wanted to know.

"Nah, only a flesh wound, but when he knew it was the sergeant who'd tried to shoot him he sure did panic."

"So did you blokes report it to anyone?" asked Charlie.

"Who's gonna believe the word of two niggers against a white officer? Happens all the time. See, nothing frightens a cracker more than a nigger with a gun."

"But what about the Aussies?" asked Charlie. "They must've seen it, too."

"They went one better. Hell, Wash knew his way around a gun. He grew up on a farm. And the Aussies knew he weren't goin' to be safe round here no more. So when they got transferred late that afternoon, they smuggled him out with 'em. Aussies didn't care if he was black, blue, pink, or purple, long as he could hit a target."

An owl sang one low note over and over. Pearl slumped over her rifle. It all seemed impossible, unreal.

"Well, where is he now?" she asked.

Tyrone gestured vaguely up the Markham Valley. "Pushin' the Japs north, up into the mountains."

"They've already got two days on us," said Charlie. "But, hey, there can't be too many Aussie units with a big black American."

"That's if Thomas lets us go on," said Pearl. "He's recommending to Rudolph that we return to Lae."

They heard a soft scratching against the gallery floor. The little puppy came bounding around the corner and into Pearl's lap.

Pearl scratched its belly. "What's the dog's name?"

Tyrone laughed briefly. "Called her after that girl he was sweet on," he said. "Man, he loved that dame. Talked about her all the time." Tyrone shifted and crossed his legs. "He called the dog Pearl."

*   *   *

It seemed to Pearl, after hearing Tyrone's story, that the mosquitoes were nipping less frequently and the heat was not so unbearably sticky. James had talked about her, had missed her. She now felt emboldened by the risks she'd taken. The puppy nestled in her arms and fell asleep, while Pearl and Charlie dozed against the wall of the hut.

Near dawn, she woke to the sound of footsteps drumming against the other side of the gallery. She gave Charlie a nudge and jumped to her feet, her fingers finding the trigger of her .303.

Dashing around a corner of the gallery, she and Charlie were astonished to see, in the half-light, two American privates running from the back of the supplies hut, carrying what looked like boxes and crates.

"Halt!" Pearl cried, echoed by Charlie, and when that didn't work she and Charlie ploughed into the mangrove swamp after them. They followed the shadows flickering through the mist, through puddles and sludge, until Charlie leaped forward and managed to tackle one, who dropped the box he was holding. Pearl was now only a few feet to the left of the second man, who was sprinting through the swamp. She raised her rifle, aimed at the soldier's leg and squeezed the trigger. The gun jumped in her hand and she watched him fall facedown in the mud with a brief cry that was almost erotic. Shocked by what she'd just done, she ran forward and turned him over. She could hardly believe her eyes: The man was clothed in an American uniform, a two-piece jungle suit and M1 helmet, but his eyes were slanted and his skin was burnt-egg yellow. The Japanese had been removing the clothes of dead soldiers and masquerading as Allies in order to steal food and medicine.

A plane was due in from Lae the following afternoon, carrying ammunition, food, and some overdue medical supplies. Scores of men had been wounded farther up in the Markham Valley during the night and they were now being borne back to the camp on stretchers by native carriers. The extra food was vital, too, given what the Japanese had stolen. Sergeant Rudolph would also be on the plane. He was flying in to supply them with more props and costumes for the show, and to check on the welfare of his men since Blue had been killed. The drummer, Marks, who'd been feverish and vomiting throughout the night, was now in the camp infirmary.

The plane was over two hours late. Most pilots were reluctant to fly in the afternoon because of the heavy clouds that obscured almost everything, including the tops of mountains. When the aircraft finally landed and taxied along the airstrip, the troubadours lined up to meet their commanding officer.

When Rudolph appeared at the rear of the plane, the three surviving band members and Wanipe stood at attention and saluted him. Rudolph jumped to the ground and ordered them at ease. James's puppy had followed Pearl out to the airstrip and sat at her feet, as if she were now part of the company. Already Pearl had grown attached to the dog, carrying her around in her pocket or down the front of her shirt. She felt that finding the puppy was a positive sign, an encouragement from James himself to continue her journey until she found him.

Rudolph offered a few words of condolence with regard to Blue, but his mumbled platitudes were hardly a comfort. While he talked, Farthing's breathing grew heavier. He was sweating moist patches through his uniform, and his face was swollen and red.

"All right, men," concluded Rudolph, "unload the supplies while I meet with Thomas."

"Yes, sir!" they chorused as Rudolph strode toward the CO's office. But Pearl ran after him, requesting a quick word, the puppy trotting beside her.

Rudolph shielded the sunlight from his eyes with one hand and squinted down at her. "Well, Willis?"

"We've refined the act. It's much better now." She picked the puppy up and held her. "I'm still impersonating a sheila, like you told me."

There was an awkward silence. Rudolph looked at his watch.

"I want to go on," she said forcefully. "Thomas is going to recommend that we return to Lae. He thinks it's too dangerous to continue on to the front."

"Things have changed a bit since the last movement orders came through."

"But we've come this far," she pleaded. "Please let us go on."

Rudolph frowned. "We've got units of mad Japs up the valley and in the mountains under no central command. Some Allied posts have lost radio contact and the casualties are mounting— and that's just the ones we know about. What's more, Blue's dead, and it sounds as if Marks has got malaria." Rudolph shook his head. "The rest of you don't look too hot, either."

"I feel fine, sir." She pulled back her shoulders and straightened her posture. "I'm ready to go on. To follow our men. With your permission, that is."

He fixed his gaze upon her. "It's not up to you, Private."

"Thomas thinks we're all idiots, that musicians have got no place in the war."

Rudolph's lips tightened. "We're all entitled to our opinions."

"He said he needed soldiers, not saps who sing and dance."

Rudolph started to say something, then stopped himself. "Go back and help the others. I'll deal with Thomas." He began walking away and then paused. "Oh," he said, turning and pulling something from his pocket, "this came for you."

He handed Pearl a crumpled envelope. It was addressed to Private Martin Willis. She ripped it open and immediately recognised Martin's neat, cursive handwriting.

Dear Martin,
All is well in peacock land. I have learned to milk a cow. There are so many chooks about I myself am almost laying eggs. You can't buy a decent corset in Katoomba and the frost has rotted my suede high heels, but apart from that I'm still the same old girl!

Your loving sister,
Pearl xxxx

Crates and boxes, tied down with thick ropes, filled the hold of the plane. Charlie, Pearl, and Farthing worked as fast as they could to unload them, stacking them beside one another in an uneven wall. Farthing was still sweating and feverish and was moving at a sluggish pace. First, there were boxes of ammunition, then tinned food, then powdered milk. Dusk was sifting through the low clouds. Cicadas chirped, a frog croaked, and for a short while their world was so tranquil that Pearl thought they could be anywhere, even back in Australia, in the bush.

They'd unloaded about only one third of the crates—mostly artillery—when Farthing grasped his stomach, leaned over, and vomited between his feet. He straightened up for a moment but then his knees began to buckle. Charlie and Wanipe caught him just before he hit the ground.

"Let's get you to infirmary," said Charlie. "You can keep Marks company." He and Wanipe supported Farthing and walked him through the camp. Pearl knew what would be next: the aching joints, rising fever, the sweats and chills, diarrhoea. She wondered who'd be next. At this rate they'd never get beyond Nadzab, especially now that Thomas had it in for them.

At about nine o'clock that night, she was resting on her bedroll, Charlie and Wanipe on either side of her, the puppy nestled into her armpit, when Sergeant Thomas himself appeared, accompanied by a grinning Rudolph. The three stood up to salute, but Thomas waved a hand.

"At ease, men," he said, fixing his eyes on Pearl.

When she returned his gaze all she could think was that this was the bastard who'd tried to shoot James. She felt an overwhelming desire to put her hands around his throat and strangle the life out of him.

Thomas pursed his lips, as if gathering himself to make a

reluctant admission. "Good work last night, Willis," he said finally. "And Styles. We needed those supplies."

The puppy shifted and yawned. This, Pearl knew, was the moment to make her move. Timing was everything—in life as in music. "Thanks, sir. But there's one other thing."

Thomas sighed impatiently, as if he'd already intuited what was coming.

"Look, that's just not possible."

"Why not?"

"Apart from all the Japs running around, you've got god-damn cannibals all through the mountains—and you can bet the headhunters aren't siding with the Allies, Private."

"We can defend ourselves," said Charlie. "You know we can."

"Half your band's come down with malaria."

"There's me and Charlie left," Pearl said. "We'll actually be more mobile than ever."

"With the dog we've got a trio!" Charlie added brightly.

"Me go, too," said Wanipe. He pointed to the other two. "Me belonga them."

The three glanced from Thomas to Rudolph imploringly. The puppy gave a short bark.

"What about it, Sergeant?" said Rudolph. "I reckon my boys have proved themselves."

19

The Markham Valley was hemmed by mountain peaks that rose six thousand feet into the sky, with streams unravelling like silver ribbons through chasms and over ridges. Sometimes the valley widened into grassy plateaus, where lilies floated on still brown water. The trio walked in single file, following the puppy, which trotted ahead through the mud with a keen sense of purpose, nosing and smelling at the ground. Their first mission was to walk to an isolated forward post about twenty miles up the river, where they would deliver some medical supplies and perform a show. They hoped to cover the distance in a single day, but the sharp bends in the river were slowing their progress.

They'd scaled down their possessions and props even further: a bedroll, netting, and a rifle each, and only a few costumes. Wanipe carried the portable organ, food supplies, and a small set of bongos made from pigskin. They were to keep in touch with Rudolph via the radio transmitters at each outpost, and would receive further orders as the front line shifted. By midday, Pearl's boots had grown heavy and her shoulders ached from the pack.

*   *   *

In order to save time, Wanipe sometimes walked into the water and led them straight across a curve in the river, holding the portable organ high above his head. When she and Charlie followed, they stumbled over the loose round pebbles on the bed of the stream.

After lunch, it began to rain so heavily that the mountains towering over them disappeared. By sunset, they'd only walked seven miles. Their uniforms were stained with the red silt that had been swept downstream from the dead volcanoes. Pearl's skin itched with mosquito bites; she was parched and hungry and beyond exhaustion.

Wanipe paused within a thicket of sago and ficus trees and announced, "Here tonight. Safe." He put down his load and began to collect fallen palms and vines. A mortar exploded somewhere in the hills to their right, and Charlie and Pearl dropped their gear and helped Wanipe with the gathering.

It took him less than ten minutes to build a makeshift lean-to, curtained with vines that made it disappear into the green tangle of the forest. Pearl squatted nearby and began a fire, while Wanipe vanished into the woods. Soon he returned with handfuls of wild sweet potato and showed them how to cook it in Pearl's upturned steel helmet, along with some bully beef. After dinner, they sat around the fire, smoking and working on new material for the show. They decided to shorten the act to a sixty-minute concert that combined music, song and dance, comedy and impersonations, with Charlie now playing the portable organ.

Later, Charlie sat cross-legged with a ventriloquist's doll that had come with the supply plane two days before. He practised talking without moving his lips, telling jokes and riddles. He then began to roll his eyes back in his head, just like the doll.

"What are you going to call him?" Pearl asked.

Charlie didn't hesitate. "Mr. Blue."

Before they retired to the lean-to, Wanipe unscrewed a metal tin and held it out to Pearl. Inside was a white gluggy substance that had the smell and consistency of lard. Wanipe dipped his hand in and rubbed it onto Pearl's face, allowing his fingers to linger against her cheek, her jawline, in what seemed like a subtle romantic gesture. "Pig fat belonga," he said. "No mozzie fly bite."

It was then that Pearl realised two things at once: Wanipe was offering her some natural insect repellent, and he knew for sure that she was female.

As she rubbed the pig fat farther into her skin, she glanced at Charlie and mouthed the words, "He knows." Charlie and the doll shrugged.

After smoking a cigarette, he sat beside Wanipe and tried to explain, in his rudimentary pidgin and a kind of pantomime, that Pearl was only pretending to be a boy, and the true reason for her presence in his country, why she was even in the army at all. Wanipe seemed concerned at first, then quizzical, until Charlie finally thought of the pidgin word for "husband." It was then that Wanipe relaxed and smiled knowingly, his mouth a flush of reddish brown-stained teeth. He took Pearl's hand and held it, murmuring, "Pretty boy. Too pretty." And then smiled and nodded and said he would help her find the man she was looking for.

It was a relief to have told another person, and the three of them spent the night together, lying side by side within the lean-to, beneath the one mosquito net. It began to rain again and Pearl lay huddled beneath the bedroll with the puppy, listening to the gunfire echoing in the mountains. It was their first night spent out in the open, without the protection of a base camp and other soldiers.

At dawn, she woke to blue mist scrolling down from the mountains and across the valley. Wanipe was eager to set off before the morning grew too hot and, after a quick breakfast of dried biscuits and tea, the three packed up and began walking north. The air was fresh at that time of day, cooler than the coastal humidity, and for a while, Pearl felt refreshed and hopeful. But by midday they were wading through swamps infested with leeches and swarms of buzzing mosquitoes. Sometimes, when the puppy grew tired, Pearl would pick her up and place her down the front of her shirt, where they could feel each other's heartbeats. She felt silly calling the puppy Pearl, and toyed with the idea of renaming her James. But the dog was a female and, after some discussion with Charlie, she settled on the simple title of Pup.

They misread the map and took a wrong turn that led them along a stream. It wasn't until they began to smell the aroma of boiling rice that they realised they'd wandered into enemy territory. They quickly retraced their steps and, over an hour later, stumbled almost by accident into the little Allied post, which was no more than a few hammocks strung between the trunks of trees and a thatched hut with walls made from fly wire. Everything was damp from the afternoon showers and the ground was covered in moss. Eight Americans were based there, three of whom had come down with dysentery and malaria and were lying inside the hut, vomiting and shitting into a halved ten-gallon drum.

One of the gunners boiled some coffee while another administered the supplies to the ill men inside the hut.

"Didn't think you were gonna make it," he said. "Japs ain't been very neighbourly lately. Lost four men last week."

Charlie asked him how long he'd been posted in the area.

The gunner shrugged and figured that it had been eight or nine weeks.

"Have you seen a small unit of Aussies," asked Pearl, "with a Negro in among them?"

"What? Like a native guy?"

"No, an American."

"A black American carrier?"

"No, we heard about a unit of Aussies with a Negro gunner."

The man poured the dark coffee into four tin cans. "Why would a bunch of Australians have a Nigra in with them?"

"So you haven't heard of him," said Charlie.

The man called to one of the soldiers inside the hut. "Hey, Lance! You heard 'bout a Nigra runnin' round with a bunch of Aussie forwards?"

Lance guffawed. "I reckon I'd remember that."

They all sipped their coffee in silence. Pearl's back was aching from carrying the pack and her face was so badly sunburnt it was beginning to peel. She was feeling sorry for herself until she glimpsed the gaunt, wasted figures of the men inside the hut, covered in sweat and dirt, struggling to sit upright against the wall so they could see the show.

They performed outside in the clearing, cavorting about in the mud. The puppy ran in excited circles, rolled in the dirt, and barked whenever anyone clapped. Charlie premiered his routine with Mr. Blue, the doll, who turned out to be a wise-cracking, slightly lewd addition to the show. He sat on his master's knee, making jokes about army life.

They played duets on the saxophone and organ, and as the sound of "Stompin' at the Savoy" rose through the trees and vines Pearl was comforted by the smiling faces, the simple happiness the music gave these dying men. It seemed to work better than morphine. Within half an hour, two of them were out of bed, swaying back and forth on unsteady legs, mouthing the words to the songs. And it was at moments like these, even though she was exhausted and starving, that she was able to push herself beyond any known limit and improvise generously on the tunes that they begged for, turning it inside out and upside down, always aware that what she was playing might be the last piece of music these men would ever hear.

During their final number, "Aunt Hagar's Blues," Wanipe began tapping his fingers in time against the pigskin drum, and Pearl was surprised by the ease with which he found the beat. A grin widened across his face as he discovered the accents within the melody.

The branches of a ficus shaking in the distance caught Pearl's eye. When she shifted into a shadow, she could make out the faces of two, then three men hiding in the tree—slant-eyed, dark-skinned, all wearing steel helmets. She felt a flare of panic and was about to dive into the mud when she noticed that their guns were not raised, but were resting in their laps, and that their heads were bowed as they listened to the song. She'd never realised that the enemy could appreciate—even need—the music as much as the Allies did. When she squinted, she could see that they were smiling.

Days folded into weeks of monsoonal rains, slippery tracks that led nowhere, the uneven rhythm of gunfire. They walked from one isolated post to another, slinking through tall kunai grass, trekking through streams, sleeping in filthy foxholes or beneath one of Wanipe's lean-tos. Every two or three days, when they reached a new post, Rudolph radioed through their movement orders. Japanese detachments were continuing to operate independently throughout the upper valley, rather than under a single central command. Battles erupted without warning or apparent strategy. Sometimes Charlie and Pearl found themselves standing in a split trench three feet wide, playing standards and telling jokes to only four or five men who would occasionally break off mid-laugh to raise their rifles and fire at the enemy. Other times they'd perform inside makeshift tents, or beneath a canvas groundsheet strung over the branches of three or four trees.

When it rained Pearl was fearful that her wet uniform would cling and betray her feminine curves, but the monotony and scarcity of army food, in addition to the miles they had to walk each day, reduced her weight so much that her body quickly assumed the taut, boyish frame of her brother. After the second month out of Nadzab, the normal flow of her period slowed to a two-day trickle. She learned to rotate two lengths of surgical gauze in order to absorb the discharge, washing and drying one while wedging the other into the crotch of her underpants. She developed tinea; large corns grew on both feet and began to bleed; her face and arms were tattooed with scratches and mosquito bites. One night a bush tick burrowed into her left armpit and Wanipe had to gouge it out with the tip of her bayonet. Her body always seemed to be aching during those months— her feet, her joints, her hands—as if the part of herself that was merely a normal physical being could no longer compete with that other aspect of herself—her stubborn will—that was totally focused upon her goal. When she discovered lice in her hair, she shaved it all off and rubbed pig fat into her scalp. Afterward, Wanipe ran his hand over her smooth, slippery head and remarked ruefully, "Not now pretty."

By this time the troubadours existed on emergency rations that were dropped from low-flying planes every five or six days. The rations were limited to two cans of bully beef a day, several biscuits, and a pack of cigarettes. A small cake of soap and three razor blades had to last almost a week. One afternoon, in mid-July, Wanipe used Charlie's bayonet to spear a wild pig, which they roasted and shared with a detachment of emaciated Americans weakened by malnutrition and lack of sleep.

Wanipe also introduced Pearl and Charlie to betel nuts, mixed with seed stalks from pepper plants, which made their mouths go numb and induced in them a goofy, loose-limbed joy. It was almost as good as several shots of whisky, and under the lean-tos in the evenings they'd sometimes sing together. Pearl and Charlie taught Wanipe swing rhythms he could play on the pigskin drum to complement their performances. Wanipe, in turn, taught them songs in his native tongue. He then learned the words to "Boogie Woogie Bugle Boy," and soon they were singing harmonies almost as tight and mellifluous as those of the Andrews Sisters. He also made a flute out of a hollowed stalk of sugar cane and played haunting, breathy melodies in peculiar time signatures like 7/4 and 12/8 that intrigued Pearl so much she tried to notate the music on a piece of paper, but it was like trying to transcribe the wind or the sound of a waterfall.

It was around this time that she had a breakthrough with her playing. Perhaps it was the discipline of having to perform under such harsh conditions, or being surrounded by so many foreign sounds, but whatever it was, in between shows she began developing a personal repertoire of melodic patterns. She had some for the blues in B flat, slightly different ones for the blues in F, a totally different one for "Hindustan" in D minor, and this repertoire kept building upon itself, like scaffolding around a building.

Charlie and his portable organ helped enormously, and allowed her to adventure into improvising on the chord changes of a given song. She was finally starting to understand what James had tried to teach her that day back in Sydney, at the conservatorium's piano. She borrowed certain phrases and licks from swing tunes and either kept them as they were or inverted them, playing against the dominant note of the chart and using a subservient one, which was like following the shadow of the tune rather than the tune itself. And the way she mixed and placed the notes during her solos now was totally her own.

Wherever the troubadours travelled, they continued to ask about the mythological Negro who'd run off with some Aussie commandos. One villager said he saw a lone black man amid a group of whites helping to carve an airstrip at the foot of Mount Wilhelm, another saw him marching along a track with a patrol toward Goroka. Another said he'd been grenaded in the Eastern Highlands.

When the fighting moved up into the Bismarck Range, the musicians moved with it, accompanying the hammer of gunfire with Benny Goodman medleys. Every now and then Pearl paused and gazed down at the valley they'd left behind, the red sash of the Ramu River stained with volcanic silt against a skirt of deep green jungle.

August passed with the roar of mountain howitzers and mortars as the Allies moved farther into the highlands, whittling away one Japanese post after another. At night, grenades exploded into a fire of orange light as tracer flares arced through the sky. Sometimes the Japanese kept screaming and yelling until dawn to ensure that the Australians and Americans could get no sleep. More than once Pearl saw a soldier stir, grab his gun, shoot a few rounds, roll over again and go back to sleep.

The mountains they now climbed grew in altitude—up to ten or eleven thousand feet. The air was thin and Pearl found she had to take deeper and longer breaths to play the saxophone. When they rested, she'd lie on her back and work on exercises for her diaphragm. She began practising circular breathing so she wouldn't have to pause so often while she performed a solo. Leaves and branches constantly dripped with water, even when the sun was shining. The troubadours, including Wanipe, performed beside rivers, in trenches, between rows of native gardens.

The puppy was developing into an alert and affectionate dog, always eager to please. By this time she'd grown to the size of one of Pearl's boots, and her ears often stood up and quivered like a bat's. Throughout the winter months, while they walked from mountain to mountain, Pearl taught her to sit, to lie, and to roll over. Training Pup became the only diversion for the musicians while they toiled between villages and forward posts. Soon the dog could play dead, fetch props during the show, and walk on her hind legs. She was fiercely protective and growled and barked if even a bush mouse came too close to the group.

Now that Pup could walk on her hind legs, it wasn't too hard to teach her to turn in a circle. At first she could only do it once, but after two days and rewards of dried biscuits, she was twirling in a series of pirouettes, dropping onto the ground, rolling over, and repeating the turns again.

The dog made her premiere at a mobile medical post carved into the side of a mountain. Mr. Blue sang "At the Jazz Band Ball" while Pearl played the melody on organ and Pup cantered and spun before the crowd of weary medics and wounded patients, all of whom cheered and whistled. Pup's one number proved to be the highlight of the show, with men calling for an encore.

Of course, the more Pup performed, the more she improved. After each show, the soldiers would always crowd around her to pat her and feed her scraps and then she was passed from lap to lap like a newborn baby. The men then invariably pulled crumpled snapshots from wallets, photos of their own pets from home—faded images of themselves with floppy-eared bassets, shaggy sheepdogs, and drooling Labradors. The owners in the pictures were almost unrecognisable as the lean, gaunt creatures that stood before her. Pearl thought that maybe the dog act was so important to these men because Pup represented all the tenderness and comfort of a world from which they'd been separated for months, even years. And as they fed the dog their biscuits and stroked her ears, it seemed as if their own capacity for affection and love were slowly being rekindled.

Wanipe now did a solo on his sugarcane flute, while Pearl hid behind a bush or inside a tent, changed into her red dress and wig, and painted on her makeup. She sang with a quality not unlike the way she now played the saxophone, which were improvisations on the principles James had taught her, refined by her understanding of the circular-breathing technique. All her reeds had split and splintered by now, and she had to make her own ones by filing down strips of bamboo.

Any spare time during their trek into the clouds was devoted to her saxophone. When she was confident the party wasn't close to enemy posts, she rehearsed this gentler way of playing, like an actor going over lines, whispering to herself. She practised before and after shows, in the harsh white light of midafternoon, at dusk, when machine guns rattled in the mountain peaks above, when the surrounding ridges purpled into shadows. She practised by streams, imitating the song of flowing water, and with each day her melodic lines became lighter and more fluid. She saw birds with narrow bodies that looked like thin pencils with wings, and impersonated their chirping on her instrument so well they chirped back, believing she was one of them.

This new lyricism had its own power, she knew, especially when she stood in foxholes, ankle-deep in mud, and played songs like "What Is This Thing Called Love?" Her new way of playing gently erased the heavy wetness of the soldiers' uniforms, the bugs nipping at their hands and necks, their hunger cramps, the distant coughing of mortars.

The music she expressed now was a curious hybrid of everything James had taught her and the suggestible, vulnerable life force that was no one else's but her own. It had the attack of a warrior and the restraint of a monk. Sometimes, when she was practising, Pup's ears would twitch, and soon the dog would be up on her hind legs, cantering back and forth across the ground, reminding Pearl of the society women spinning and twirling over the polished dance floor of the Trocadero Ballroom. She seemed to herself to be another person altogether to the girl she had been the year before, confident to the point of recklessness, with the childish notion that she could find one man in the hundreds of square miles that were the jungles of New Guinea. Back then, she'd been sure it was fearlessness and love that had spurred her on, but now she suspected it was something less noble—naivety, perhaps, or even stupidity and arrogance.

They were struggling along a path, on their way to a base hospital, when they stumbled upon a pygmy trader. He was no more than four feet high and his nose was pierced with a U-shaped bone. He was poised behind a tree, brandishing a bow and arrow. Wanipe held up his hands and explained, in rudimentary pidgin, that they weren't enemies. He put down the portable organ and played a few notes. The trader became intrigued by the organ, lowered his arrow, and crept forward. He played a few notes, too, and laughed, and then Charlie played him a chorus of the blues. They shared some tobacco with him and, as they sat on their haunches and smoked, Pearl, as usual, raised the question about the black American who'd run off with the Australians to fight. The pygmy's eyes widened then, and he began nodding quickly and pointing to the top of the mountain. "Big black," he said. "One black. Big. Big." He waved his hand in the air, indicating the staggering height of the man.

"You've seen him?"

The pygmy pointed to the clouds crowning the mountain. "I see." He began shooting from an imaginary rifle, gunning down a group of invisible Japanese.

"Will you take us to him?" asked Pearl, already calculating that a trip to the summit wouldn't be too far out of their way. "Can you show us where he is?"

The pygmy looked doubtful.

Wanipe said something in another language, and the two bantered back and forth. The pygmy blew smoke from his nostrils and shrugged, pointing to the string bag at his feet filled with trinkets and shells.

"Big hike. Two day," Wanipe explained to the others. "He climb for smoke."

And so they secured their guide to the top of the mountain by trading a handful of tobacco and two razor blades.

Even though she was weary and hungry, Pearl now crawled over rock faces, slipped in the mud, and grasped at vines as she trekked stubbornly into the clouds. The air grew cooler; the rainforest thinned. They toiled along a narrow track that wound over spurs, plateaus, and streams. Sometimes she grew dizzy with the altitude. By nightfall, they'd climbed so high that the trunks of trees were covered with lichen and the ground was blanketed with leaf mould. Eerie, swirling mists moved down the slopes, so thick sometimes that they couldn't see an arm's length in front of them. It was there, enveloped in this silvery vapour, that they made camp for the night, beneath a canopy of damp branches. The trio shared their bully beef with the pygmy. To reciprocate, he pulled out a wooden pipe, then lit it and passed it around. When Pearl inhaled she tasted the smell of burning rope and her muscles went so limp they felt as if they were dissolving into the mist. Charlie began giggling and Wanipe burst into a rendition of "Beer Barrel Polka," forgetting half the words to the song. The last thing she remembered was resting her head on her backpack and feeling as if she were rising out of her own body.

When she woke at dawn she found Wanipe and Charlie sprawled on the same groundsheet, asleep. The pygmy was nowhere to be seen, and when she looked around she realised that Charlie's organ had vanished, too.

20

It was still misty and cool and there was the constant sound of dripping water. Branches on either side of the path sometimes joined and intertwined, forming lush wet steeples above their heads. The odds of finding James at the summit were slim—the three doubted the pygmy had even encountered him—but they'd come this far out of their way, and decided to continue on, over the top of the mountain, and make their way to the medical base from there. Wanipe was angry with himself for being hoodwinked by the trader, for getting high and letting his guard down, and so he led the way up the steep incline with a grim, determined stride. The mist grew so thick they found themselves circling the same terrain for hours. By mid-afternoon, Wanipe confessed that he was lost and they began scouring the area for a path they'd missed, the one that would take them all the way to the summit.

Finally, the sun came out and the air cleared a little. Soon they discovered a narrow track that gradually sloped upward through the trees. They walked for another hour or so, until they glimpsed the conical shapes of roofs pointing into the clouds, a cluster of about eleven or twelve huts that stood on a plateau of the range. There was one long house thatched with palms. The tiny village was ringed with vegetable gardens, bordered by flowers the colour of butter. They saw two small children on the track, chasing a fleet-footed baby cassowary. The infants were grabbing at the escaping bird before they stumbled into Wanipe and fell over. When they righted themselves they caught their first glimpse of Pearl and Charlie. The taller one froze, and then screamed, as if he'd seen a gruesome monster. Suddenly, the cassowary was abandoned and the children were fleeing back to the village, screaming one word over and over in their own dialect.

Wanipe was as confused by their reaction as Charlie and Pearl. The three of them were now wary about continuing on to the village; as Thomas had warned them, there were cannibals scattered throughout this part of the country, and it was rumoured that some of them had sided with Japanese forces, uniting against all the white invaders. But they barely had time to discuss their next move because a whole group of naked villagers began teeming down the track toward them. A wave of panic shot through Pearl, and she was suddenly terrified to be one of only two white people outnumbered by so many blacks.

Wanipe, however, pointed out that the villagers held no axes or spears. He told Pearl and Charlie not to move. Suddenly about fifty people were mobbing them, all jostling to get a closer look, exclaiming to one another in their own tongues in high, hysterical voices. Two tall men ventured forward and touched Pearl's face, rubbed Charlie's neck, and then looked at their own hands, as if they expected to find something that hadn't been there before. They tried it once more, whispering to each other, and Wanipe explained to Charlie and Pearl in his halting pidgin that they were attempting to rub off what they thought was white paint.

When no white paint appeared on the fingers of the men, a hush descended and they all stood back in a kind of wide-eyed reverence. Pearl found it hard to believe they'd never seen white people before, but Wanipe assured her that it was true. And when the two taller men stepped forward again and plucked hairs from the heads of Charlie and Pearl, Wanipe explained the villagers probably thought they were ghosts or even two great gods from the sky.

Whatever form Pearl and Charlie had taken in the eyes of these villagers, it was no doubt miraculous and divine. Children and women pressed forward to touch their hands while men plucked hairs from their arms and heads. Even though Wanipe was as black as they were, the villagers also regarded him with awe and respect, perhaps as some emissary between their own world and the worlds of ghosts and gods. They tried to communicate with him but their languages weren't the same, and even that disparity seemed to afford him some otherworldly status in their eyes, confirming the trio's supernatural difference.

One of the taller men lifted a necklace over his head and proffered it to Charlie. It was made of thin bamboo slats and bright red feathers. Charlie smiled and nodded and took the necklace, looping it over his own head. Then the second tall man offered his to Pearl, which she accepted with a smile and a nod. Wanipe received one made of polished bones from a woman. Pearl thought for a moment, wondering what they could offer in return. She took off her backpack and rummaged in a pocket and pulled out three packets of razor blades that she'd been carrying for weeks.

Later, at the village, Pearl and Charlie showed them how the blades effortlessly sliced sweet potatoes, carved bamboo, etched wood, and removed hair, and with these demonstrations the pale white couple assumed an even higher mythic status, two magical ghosts who'd appeared to help them. Several men slaughtered a pig in their honour and began roasting it in an open pit in the centre of the village, while children and women dragged Pearl and Charlie from hut to hut, wanting to show them where they each lived.

It was night now, and a bonfire raged in the darkness. The aroma of sizzling meat and smoke wafted through the clearing. Sweet potatoes were thrown upon the embers. Children ran in circles, playing with Pup. A group of men produced drums made from hollowed tree trunks. They assembled in a circle around the fire and began beating with their hands complex, circuitous rhythms that flipped and somersaulted into time signatures that neither Pearl nor Charlie could grasp, let alone follow. Their accents fell in odd places in an order of beats that seemed impossible to count, though not one man hesitated in its execution, in the perfect synchronicity. It was as if they were imitating the way the rain had drummed against their roofs on a particular night, or the noise of a herd of wild pigs running down the mountain.

The night grew more convivial, and the trio forgot about

their journey, their stolen organ, their orders to reach the next post. Everyone feasted on the pig and sweet potato, a welcome change from the monotony of army rations. Afterward, the villagers shared betel nuts, spitting their red saliva into the fire, while bare-breasted women in skirts of grass and vines sang in soprano voices, their hips swaying from side to side. Wanipe pulled out his bamboo flute and accompanied the women as they danced around him.

Pearl disappeared into a nearby hut. She discarded entirely the smelly khaki uniform and dressed herself in the long red evening dress. She propped the blond wig on her head, but instead of painting on a mask of thick, garish makeup—of pretending she was a man impersonating a woman—she applied a subtle sheen of colour to her lips and cheeks, using a stick of charcoal to line her eyes. She plucked a flower from a bowl in the corner of the hut, stuck it behind her ear, and discarded her army boots. The disguise—or lack of it—was invigorating, and for the first time the outfit didn't feel like a costume.

The villagers gazed at her with expressions of confusion and disbelief as she took her place beside Charlie. Perhaps they thought Pearl had conjured herself from a man ghost to a woman ghost, because one of the native girls rushed up and cupped her hands around Pearl's breasts, but they were so small the girl backed away, still puzzled.

Pearl stifled a laugh and turned to Charlie. "What about 'Sophisticated Lady'? Y'know that, Charl?" Charlie's eyebrows rose. Pearl had never sung a ballad before, and certainly not this one. And, as she never tired of pointing out, she hated ballads.

Charlie played a four-bar introduction on the harmonica,

and Pearl lifted the hem of her dress and turned toward the audience. The voice she began to sing in was distinctly different from the one she used to entertain the troops—lower and more controlled, a kind of mesmerising lilt.

It was a delicate, feminine song usually sung by female vocalists. She was happy to be relieved of the pressure of always having to pretend she was her brother, of constantly being on her guard. And the times she most feared for herself was during the female impersonations, when the swing of a hip or the flash of a leg could betray her true identity.

Here, among these villagers, she enjoyed an exhilarating anonymity: She had no name, no nationality, no sex; she wasn't even human, but some supernatural creature free to shift shape, to sing and move in any way she wished, and she found herself sauntering around the fire, gazing into watchful eyes, her voice modulating up from the tones she'd once sung in, inventing themselves into something uniquely her own.

When she held her last note, it was the only sound that could be heard on the side of the mountain, and when it ended everyone sat in a captivated silence. At first she wondered if she'd offended them, or if they'd been disappointed in her performance. But Wanipe finally broke the silence by clapping slowly and, one by one, the others joined in until the whole village exploded with the sound of applause.

After that, the show slid into one long jam session of native drums and flutes, traditional dancing and soft shoes, four-four jazz rhythms on saxophone and harmonica played against the complicated time signatures of the village musicians. Women were suddenly bedecked in headdresses made from the plumes of birds of paradise, and men rubbed pale mud onto their faces and arms until they too looked like ghosts from the sky. Children ran up to Pearl, lifting the skirt of her dress to see if she was a boy or a girl, and finally she didn't care anymore and lifted the hem above her waist and danced about with the other women, flashing her bum and the triangle of blond pubic hair. After that, she played her alto behind the relentless beats of the drums, trying to find a way into them, and be at one.

21

The next morning, two elders led the trio back along the top of the ridge to help them get their bearings. A small group of children followed along behind. The elders tried to shoo them away but they refused to return to their village until Charlie gave them his tiny hand mirror. When they reached a chasm lined with limestone and ferns, the men pointed to a track that led down to a valley patched with native gardens and kunai grass. On the other side stood another ridge of slate-coloured mountains, the tops ringed by clouds, with rivers running out of them, as if they flowed from heaven. It was a poignant parting for all of them, and already Pearl was nostalgic for the most fun she'd had since her journey had begun. In a way, it reminded her of home, her own family, when they'd push back the furniture, crowd around the piano, and sing, dance, and perform for one another. Now that she wasn't performing she had turned back into a man, wearing a khaki uniform, steel helmet, and army boots.

They were on their way to the mobile medical unit stationed about eight miles from the foot of the mountain, and were hoping to make it by dusk. Marks and Farthing would be flown in from Nadzab on a supplies plane to rejoin the band after three months of rest and treatment.

The descent took them down another steep track, and they paused regularly to ease the cramps in their legs, the splintering pains that the Allies had nicknamed "laughing knees." Coming upon the mounds of three Japanese graves freshly dug into the side of the mountain, they noticed the site was marked with nothing more than a piece of sapling and some carved ideographs.

After they passed the graves, Charlie complained that he was feeling sick. At first Pearl thought it was vertigo and told him to stop looking down at the valley. Sometimes the incline was so vertical that Wanipe had to carry the dog in his pack. The track snaked around limestone slabs, over streams, between the thick aerial roots of trees. Every one hundred feet or so they'd have to pause and rest because of the cramps forking through their legs like a series of electric shocks. It was during one such break that Charlie suddenly bent over and vomited. Pearl and Wanipe traded worried looks; they both knew what Charlie's symptoms implied, but neither wished to admit it. They heard the whistle of a shell and then the distant purr of Bren guns. Charlie began to suffer from dizzy spells and was having trouble keeping up. They stopped again, passing him water.

While Charlie rested, Pearl and Wanipe bathed in a stream that coursed down the range, washing mud from their hands and faces. The water was cold and bracing. Pearl still wore her uniform and scrubbed it with a cake of soap. It had begun to rot from the daily rain and perspiration but she still tried to keep it clean. When Wanipe emerged from the water, he disappeared off the track and into a thicket of trees. Pearl and Charlie waited fifteen minutes, half an hour, and still he didn't return. Pearl was growing anxious, but said nothing to Charlie, who was resting against a fallen log, looking up at the sky, where dark clouds were gathering.

Wanipe finally came striding into the clearing. Cupped in his hands were several betel nuts that he'd traded for with a pack of cigarettes. He told Charlie to chew on them: They would stave off the cramps and give him energy.

As the party set off again, it began to rain and the track grew wet and slippery. The nuts did indeed revitalise Charlie, and he was able to walk at a fairly even pace. Even so, the afternoon storm slowed their progress, and Pearl suspected they wouldn't make the medical unit by sunset, that there'd be another night spent in the damp jungle, with Charlie sick and snipers about and virtually no rations left. They laboured on for another twenty minutes, watching the sun fade behind the jagged mountains that were now grey and austere in the twilight.

Wanipe and Pearl built a lean-to out of vines and palms, then settled Charlie on a bedroll inside it, with a blanket and plenty of water from a nearby stream. They were hoping a long rest would revive him enough to make it to the hospital base the next day, but Charlie was up half the night, vomiting and shitting outside.

By morning, he was so weak he could hardly walk. He stuck his head out of the lean-to and began dry retching, having nothing left in his system to expel. Wanipe and Pearl briefly considered making a stretcher from a groundsheet tied to two branches and carrying him the rest of the way, but they knew they couldn't manage both Charlie and their own gear. Charlie lay back down on the ground and suggested that they go ahead without him, that they could return later that day unencumbered by instruments and supplies, with a proper stretcher and a couple of other people to help them.

This alternative seemed more plausible, though Pearl was uneasy about leaving him alone, particularly since he was so ill and weak. She insisted he keep the last of the emergency rations—a few biscuits and the last remaining antimalarial tablet—and refilled his canteen of water from the stream. When it came time to go, she found excuses for delaying their departure, placing a wet rag on his forehead to cool his fever, rummaging in her backpack to leave him the last of her cigarettes, making a pillow with her own blanket and slipping it beneath his head. She and Charlie had been inseparable since that chilly dawn down at the Woolloomooloo wharf the year before; he'd shadowed her every move, as she had shadowed his. She felt guilty, somehow responsible for his illness, as if she herself had accidentally caused the contamination.

"I wouldn't have got this far without you," she admitted.

"Come on, soldier," he chided.

"I mean it, Charl. You've been the best."

She was still fussing over him, smoothing his blanket up to his chin.

"Hurry up and piss off," he urged gently. "I want a real doctor looking after me tonight, not some dickhead jazz muso."

She laughed in spite of herself and tweaked his nose. He

smelled of stale vomit, but she leaned over and kissed him on the lips. He kissed her back, and she felt the sweat from his upper lip bead her own.

The tracks were always longer and rougher when she walked on an empty stomach; the sun was hotter and her backpack was heavier. Sometimes she grew dizzy and spots whirled in front of her eyes like bright, nervy insects, but she didn't stop walking for fear that she'd never start again. By midmorning she and Wanipe could hear grenades exploding in the valley and the hammer of machine guns. Pup was suddenly anxious at the sound of them and ran in circles, barking back. They followed a river north for about two hours and finally the mobile hospital appeared, a camouflage of green tents and a couple of circular huts between clusters of trees cloaked in leaf mould and vines. A narrow airstrip lay behind the camp, though no planes were on the runway.

"Malaria," declared the CO, Nevins, when Pearl described Charlie's symptoms, explaining why they hadn't arrived two days ago, as scheduled. He was a squat, pear-shaped man with tobacco-stained teeth and a nasal voice. "Don't worry about him being left with so little food. He won't keep anything down anyway."

While Nevins organised two carriers and a stretcher to accompany them back to the lean-to, Pearl and Wanipe found the mess tent, where they each ate a plate of bully beef and boiled taro from a local garden. After her stomach was full, Pearl felt a sense of warmth moving through her body, a kind of tranquillising of her muscles.

When she reported back to Nevins in his hut, the party's movement orders had been phoned through from Lae, and he had them written out on a piece of paper.

"There's a couple of units somewhere up on Mount Hagen, about forty miles from here," he said. "They've been isolated for weeks. We're the closest post." He looked up from the report.

Pearl, standing at attention, nodded uneasily.

"One lot are guarding the airstrip. The other lot seem to be missing. They're our most forward unit, Private. But two days ago they lost radio contact and we don't know where they are."

Pearl knew what was coming, but dreaded it nonetheless.

"I've asked some of my men to try to locate them, but to tell you the truth, son, I've got a textbook snafu on my hands here. More than twenty wounded to every medic." He paused and offered her a cigarette, which she accepted.

"You can still do your little show for the troops up there. You'll just have to find them first!" He chortled and some smoke escaped through his nostrils.

She looked down at her muddy boots, ambivalent about going on to Hagen without Charlie, even in the company of Farthing and Marks, who were due to arrive the following morning on a plane. As far as she was concerned, it wouldn't be a show without Charlie. Perhaps the Hagen trip could be put off until he'd recovered; perhaps with the right medication and treatment the malaria would subside.

Nevins eyed her rotting shirt and trousers. "And you might as well go to the requisition hut and get a new uniform. That one's falling off you."

She obediently collected the new uniform before setting off

to pick up Charlie, but decided not to bother changing into it until she'd returned to the medical post. A stretcher was found and they set off at once with two carriers, each with a bone as long and as wide as a cigarette piercing the base of his septum.

The trek back took less time now that Pearl and Wanipe walked on full stomachs and were unencumbered by their backpacks and instruments. The only things they carried now were their rifles. The gunfire in the hills stuttered intermittently, growing louder and more frequent as they headed south, causing Pup to whine with anxiety. Pearl wondered why she was the only one from the original troubadour band to have been spared from contracting malaria, when one by one the others had been struck down as surely as victims of a plague. The only thing she could put it down to was all the quinine she'd been forced to take back in Sydney, when Hector and her mother had been convinced she was going mad.

Sunlight filtered through swirling mountain mists, making the forest seem otherworldly. A small bird of paradise crossed their path, its plume a fan of iridescent blue. There was a hint of smoke in the air, the aroma of burning wood, and water dripped from the leaves of trees, even though it hadn't rained all day. They could hear a flutter of wings above the branches, and the high-pitched voices of native birds carolling to one another.

Once they reached the foot of the track that wound up through the mountainside, Pearl pointed to the clearing, to the lean-to which was now only about fifty yards away. The four trekked up the path together in single file, the excited dog at her heels. She could smell the vague stench of vomit and as she got closer she saw flies buzzing around the hole Charlie had retched into the night before. But as she got closer still, she saw a long slick of blood trailing through the flattened grass and disappearing up into a thicket of trees. She bolted toward the lean-to, and there was confronted by a scene so shocking and grotesque, so utterly impossible, that everything inside her suddenly stopped: her breathing, her heartbeat, her sense of hearing.

Charlie was lying facedown on the ground, arms splayed. His buttocks, the backs of his calves and his thighs had been sliced off. Tendons and blood still oozed from his open flesh and pooled against the blanket, while hundreds of flies swarmed across and around him, hungry for his remains.

22

She awoke to the sound of a man shouting orders and the rhythm of marching feet. She could hear them turning when they were told to, stopping, starting again, like some lead-footed chorus line. Her head throbbed in time with the tempo of the march and for a while she wasn't sure if she were dreaming it or not. She tried to open her eyes but the right one hurt badly.

When she opened her left eye and saw the morning light, her most recent memories flooded back, along with a throbbing headache. The trek back to Charlie. His tortured body. The way something had snapped inside her and how, gripped by a kind of fury she'd never known before, she'd wailed, stabbed the air with her rifle and run into the thicket of trees, following the trail of blood. She shot at everything she saw: trees, bushes, rocks, the sky. The last thing she remembered was Wanipe tackling her from behind, her head slamming against a rock, and then everything went black and silent.

She now found herself looking at the thatched ceiling of a hut. Wanipe was sitting beside her, like a guard.

"Wake," he murmured. "Wake." The dog jumped up and nuzzled her neck. Wanipe slipped his hand beneath Pearl's head and raised it. He lifted a canteen to her lips and she drank the water down thirstily.

"Well, that was a stupid thing to do, Willis." Her CO, Rudolph, was standing over her. She hadn't seen him since they'd left Nadzab.

She groaned with shock. "The Japs killed Styles. They ate him. They *ate* him."

Rudolph gnawed on his bottom lip but said nothing.

The sun was now shining directly into Pearl's one good eye and she was forced to close it. Her head was pulsing. She moaned again, trying to get the image of Charlie's ravaged body out of her head. If only she hadn't left him at the clearing that morning, if only she and Wanipe had carried him to the hospital.

"What would happen if we all just acted on instinct," continued Rudolph, "did what we wanted to do? This army runs on strict discipline. We can't have men running off willy-nilly, acting on their own interests. Being a soldier's not so different from being a musician. To do it well, you've got to follow the rules. Remember your training, soldier." He paused, obviously waiting for a response.

She kept her eyes shut, craving oblivion again.

"I know you can hear me."

She cracked open her eyes. They were welling with tears. Sunlight angled through the doorway of the hut, throwing Rudolph's shadow across her body as she lay on her bedroll.

"The good news is that all you seem to be suffering from is concussion."

"So what's the bad news?" she choked out.

"Farthing and Marks have taken a turn for the worse. They're now on a hospital ship heading back to Sydney."

She licked her dry lips. "They're still alive . . . "

"Barely. I've only flown in on the supply run. You think you and the native can handle the Hagen mission on your own?"

The Hagen mission. She'd forgotten all about it. With Charlie gone, she certainly didn't feel like carrying out the orders. She hadn't been trained in combat, could barely hit a target. Hagen was the highest and one of the most remote mountains on the island.

"We've got to find that unit," said Rudolph. "There's been no radio contact for days."

She tried to demur, but Rudolph wasn't listening. "Of course, you can rest up today. There're some Americans holding the airstrip up there and they've got a radio. But they've lost most of their men and can't leave the strip. When you find the lost unit, you just have to lead 'em back to the strip and radio back here to camp."

She shifted, trying to think of a way out. Nearly all her muscles ached.

"I'm told that it's an Australian unit," continued Rudolph. "The rumour is that they're being led by a crash-hot black bloke!"

Pearl propped herself up on one elbow, wondering if she'd heard right. "A Negro with a group of Aussies?"

Rudolph shrugged. "Probably just a native. Now come on, Willis. I want you up and out of bed by tomorrow. It's not like you've got malaria."

Rudolph sat down by the doorway and lit a cigarette, drawing on it heavily.

Pearl stared at the ceiling and considered her options. Of course, it was possible that James was up on Mount Hagen with the Australian unit, but highly unlikely. In fact, there was no guarantee that he had even survived his desertion from the U.S. Army. Still, she'd come this far, with so little encouragement.

Pup leaped onto the bed, tail wagging, and licked Pearl's face. In her innocent optimism, the dog suddenly made Pearl feel ashamed of her own self-pity and resignation. Charlie would have urged her to go on, to follow this lead.

The next day, in the mess hall, Rudolph placed his tin plate of food beside hers on the trestle table and clapped her on the back. Though nothing was said, Pearl sensed it was a kind of forgiveness, an absolution from her dangerous, random shooting rampage of the day before. She realised then that Rudolph was more of a musician than a military man, more of a creator than a destroyer, just like her, and like James.

They sat in silence, staring down at their plates as they ate. She and Wanipe were due to fly out to Hagen after lunch and she was feeling uneasy about the challenges of this next mission. Her old uniform stank and the seams were fraying around her legs; the knees had worn away and two buttons were missing from the bottom of her shirt, and yet it felt like a second skin, the one that had protected her from the heat of the tropics, the sting of mosquitoes, the daily rainfall, the mists of the highlands and the eyes of Allied soldiers.

Rudolph paused and wiped his mouth with the cuff of his shirt. "You know, Willis, you're a bloody good muso. You might have a real future ahead of you when you're sent back home."

"*If* I'm sent back home."

"You're up for a furlough. While you're up in Hagen I'll do the paperwork."

The pain in her hip and head suddenly worsened. Some sensation inside her—instinct or fear—made her apprehensive of going back to that other world. How could she fit back into the shape of her old life when she was now straining and growing into something new and completely different? Playing for the troops had become acutely necessary, not only for them, but for herself as well. The thought of performing dance music at Sydney society balls seemed trite, a waste of time. It made no essential difference to the lives of those people, to the axis of a single day. She realised that she'd now rather stand in a stinking foxhole and play for a handful of exhausted soldiers than sit on the revolving stage of the Trocadero and perform for hundreds of couples bedecked in beaded gowns and tuxedos.

"I don't know," she muttered.

Rudolph shrugged. "It's up to you, Willis. But either way you're overdue for a furlough after Hagen." He wiped his mouth and took his plate back to the front of the mess for a second helping.

The Stinson that was headed for Mount Hagen was due to take off just before the supply plane that would fly Rudolph on to Bundi. Pearl and Wanipe's aircraft was being loaded with boxes of tinned food. The missing men would no doubt be starving and suffering from malnutrition.

While Wanipe gathered their few remaining belongings, Pearl fed Pup at the back of the mess tent. She was still sore from her collapse, and the chill in the wind caused her joints to ache. The plane was due to take off in about ten minutes. She barely had time to gather her new uniform and boots and scout about for a private place to change. Every tent was full; each hut held at least three wounded men. She rushed down to the river. East of the camp, it was hemmed by bushes and tall, gnarled trees. On the sandy bank, she glanced about to ensure she was alone, then quickly pulled off her boots and stripped herself of the clothes reeking of sweat and mud.

She was just slipping her arm through the sleeve of the new shirt when a wet and naked man, towelling himself, walked out from behind a slab of limestone. The two stood stock-still, staring at one another. He had strands of black chest hair glistening with river water, a protruding potbelly, skinny legs, and a finger of flesh that hung limply between them; she had a black eye, tiny breasts, a slim waist, and narrow, boyish hips marked with bruises, a patch of fair hair between her thighs.

Rudolph staggered back a little, shocked, as if he'd just seen a vision of his own death.

She began to tremble. "Sir, it's not what you think . . ."

"I'm not thinking anything. I don't know what to think."

She slipped her arm into the other shirtsleeve. "I'm not Martin Willis."

"That's bloody obvious."

"I'm Martin Willis's sister. His twin. Pearl."

She wanted to explain, but where to begin?

"He gave me his papers. His uniform. Everything. I cut my hair like his. Blue and Charlie Styles knew. No one else."

Rudolph, still wide-eyed, was staring at her pubic hair. "You mean to tell me that for—what?—for eleven months you've been in the army, masquerading as your brother, and nobody found out?"

"Styles did, sir. Right away. We told Blue about it. And Wanipe. No one else."

"Farthing? Marks?" His voice was growing more incredulous.

"No, sir. No one."

Rudolph took a deep breath. He looked overwhelmed. "I'm going to have report this right away, Willis. Or whatever your name is. I can't—"

"No, sir, please—"

"I can't have a woman under my command!"

"But you already do."

"If the brass found out about this they'd have me—"

"That's exactly what I mean," she countered, slipping her legs into the trousers and pulling them up. "How's the brass going to react when you tell them I've been posing as my brother?"

"Well, that's your problem. Not—"

"With all due respect, sir, it *is* your problem."

"You're going to be court-martialled. You *and* your brother."

"I'm going to Hagen," she declared. She took a few steps toward him and lowered her voice. "I've been under your command for almost a year. No offence, sir, but how's it going to reflect on you—on your leadership, on your military record—

when they find out you can't tell a boy from a girl?" She thought of James trekking around Mount Hagen, lost, with the band of Aussie commandos. "I'm going to Hagen," she repeated, "and no one's going to stop me."

Rudolph must have realised he was still standing naked in front of her, for he abruptly pulled his towel over his exposed genitals. "Fuck you," he growled. "And fuck your dog, too." On the airstrip an engine began to purr.

23

Mist crowned the summit of the mountain. It was hard to see where the earth stopped rising and the clouds began. From inside the plane, with her one good eye, Pearl could see dozens of streams cascading through gorges, toward the plateaus and valleys below. The peaked roofs of native huts sat farther down, on an uneven terrace, against the green and straw-coloured rows of a garden. She was wedged next to Wanipe in the back of the Stinson, between him and several boxes. She held Pup close to her, against her chest, where she could feel the dog's warm breath against her skin. Pearl's ears hurt so much that they felt as if they were filled with water and would burst at any moment.

Pearl's altercation with Rudolph less than an hour before hadn't ended well: He'd remained angry, affronted, shocked. But perhaps the hardest thing for him, she knew, was the humiliation he would face if her true identity were ever revealed; the consequences for him as both a soldier and a man would be devastating, which was why he'd finally relented and allowed her to board the plane.

There was an airstrip on the east side of the mountain, but, due to the heavy cover of mist, the pilot was unable to locate it. Instead, he flew beyond what they could see of the cloudy summit, circling around the jagged spurs and precipices. As the aircraft scooped and dipped and shuddered, Pup cowered closer to her mistress.

Suddenly a straight brown gash appeared in the west side of the mountain. At first it looked like an abandoned garden, but as the plane dropped toward it Pearl could see a landing strip carved between stunted trees. The Stinson shook as the nose edged downward. Pearl's breath seized inside her, her muscles tensed. One ear popped, and then the other. The pilot cut the engine and the plane swooped down. When she felt the thud of the wheels against the ground she let out a loud whoop and the dog answered back with three short, happy barks.

A group of American soldiers unloaded the plane quickly; the pilot was nervous about the cloud cover and mist and wanted to return to base as soon as possible. As they stacked boxes of food to one side of the strip, the Americans explained that, in defending the airstrip over the past few weeks, they'd already lost nine men. After the job was done the pilot climbed back into the cockpit, started the engine, and taxied the plane in a circle. Within moments, he was lifting off the mountainside, and the plane disappeared behind a rocky, Z-shaped ridge.

The temperature was much cooler up on the mountain, with wind singing through the lichen-covered trees. The thin air made Pearl feel giddy and slightly intoxicated. Pup trotted about the surrounding area, nosing at flowers and dew-covered ferns. Mould grew between tufts of snow grass and clusters of blue and violet blossoms. Mist crawled down from the peak of the mountain and circled them like ghosts. Pearl was glad she was wearing the new uniform—she would have been frozen in the old one. Wanipe had prepared for the journey by dressing in a uniform, too, though he refused to wear boots. The Americans were already hoeing into the tinned food, not even bothering to heat it up.

Pearl was still sore and bruised; her right eye continued to throb. It seemed impossible that Charlie had been killed only two days ago. She kept expecting him to sneak up behind her and pinch her on the bum, or call out, "Hey, Willis, what's for tea?" And the longer she watched the Americans eating and trading jokes, the more keenly she felt his absence and its awful permanence.

When the missing unit had last radioed, they'd reported that they were three miles east of the landing strip, farther up toward the summit. When they'd lost contact with their CO several days before, the men had been holding the crest of a ridge against a small band of Japanese. Pearl and Wanipe had been told there were twelve Australians in the unit, though their numbers may have dropped; no one could be certain that they hadn't all been killed.

That night, they camped with the Americans close to the landing strip, beneath a lean-to of bracken and ferns. At dawn, after they woke, one of the GIs loaned her a walkie-talkie so she and Wanipe could keep in touch with them. It was so heavy that Wanipe had to carry it strapped to his back. They set off into the sunrise and, a couple of hours later, located the ridge the soldiers had fought to hold. They searched the surrounding area for Allies—dead or alive—but found only the smoked corpse of a local man, who sat strapped to a chair on a bamboo platform.

Nearby, however, Pup found the ashes of what looked like a recent fire and she nosed around in the soot until the metal button of a uniform glinted in the sunlight. Pearl picked it up and rubbed it against her trousers, noticing it was exactly the same as the button on her own jacket.

The days passed in spirals of mist and foot tracks that seemed to lead nowhere. They followed sparse trails of rusty tin cans, the occasional blunt razor blade, two broken boot-laces, and several charred matches. Sometimes, they happened upon isolated gardens, bordered by pigpens and beds of sweet potato. The villagers were shocked by the sight of Pearl, whom they thought was some ghost or otherwordly god, as had the villagers back in the Bismarck Range.

She kept in touch with the Americans at the airstrip via the walkie-talkie, and they in turn communicated with the mobile medical base and with Rudolph, who was now back in Lae. But the higher she and Wanipe walked toward the summit, the thinner the air became, and with it she felt her resolve diminishing. Several days after discovering the button in the ashes of fire, the thin, unpromising trail of bootlaces and matches ran out. She developed a bad cold; her throat grew dry and raw from coughing. As they were climbing a steep ridge, she lost her footing and her rifle slipped from her shoulder and dropped into a chasm so deep she heard only a distant echo when it hit the ground. Pup was whining and irritable until Pearl discovered a tick in her hind leg and dug it out with a razor blade. Wanipe cut his foot on a rock as they crossed a stream, and within two days it had become infected, ballooning into an angry purple lump. Every time Pearl urinated, she caught the flow in her cupped hand and rubbed it into the wounds on Pup's leg and Wanipe's foot, as it was the only disinfectant to be had for forty miles.

During their thirteenth day on Mount Hagen they encountered a family who were not shocked to see a white ghost. The father, a small man with a broad, flat nose pierced with a hook-shaped bone, smiled and greeted Pearl and Wanipe as if they were neighbours. He and his seven children ushered them into a wide hut, one wall of which opened onto a deck overlooking a waterfall and ravine. There, they sat on straw mats and, while the children chased and played with Pup, the father offered Pearl and Wanipe gold-lipped pearl shells rimmed with red clay and iridescent feathers from a bird of paradise. At the same time, he produced two razor blades and a box with only five matches inside, holding them up and pointing to Pearl, and then to himself, repeating the gesture several times. He wished to barter for additional blades, she realised with a rising sense of excitement; the unit of soldiers she and Wanipe had been tracking must have traded the matches only days before.

She handed over all but one of the blades she had, and two of the three boxes of matches in her pack. She also added some dried biscuits and a shard of a mirror that she used when she applied makeup for the show. The father was overjoyed, and the mirror was passed between the excited children as if it were some rare form of magic.

Then came the hard part: attempting to communicate with

him to find out which way the unit had gone. Wanipe tried a few words from the different dialects he'd picked up during his trading days, but the father just looked quizzical and answered back in his own tongue. Pearl picked up the blades and match-box he'd shown them originally and with her hands shaped the outline of a man. She then shrugged and pointed in various directions from the deck of the hut. She repeated the gestures several times until the father smiled, strode across the deck, and pointed to a rocky crest of limestone to the west.

They gave the man back his shells and feathers and instead took ten sweet potatoes and two pig's feet. The children were sad to see them go and followed them across the heath of alpine grass and snow daisies for almost a mile, skipping along with Pup and throwing sticks for her to fetch. After a while, they grew bored and began straggling back home.

It was sunset by the time Pearl, Wanipe, and Pup reached the limestone crest, which was a long plateau of rock overlook-ing what seemed to be a gorge. They were unable to gauge the depth of the drop, nor what lay beyond it, for great rolls of mist were purling toward them. The plateau was wet and mot-tled with moss; there were ridges and indentations against the rock wall behind them. They followed the embankment until Wanipe found a cave for them to shelter in for the night. The pig's feet were a welcome change from the monotony of bully beef and biscuits that had been their staple diet for so many months. Pearl hugged Pup close to her, but she didn't rest well on the hard floor of the cave, and the evening was fractured by nightmares during which she was forced to solo with a band playing at an impossible tempo. She blew and blew into her mouthpiece, moving her fingers briskly against the keys, but the instrument made no sound, no matter how hard she tried.

Morning dawned with the plaintive song of a bird, a relentless pitch of longing. While Wanipe slept, Pearl crawled out of the cave and stretched. Patches of frost clung to the limestone, glistening silver against the moss. Pup nosed around the plateau, chasing a beetle. As the sun rose, the fog in the gorge began to lift in places and slowly pockets of a deep valley emerged, as if out of a dream. It was clustered with pale green bushes and withered trees that grew against the terraces sloping downward, like a staircase made for giants. She could see the silver wings of a small crashed plane farther down in the valley. The bird that had awakened her kept twittering, and she followed the sound to a nest about fifteen feet away, built into a recess of the limestone, a wreath of twigs and leaves out of which grew an arbour of sticks, feathers, the veined translucent wings of an insect, and what looked like strands of blond human hair glinting in the sunlight. The tiny bowerbird stood beneath the arch, pale blue feathers ruffled, chirping urgently at the rising sun.

She was just returning to the mouth of the cave when, out of the corner of her eye, she glimpsed something moving on one of the lower terraces, about half a mile away. She edged to the lip of the precipice and, squinting, saw two, then three figures walking east toward the early light. They were too far away for her to tell if they were natives, Allies, or Japanese, and she scrambled back to the cave to grab her binoculars. As she rummaged in her bag, she called to Wanipe, alerting him to the presence of strangers. He sat up, startled, registered what she was saying, and together they crept out onto the shelf of rock, lying on their stomachs to conceal themselves.

It was a minute or so before she spotted them again through the magnification of the lenses, and when she did it felt as if her heart began to spin in wild revolutions. She spotted three, then four men in jungle-green uniforms and black berets, their faces covered with camouflage netting. But the real shock came when, a few lengths ahead of them, she saw a dark-skinned man dressed in the same clothes, shouldering a rifle and bayonet.

"It's them!" she cried. "It's the unit!" She leaped to her feet, passing the binoculars to Wanipe. For a few crazy moments she fancied the dark-skinned man was James—for who else could it be, with skin the colour of milky coffee, wearing Australian army fatigues? She felt so much blood and adrenaline course through her body she thought she would levitate. But then it occurred to her that the man in question was probably a local guide, and all the air abruptly left her body. Wanipe himself dressed in a similar uniform to hers and there were bound to be other guides who did the same.

Wanipe gave a low cry and waved her back to the ground. She put down Pup and dropped to her stomach. He passed her the binoculars and pointed to a nearby terrace, about three hundred yards away, also ringed with mist. At first she glimpsed only a line of gnarled trees, tufts of pale flowers, and the cabin of the crashed plane. Then the lenses caught the image of a Japanese man in a worn khaki uniform; his head was bowed and he was looking at the ground, as if he were tracing the path of a small animal. The lenses then caught another man behind, then another, and another, until it became obvious that there were about twenty Japanese stealing across the upper part of the valley, all armed with rifles. They were short and emaciated, shoulders hunched, but they were heading east, in the same direction as the Australians, and it was clear that they outnumbered the latter by at least three to one. The only things that separated the two groups were three terraces, and about six hundred yards.

Perhaps the Japanese were tracking the Australian unit, or maybe it was sheer coincidence that they were in such close proximity to their enemy. Either way, it was only a matter of time before the Aussies would be taken unawares, for the Japanese, like Pearl and Wanipe, had the advantage of being higher up in the valley and having better sight lines. Her heart drummed in her chest and an uncontrollable trembling overtook her body. She could no longer hold the binoculars steady and the image of the Japanese unit began to shudder, like a film being run through a faulty projector. She passed them back to Wanipe and made for the cave to grab the walkie-talkie, at the same time attempting to calculate their location, which she figured was roughly four miles east and six miles north from the airstrip where they'd landed. Or was it six miles east and four miles north? They were much closer to the summit, she was certain of that. She called the Americans back at the airstrip, but there was a lot of interference, like the sound of breaking waves. She yelled that the lost unit had been located, that there was a band of Japs tailing the Aussies and they'd need reinforcements as soon as possible. The tidal sound of the interference rose and crashed in her ear.

"Reinforcements, for fuck's sake!" she yelled again. And then the connection went dead.

She punched the air with frustration, wanting to slam the transmitter against the ground. Instead, she grabbed Wanipe's rifle and crawled back outside. She raised the binoculars to her eyes. The Australians were making slightly faster progress than the Japanese; they seemed to be heading for a stream farther east that surged through a chasm of the valley in currents of glistening stars. But the lead was only a minor advantage, because the only thing protecting the soldiers from what would soon be a bloody onslaught was the mist still scrolling up through the terraces of the gorge. With only one rifle between her and Wanipe, she felt a crushing sense of impotence; she was powerless to stop what would happen. She had to do something, she decided, something to distract the enemy and at the same time alert the Australians to their proximity. She swung the binoculars back to the twenty-strong unit and saw that the men were sliding down the slope to the next tier of the terraces.

Before she had time to consider the consequences, she was back at the cave, piecing her battered saxophone together, inserting her last reed. Her hands were shaking so much she could barely fit the mouthpiece onto the body, and she suddenly had the desperate urge to piss.

"Here," she said to Wanipe, handing him the saxophone. "You sit here and blow, blow hard. The Japs'll turn around and follow the sound. I'll take the rifle down lower into the gorge and fire at 'em as they come toward us."

Wanipe frowned and narrowed his eyes as he considered the plan, then shook his head.

"But we've got to do something!" she wailed. "They're almost upon the unit!"

Pup, sensing the tension between Wanipe and her mistress, began barking and wagging her tail.

"You play," he said, holding up the saxophone. "I shoot."

"I'm the head of this unit."

Wanipe shook his head again, glancing quickly through the binoculars. "My gun. I shoot. You music. You saxophone." He put the instrument on the ground and, before she could stop him, wrenched the rifle out of her hand and began racing across the plateau.

She called after him, but he was already disappearing down the steep incline that led toward the valley, Pup trailing him excitedly as if it were all an exhilarating game, yet another show they were performing.

Pearl cursed herself as she picked up the saxophone: "Fuck! Fuck! Fuck!" The mist was thinning even more with the rising sun, and when she squinted she could just make out the line of Japanese soldiers threading through the bush. They seemed small and harmless against the magnitude of the valley, and the disjunction between the illusion they presented and the threat that they posed made her shudder. She could see Wanipe's head bobbing between the bushes and trees that grew out at an angle from the side of the gorge. He positioned himself behind a boulder about fifty yards down into the valley. He raised his arm and waved to her and she waved back, knowing her time had come. She moved away from the ridge and kneeled in the mouth of the cave for both protection and amplification. She lifted the saxophone, and the mouthpiece was like a block of ice between her lips.

Pearl made herself believe that it was indeed James down in the valley with the Australians, trekking toward the stream, and that with her saxophone she could save them all. With the right combination of tempo and sound she could make the mist in the gorge thicken, protect Wanipe from enemy bullets, cause the Japs to retreat, draw the Allies back to safety, transform all the misery and loss they'd endured.

Her fingers found the keys of her instrument. She drew in a deep breath, and began to blow hard. Suddenly, instead of playing a familiar tune, a primal wail surged out of the bell of her sax and echoed throughout the valley. From the opening of the cave she could see the Japanese unit suddenly pause. Then they began ducking and pointing their guns in all directions, unsure where the noise was coming from. The first rifle shot exploded. A machine gun stuttered and she could hear bullets ricocheting off the limestone chasm below. She inched back a little and continued to blow, her fingers moving randomly across the keys in one long, primeval howl. The mist was clearing, and from where she knelt she could just see a few of the Aussies cantering back along to the western side of the terrace they were on, moving in behind the Japanese, positioning themselves for an ambush. She glimpsed a Jap drop backward, roll down the slope of a terrace and disappear. Gasping occasionally, she tried to play even louder in an attempt to distract the enemy from Wanipe's position. Two bullets whistled over the ridge, and she ducked as they hit the cliff face. Another bullet ricocheted off the top of the cave, and she squeezed her thighs together, gathering her nerve.

She drew air down deep into her lungs, her groin, and

before she knew it she found herself playing faster and faster, even though she hadn't begun with a particular tempo or even a melody. She was playing nuances and half-tones— tones within tones—sounds she'd heard from squawking tropical parrots, squealing pigs, the cries of mating birds of paradise. A machine gun rattled an uneven rhythm behind the wild runs she played, and she could hear the closer rhythm of Wanipe's rifle reporting back, as if they were all involved in some crazy cutting contest, playing chorus upon chorus until the weaker musician slunk offstage in exhausted and embarrassed defeat.

She couldn't see the battle, but could hear the advance of the enemy by the higher pitch of their booming rifles. A bullet skimmed the top of her helmet and zigzagged through the cave, and she ducked to the right, pressing her back against the wall.

She was startled to hear the voice of a man laugh and cry out, "Digger! Digger! Where are you?" in a clipped Japanese accent, farther down the gorge, to her left. She leaped from the mouth of the cave to the recess in the limestone to her right, again trying to distract the enemy from Wanipe's position. As she wedged herself into the V-shaped niche she noticed the bowerbird had fled its sanctuary of twigs and treasured things. A grenade arced through the air, and part of the cliff suddenly exploded and fell away into the valley in a cascade of rocks and dust and, as the debris began to settle, she could see clearly now the advance of about five Japanese up the rise of the gorge and the darting movements of several Australians behind them. She couldn't tell whether part of the enemy unit had already been shot down, or if the Japanese, knowing they were surrounded, had split up into smaller groups.

The recess she stood in formed a small echo chamber and her saxophone was wailing now as her fingers moved in a frenzy across the keys. She didn't know how long she'd been playing at this lightning speed—five minutes, ten . . . Two Japanese, close to Wanipe's position, fell backward one after the other. Then an Australian, farther down, dropped from the bough of a tree and landed facedown in the mud.

She thought she saw Pup skittering through the undergrowth to her right and, still blowing relentlessly, she leaned out of the recess to check. It was then that she saw him, about twenty feet away along the ridge: a thin Japanese man with matted hair down to his shoulders, knees slightly bowed, rifle brandished, the barrel pointing directly at her face. Fear shot through her, and yet her lungs ballooned with the chill morning air and her fingers danced back and forth over the keys. The man shouted something and took a few steps closer. A gust of wind blew up and sang around the cliff, and Pearl found herself modulating in harmony with it. The man shouted again, shaking his rifle. She saw the anger in his eyes and hoped if she just kept playing he would finally put down his rifle and back away. Somewhere close by she could hear Pup barking. As she stared into the fierce brown eyes of the enemy, the infernal noise she was making became a plea. He yelled again and ran forward, and for a split second she glimpsed a soldier behind him, also raising a gun—the black man in the Australian fatigues. He was thin to the point of emaciation, his frizzy hair was much longer and his skin had greatly darkened. She was so shocked that for a second she almost stopped playing but their eyes locked and the look he threw her implored her to continue, and on she blew as a grenade exploded in the valley and the man screamed at her to stop. A volley of rifle shots thundered around her, and still she kept playing as she felt a blinding light flash against her skull, an electric pain bolting down her neck, and even as she found herself dropping down what seemed like a very deep well, her saxophone whimpered a good-bye.

Rain drummed onto metal like wire brushes against a cymbal. She could hear triplets, paradiddles, shuffles, a beating heart. Was it music in the weather or weather in the music? . . . A chorus line of crotchets and semiquavers dancing on a lake . . . Or were they merely raindrops rippling the surface of the water? The drumming was growing louder, and she felt a stab of pain near the base of her skull. Then she heard the sound of barking. When she shifted she found the surface she was lying on was hard and that she was cold and shivering.

Pearl groaned and half opened her eyes. She was surprised to find herself looking at a tangle of wiring and realised she was staring at the cabin ceiling of a plane. For a moment she thought she was flying—or being flown somewhere—but the plane wasn't moving. And then it dawned on her that she was still alive and breathing, and that the barking dog had been Pup, who was now nuzzling her neck and licking her face. Then she sensed a particular smell, something raw and earthy, as familiar as cut grass or the scent of her own sweat.

"How's my Sunshine?" she heard a man ask. "How's my baby?"

At first she thought he was a ghost or apparition, lounging beside her, his head propped in one hand, gazing at her. He was gaunt and his hair was longer and threaded with silver, but he still smelled the same—that hint of a ripening lime. When he touched her face, she suddenly felt blood rushing through her veins and a ringing in her ears. Was she imagining all this? Could it be real? Where were they now and how had they wound up together inside the cabin of what looked like a crashed plane?

He took her in his arms and kissed her eyelids, her earlobe, her neck, while the dog leaped about them, wagging her tail. "Baby," he murmured. "Your friend told me all about it. Wanipe. He told me everything."

James supported her head and held a canteen of water to her lips. She took a sip, spluttered, then drank some more. "Don't know how you did it. Pretending to be Martin. Comin' all this way . . ."

Pearl glanced at his thigh, bound with a bloody cloth, and cried out, as if she'd suddenly been knifed.

"Whoa, baby"—he dropped the canteen of water and slipped his arm around her—"it's all right. Just a flesh wound."

She touched the side of her head then and realised it was also bandaged. "Sunshine, you lucky to be alive, too. Bullet skimmed your ear. Half an inch closer and you'd be up in heaven now."

She glanced about, her heart hammering. She was overwhelmed by so many emotions—relief, ecstasy, confusion— that she briefly choked on her own breath. "But how? How did we get . . . ?" She pressed her face against his naked chest.

James held her close, stroking her hair or, rather, running his hands across the surface of her clipped blond spikes. "Baby, it's all right," he murmured. "You just collapsed. Collapsed from shock, I guess."

"Where's everyone else?" she breathed. "Where's Wanipe?"

When she looked directly into his eyes she realised that they were another aspect of him that were exactly the same: that pale, slightly rheumy grey-blue.

"Every day," he murmured, "every night. I can't get you outta my head, Pearl. I thought maybe going away would make things better, but . . . "

He shook his head and sat up. She watched the rain drumming against the cracked window of the cockpit. He began rolling a cigarette, head bowed, as if he'd run out of breath and could no longer talk. "Can't believe you're here." He glanced at her, half grinning, shaking his head. "You *are* here, right?"

"I think I'm here." Down near the cockpit she could see splintered wooden boxes and ammunition. "But where are we?"

He finished rolling the tobacco and explained that they were resting in the crashed Japanese supply plane because the others had stored the corpses from the battle inside the nearby cave. Besides, it was warmer and drier in the plane. She'd been out cold for about two hours; Wanipe and the five surviving Australians were off hunting for food; the Japanese unit had been wiped out, so she needn't worry about the reinforcements. They'd probably arrive when the weather cleared, when the pilot had better sight lines.

The mist coiling around the plane was so thick that she could barely see anything outside. A light rain was still falling.

They shared the cigarette he'd rolled and she marvelled at the fact that they were both still alive, in the same cabin, together, after all this time and distance.

"Baby, you're a star," he murmured, shaking his head. "The brightest one in the sky. At first, when I heard that horn—hell—when I heard that sax I thought I was going nuts." He lifted his index finger to his temple and drew little circles in the air. "But the others heard it, too, and before we knew it the Japs came out of nowhere, guns were firing, and then I see my goddamn dog all the way from Nadzab running straight toward me!"

He stubbed out the rollie and drew her to him, enfolding her now, as if to protect her.

"Sunshine, you saved our lives, you and your horn."

She could feel her cheeks flushing and then a deeper burn, lower down, between her legs.

And then their muscles melted into each other and his tongue found her mouth; her hands traced his bony rib cage, the ladder of his spine, while his fingers pulled at the buckle of her belt. He couldn't move much, due to his wounded leg, but as the dog sat at their feet, watching, she rolled herself on top of him, looked directly into his wide grey eyes, pushed his cock inside her, and made love to him as gently as the rain was falling.

Afterward, James pulled an old army blanket over them and they rested in each other's arms. The dog nosed her way under the blanket, too, and nestled between their legs, licking a graze on Pearl's knee. James ran a finger behind her ear, murmuring,

"Baby, I more than love you. There'll never be a word"—he gently kissed her right eyelid, then her left—"to say how much."

She pressed her face into the hollow of his collarbone, blinking back tears. "Don't ever leave me again. I couldn't—I just couldn't—"

"Shh . . . " he whispered, stroking her face. "Put it this way, baby. The day I ever leave you again, it'll be in a wooden box."

They held each other, listening to the rain, the dog now curled up in the crook of Pearl's legs. She heard James's breathing slow down and sensed him drifting off, still hardly believing they were together again, after so many months, after so many miles. She wanted to stay under the blanket with him, and the dog, forever, where no one would guess their many secrets or question the depth of their love.

The rain gradually softened and the mist thinned. James rolled onto his back. Thirsty, she raised herself on one arm and grabbed the canteen, but there was no water left. James shifted and groaned.

"You okay?" she asked.

"Leg's gone to sleep," he murmured. "Baby, help me up?"

She scrambled to her feet and helped hoist him into a standing position. "Over there," he said, nodding at the pilot's seat. "Need to sit up for a while." With her arm tight around his waist, she walked him into the cockpit and helped lower him into the seat. All the dials on the panel were smashed and the joystick was bent into a mangled question mark.

"Thanks," he said, and squeezed her hand. He pressed a few buttons on the panel and glanced up at her, half grinning. "So, Captain, where're we flying off to today?"

"Oh, I don't know." She walked back through the cabin and picked up the empty canteen. "What about the moon? Or even Venus. Any planet that's not at war."

He pushed more buttons and shoved the gearstick around.

"Just wait a sec, Lieutenant," she said, returning to the cockpit. She held up the canteen. "Before we depart we need more supplies."

He raised his hand in a solemn salute. "Aye, aye, Captain. You requisition the water. I'll prepare for takeoff."

She grinned and returned his salute. Then, shouldering his gun, she opened the hatch and jumped to the ground, with Pup following her. As she walked away she turned to wave at him, and he waved back, his head framed by a half-circle of cracked glass.

The rain and some of the mist had lifted, but as she sprinted down the side of a terrace, there was no sign of Wanipe or the other Australians. She heard a gurgling sound and followed it across a glen freckled with tiny flowers, the dog trotting along beside her. Sometimes, she saw blood splashed against rocks and blades of grass and wondered whether it had been spilled from enemies or Allies. Of course, as it was sinking into the earth it all looked the same.

When she glimpsed the stream she rushed toward it, and as she did she was possessed by a similar rush of excitement, the promise of spending the rest of her life with the only man she'd ever love. The dog leaped ahead, barking madly, as if she, too, were thrilled by their reunion.

Pearl and Pup reached the bank, where they glimpsed Wanipe and the rest of the Australian unit, who were wading across from the other side. They waved and called to each other, and the dog, recognising Wanipe, began howling a greeting and dancing on her hind legs. Pearl splashed her face with the clear, freezing water and refilled the canteen.

As she waited for the others to cross the stream, she noticed through the thinning mist two or three American soldiers moving stealthily along the terrace above. She was so relieved that the reinforcements had finally arrived that she left Wanipe and the others behind and began striding back to the plane.

As she skirted around bushes, she could see the wings and tail of the supply plane glinting silver. When she squinted she could glimpse the outline of James through the cracked glass. She saw him raise his hand again and give a brief wave. She responded by jumping like an excited child and punching at the air.

Then there was a deafening boom and the mountainside exploded. She fell to the ground as dirt, shattered glass, and bits of metal rained through the air. Another boom thundered. Pearl lifted her head to glance up at the clearing, and what she saw seemed impossible: The plane she'd waved at only moments before no longer existed; all that remained were clouds of smoke.

She jumped to her feet but Wanipe had already reached her and was trying to hold her back. She broke away and raced up the track toward the clearing, the dog running ahead of her, barking. Seething with rage, she hugged the rifle as she rushed up the path. She was ready to kill someone, to put a bullet into the man who'd grenaded the plane. She heard a branch crack but all she saw were the tops of two steel helmets moving through the undergrowth. She caught flashes of their jungle-green uniforms as they stalked toward the remains of the plane, guns cocked.

"Jap boy's dead now," called one of them in an American accent.

She stood stock-still, unable to move, as if she'd turned to granite. Without twitching a muscle, she watched the black smoke billow up from the plane, until she heard a bloodcurdling cry echo through the valley and realised it was her own.

Coda

"Mum and Dad never found out the truth," says Pearl on the last tape. "Really, no one knows the whole story—well, not anyone who's still alive." She pauses, and I can hear her wheezing, as if struggling for breath. Ice tinkles in a glass. She clears her throat and takes a sip of whatever she's drinking, probably vodka.

I feel as if I'm welded to my chair, unable to move. I'm imagining the exploded plane, fire and smoke wreathing the air, and the man she'd just made love to now no more than blood and splintered bones scattered across the valley. My breathing's so shallow I feel light-headed, dizzy, as if I'm gazing at a street from the top of a skyscraper.

I have to force myself to concentrate as she moans softly and takes another sip of her drink. "Wait, darling," she murmurs, "there's more."

On the plane back to Sydney, Pearl was lectured to by Sergeant Rudolph, who wanted to get her out of the military and back into civilian life as quickly and quietly as possible.

"It was an accident, Willis!" he kept repeating, exasperated. "No American would want to kill one of his own."

Pearl was still wearing her uniform, still pretending to be her brother; it had been only thirty-two hours since the reinforcements had blown up the crashed Japanese plane. Pearl, still in deep shock, was clutching the dog to her chest and refused to let her go. She would never believe that James's death wasn't deliberate, that it had all been a terrible mistake. "James was good enough to die protecting Australia, but not good enough to live here," she told Rudolph bitterly. They were the last words she ever spoke to him.

Once they landed in Sydney, Rudolph rushed through the paperwork, and within two hours Private Martin Willis had been honourably discharged from the Australian Army and was handed fifty pounds in deferred pay. Pearl promptly took a train to the Blue Mountains, turning up at the farm at sunset with her backpack and dog. After she banged on the door, it swung open and Martin appeared, dressed in a pair of overalls, his hair long and matted. He took one look at Pearl and exclaimed, "Christ, what happened to you?" They hugged tightly and then both burst into tears.

The next day, they switched identities again and turned up at their Potts Point home together, shocking the daylights out of Clara and Aub. And the twins kept each other's secrets: Martin maintained that he'd been away in New Guinea for a year, while Pearl told them she'd run off to the mountains to live with Pookie and Nora Barnes. Their parents were so thrilled that the twins were both alive and healthy that they welcomed them back into the home with a lot of sobbing and open arms and untold bottles of beer.

*   *   *

"Don't worry, darling," says Pearl toward the end of tape twenty-three. "There's a happy ending to this story, after all." I hear the tap of her glass against a table and then she sighs. "Seven weeks after I got back to Sydney . . . " She clears her throat. "Seven weeks later . . . I found out I was pregnant."

At first I think I'm hearing things. I hit the Pause button and rewind for a couple of seconds, then press Play again.

"—after all . . . seven weeks after I got back to Sydney . . . Seven weeks later . . . I found out I was pregnant. Mum hit the roof at first. But after a while she figured out a plan and packed me off to a country home to give birth. To give birth in secret."

I hit the Pause button again and pour myself a double whisky. I down it in two gulps and pour myself another. I think I know where the story is going now and I'm starting to get jittery. My hands are shaking and I can't feel my legs. I steady myself against the desk and sit down again. As I go to press Play again, my finger trembles like a divining rod.

"When I first saw you," she says, "all I could see was your father. His beautiful blue eyes and those long black lashes. That's why I called you Jimmy. You were the spitting image of him."

I gulp down my second whisky.

"It was Mum's idea. She made me do it." I can hear her weeping now, her voice cracking. "It was the only way she'd let me keep you. Back in the forties, you know . . . People could turn a blind eye to a soldier coming back from the war with a bastard kid—even a black one. But not if . . . not if you were a woman."

She falls silent, and all I can hear are the wheels of the cassette player turning. At first I think this is the end of the story, that she has nothing more to say. But after what seems like a long time, she coughs and sips her drink again.

"There were so many times," she murmurs, "when I wanted to—when we both wanted to, Martin and I—to tell you the truth . . . " She chokes up, then recovers herself. "We were going to tell you after Mum died. But by that time—Christ, you were at uni on an Aboriginal scholarship and it just seemed . . . I don't know. We couldn't bring ourselves . . . " I can hear a catch in her throat, a soft hiccup. "And once you became a writer— well, things just got out of hand. I know this must come as a terrible shock, which is why I asked Brian to wait a year after my death before he, before he came looking for these tapes." She blows her nose, sighs. "But I want you to know, Jimmy, you're my beautiful boy. I want you to understand the deep love that made you. The deep love I'll always have for you . . . "

Her voice trails off, and I'm so stunned I feel the start of a migraine pulsing at the base of my skull. Right now I don't love Pearl back—no, not at all. My first reaction is to lurch around the house, smashing things up—her favourite vase, her set of china, Clara's crystal champagne flutes. All those years I spent wondering about my real mother, where I came from, and why. All those years I imagined my teenage mother giving birth to me, the one with the long, black lustrous hair. The one who came from a mission outside Dubbo.

And what do I tell my own son, and my ex-wife, and all my Redfern mates? I've always been a bit of an outsider but this news makes me feel like a fucking alien.

What kind of family could keep a secret that long? All to protect Pearl's future, and the Willis name.

And speaking of names . . . Fuck, that's right . . . I've been named Australia's First Indigenous Crime Writer. That title is plastered all over my backlist—over two hundred thousand copies worldwide. I've just picked up a Deadly Award for services to Indigenous literature.

It probably won't be long before I'm outed as yet another literary hoaxer—joining a long list of bullshit artists, from Helen Demidenko to James Frey. Just another impostor riding the Aboriginal gravy train . . .

It's not until I smash an antique porcelain bowl in the kitchen, not until one of the builders, Omar, grabs my arms from behind to restrain me, that I begin to calm down a little.

Omar sits me on a chair, pulls a cold beer from the fridge, and hands it to me without a word. I offer him one but he shakes his head and returns to his work in the basement. After two more beers I feel as if I'm coming to my senses. I start to get some distance and can see the story from Pearl's point of view.

I realise that if she hadn't gone along with Clara's ruse, she would've been forced to give me up for adoption—being a single mother with a black kid in the forties would have meant she'd be constantly ostracised. And I imagine, given the obsessive love she had for James, there's no way she would've been able to give me up. I was the only part of him that remained alive and growing.

Now, looking back on my early childhood, I see events in an entirely different light: Pearl's insistence on bathing me

every afternoon before dinner, her making up fairy tales for
me at night until I fell asleep, our many special outings, just
the two of us, when she'd take me to the beach, to the cinema,
to outdoor concerts, to football, her Eskimo nose kisses, and
many surprise gifts. These weren't the actions of an attentive
aunty but quiet demonstrations of a mother's love. And now
her many quarrels with Clara over the years about how I should
be disciplined—or not—make much more sense. If I'd been
adopted, I would never have known Pearl, let alone the rest of
the family. And she would never have known me. And I also
realise that Clara would've held it over Pearl for all those years,
like a veiled threat.

I'm beginning to believe there might be a way around the
dilemma I now find myself in. It's possible that during the
whole process of my writing this book, listening to the tapes,
transcribing the stories, Pearl has been subtly preparing me for
the inevitable shock. It's quite a thrill to realise now that all that
show business blood runs through me, from both my mother
and my father. I'm now the son of the woman who impersonated a man for a year, nephew of the man who became a
woman for the same length of time, grandson of the lady who
performed a half-man, half-woman routine. Why, masquerading is in my family's cell structure, woven into our DNA. And
this manuscript could sit in my filing cabinet for years, until I
die, without anyone ever knowing the truth.

I pour myself a whisky and think about the possibilities. But
by the time I drain my glass I'm starting to reconsider.

If my Herman Djulpajurra series continues to be well written and compelling, I don't see how it matters to the public

and the press that my father was a black American rather than a black Australian. As the saying goes, I'll have to face the music, but I think I might wait a few days before I turn the volume up. And when I do, I'm going to ask my American agent, Barney, to extend my next U.S. author tour to the South, to Louisiana, to the birthplace of my father. Maybe I have family there.

Looking back on it, I can now see that all the longing Pearl still felt for James, the yearning that stayed with her for the rest of her life, she channelled into me, and what she had left over she poured into her saxophone. Clara, Aub, and Martin raised me as their own, and one of them always looked after me when Pearl was rehearsing or when she worked at night. When Pup died, when I was about six years old, Pearl and I were so bereft that Aub stuffed her and replaced her eyes with tiny balls of amber glass. He then glued the dog to a small wooden platform on four wheels and tied a length of rope to the front, so I could drag Pup through the house and pretend she was still alive. She still sits on a shelf here in my study and now, as I pat her, I can imagine her as a puppy folding into the armpit of my father or leading my mother through the highlands of New Guinea. God, I'm getting teary. Better pour myself another drink.

As the years passed, I saw Pearl's lovers come and go, but I can't remember any one man lasting longer than six or eight months, and for the rest of her life, it seems to me, no one else was able to fill that part of her that yearned for the father of her son.

Pearl eventually got on with life, forming a band that included Martin and Nora Barnes. The ensemble toured the country well into the late fifties, playing nightclubs and concerts and sometimes winning band competitions. Her band recorded acetates after the war that, even now, in a new century, still sound startling and unique. When I listen to them now I can hear James Washington's jazz style slipping out between her riffs, a brief musical blending of those two human beings.

I'm trying to look on the positive side. I guess writing this book has allowed me to understand the complexities of my mother and my background better than I ever have before and, by doing so, I begin to understand myself more clearly—a person who's never felt completely at home in either black or white society. And as I listen to her saxophone soaring through the speakers, I begin to cherish the good things she left me with— the lyrical melodic lines of her ballads, the wild dips and runs of her twelve-bar blues, the stories she has told me, which have altered me forever, and have become my own. And finally, the best thing she willed to me was the great love she had for the father I never knew, the way she conjured him up like a piece of music, created him out of nothing, and kept him alive, just as I now breathe life into her.

Acknowledgments

This novel was written with the assistance of the Literature Board of the Australia Council. Many thanks for the support. It was also written with the support of the 2002 University of New South Wales Writer's Fellowship, which provided priceless resources to further my research. In particular I'm indebted to Professor of History Sean Brawley, whose lectures in the class The Pacific War: World War II in the Asia-Pacific World War at UNSW were both inspiring and revelatory. Dr. Brawley also gave me vital feedback during the writing of an early manuscript.

I'm also indebted to Professor Bruce Johnson, formerly of the UNSW English Department, for assisting my research into Australian jazz, and who has been an unswerving supporter of this work.

Also assisting me in my research on the history of Australian jazz: Thanks to all the commentators on the Australian Dance Band discussion forum, particularly Dennis King, Bill Forrest, John Whiteoak, and saxphonist Bob Bertles for their insights and suggestions.

I'd also like to acknowledge the 2009 Scholar in Writing Program at the University of Technology, Sydney, for support during the completion of this book.

For critical feedback, thanks to Dan Conaway, John Dale, Jane Gleeson-White, and Ivor Indyk.

Special thanks to my Australian agent, Gaby Naher, and my Australian publisher, Jane Palfreyman, both of whom offered detailed critiques of many drafts.

Thank you to Siobhán Cantrill, a meticulous senior editor, and a joy to work with.

The definition of a great editor is one who intuits an author's intentions and helps her realise them. Ali Lavau, you are one of the best I have ever encountered.

Excerpts from this novel first appeared in the following journals: *Extempore 2: Writing/Art/Jazz/Improvisation,* Miriam Zolin (ed.), and in *HEAT,* Ivor Indyk (ed.).

This novel was begun on 3 July 2000 and not completed until 25 January 2011, almost the length of my entire relationship with my husband, Louis Nowra. My thanks for his critical rigour and unending patience over the years. The love in this book is a consequence of my love for him.

The following works were important to my research: *All on One Good Dancing Leg,* by Joan Clarke; *Sweethearts of Rhythm: The Story of Australia's All-Girl Bands and Orchestras to the End of the Second World War,* by Kay Dreyfus; *Black Roots White Flowers: A History of Jazz in Australia,* by Andrew Bisset; *A Showman's Story: The Memoirs of Jim Davidson,* by Jim Davidson; *Meet Me at the Trocadero,* by Joan Ford; *A Yank Down Under: From America's Heartland to Australia's Outback,* by Ray A. Wyatt; *Jungle Fighters: A G.I. Correspondent's Experiences in the New Guinea Campaign,* by Jules Archer; *New Guinea Diary,* by George H. Johnston; *Somewhere in New Guinea,* by Frank Clune.

Love in the Years of Lunacy
Mandy Sayer
A Readers Club Guide

INTRODUCTION

Set in the Kings Cross neighborhood of Sydney in 1942, *Love in the Years of Lunacy* is a war-torn tale of love and jazz. Pearl, just shy of her eighteenth birthday, is the impetuous daughter of showbiz musicians. She plays saxophone in an all-girl jazz band at the Trocadero and occasionally sits in on underground gigs with her twin brother, Martin, who also plays the sax. When the enlisted American G.I. James Washington breezes into the Booker T. Washington Club one night and brings down the house with his tenor sax solo, Pearl is hooked. Their budding romance unfolds against the blacked-out nights and rumor-filled days of a city in the grip of war. In the face of mid-century attitudes about race and gender, and the looming threat of the Japanese, this is the story of two young musicians in love, and their struggle to stay together against increasingly unlikely odds.

QUESTIONS & TOPICS FOR DISCUSSION

1. The book's title draws on Gabriel García Márquez's novel *Love in the Time of Cholera,* also about a young woman who is forbidden from seeing the man she loves and instead marries a doctor, a very rational and organized man. In what ways does this novel portray love and rationality as opposing forces? How does it explore the idea of love as

an illness? If you've read the Marquez novel, how do you think it compares to *Love in the Years of Lunacy*?

2. In Pearl's instructions to her nephew, she tells him that she has always been better with music than words, and asks him to "pretty up" her story, to "make it sing." What is the importance of the narrator being a novelist? How do you think the story is affected by his ability to make it sing, and how might it be different if Pearl wrote the book herself?

3. After Pearl loses her virginity to James during the air raid, James says: "This is all new for me. And I guess it's new for you, too. So let's keep this to ourselves, okay? At least until we know each other better." Were you surprised by this admission? Who does he want to keep their romance a secret from?

4. During her first lessons with James, Pearl says they "excited her more than a roller-coaster ride, especially when James put his arms around her from behind, placed his hands on hers, and applied pressure to her fingers against the saxophone keys." How are music and physical pleasure connected for Pearl? Why do you think there is such a strong bond between the two?

5. James tells Pearl, "You gotta learn how to improvise. Take risks." How does the theme of risk-taking play out throughout the novel?

6. Pearl attempts suicide after James breaks off their engagement and their plan to run away together. This period also finds her without Martin for only the second time in her life. In what ways does Pearl rely on Martin for her confidence and sense of self? How much do you think his absence contributed to her depression?

7. Hector recommends that Pearl avoid any "extreme behavior" as part of her recovery, including late nights, drinking, or associating with musicians. It becomes clear, however, that Hector disapproves of these things even once she has recovered. Do you think Pearl makes the right choice to end their relationship? If James had not reappeared that night outside the Trocadero, do you think Pearl could have lived a happy life with the Master of Lunacy?

8. Were you surprised by Pearl's plan to take Martin's place in the army? Do you see her decision as a rational act or an act of passion? Is it possible for her plan to be both?

9. Once Pearl's unit has seen more than enough of the war, and suffered losses of its own, her mission becomes greater than just finding James. What does the music they play provide for the soldiers? What does playing for them provide Pearl?

10. It's clear that Pearl has won the respect of Sergeant Rudolph as both a soldier and a musician. Why do you think he is so angry when he discovers that she is a woman, impersonating her brother Martin?

11. The forces that bring Pearl and James together seem to be equal to the forces that continually kept them apart. If they had both survived the war, do you think they could have found a way to stay together?

12. Were you surprised to find that Jimmy, the narrator of this story, was in fact Pearl's son, not her nephew? Do you agree with her decision to keep this truth from him?

13. In the opening lines of the novel, Pearl says to Jimmy on the recording, "I want you to play these tapes one by one,

and as you listen, write down the story I'm telling you. In writing our story—the story of Martin and me—you'll also be writing your own." How does this prove to be true in more ways than one? Why do you think Pearl asks Jimmy to write her life story? And which years and whose lunacy do you think the title of the novel refers?

ENHANCE YOUR BOOK CLUB

1. Put together a jazz soundtrack for your book club, including some of the greats that James Washington played in the novel, including Count Basie, Lester Young, Benny Goodman, Jack Teagarden, Chick Webb, not to mention Artie Shaw—the favorite of James, Pearl, and Martin—who toured the Pacific Theater with his Navy Band throughout WWII.

2. Mandy Sayer acknowledges a number of books that helped her research *Love in the Years of Lunacy*. To learn more about the jazz world of this era, consider checking out *All on One Good Dancing Leg*, by Joan Clarke; *Sweethearts of Rhythm: The Story of Australia's All-Girl Bands and Orchestras to the End of the Second World War*, by Kay Dreyfus; *Black Roots, White Flowers: A History of Jazz in Australia*, by Andrew Bissett; *A Showman's Story: The Memoirs of Jim Davidson*, by Jim Davidson; *Meet Me at the Trocadero*, by Joan Ford. Another alternative for some background material is the Ken Burns' acclaimed documentary, *Jazz*.